MW01135202

A
THOUSAND SLIPPERS

Written by

John Michael McCarty

Inspired by True Events

"*A THOUSAND SLIPPERS* IS AN INGENIOUS AND INTRIGUING STORY with a counterpoint between a Japanese airman on a submarine in the early days of World War II and a colorful cast of characters in San Francisco...a delightful read."
        -San Francisco Museum and Historical Society

"ARMED WITH A SHARP WIT, John McCarty weaves iconic characters through a historic maze with such ease and color that we simply shake our heads in a whaddya-know kind of wonderment. The author writes with a descriptive flare that is easy on the eyes and tickles the nostalgic bone. His novels turn pop-culture and local antiquity into a fun and informative journey, a canny blend of lunatic farce and self-assured banter. Mr. McCarty is emerging as one of our truly distinguished local treasures..."
        -Russian River Times

"THE AUTHOR OFFERS A FASCINATING PEEK INTO THE MINDS AND ACTIVITIES...from another time period."
        -The Windsor Times

"JOHN MCCARTY TRANSPORTS THE READER BACK...with delightful and colorful characters. The author has an uncanny talent for creating quirky but well-rounded characters...a great escape and a fast page turner."
        -Jeane Sloane, national award winning author: *She Flew Bombers.*

A THOUSAND SLIPPERS. Copyright © 2014 by John McCarty. Printed in the United States of America by CreateSpace. No other part of this book may be reproduced in any form or by any electronic or mechanical means including information storage and retrieval systems without permission in writing from the author, except by a reviewer, who may quote brief passages in a periodical.

For more information regarding John McCarty's novels, visit http://www.johnmccarty.org. To contact the author directly or to signup for free monthly notices on his events and new publications, go to john@johnmccarty.org.

Cover design: Ron Friedland

Distributed in the U.K. and Europe by Amazon.com
7290B Investment Drive, Charleston, South Carolina, U.S.A., 29418

ISBN-13: 978-1492866312
ISBN-10: 1492866318

The author wishes to express his gratitude to the Fulbright Association, the San Francisco Historical Society, Redwood Writers, Mochitsura Hashimoto (author of *Sunk*), William McCash (author of *Bombs Over Brookings*), Dee Tilson, Bob Thorpe, Charlie Wheeler, Andrew Goldstein, Patricia Morrison, Al and Charlene Peterson, Deb's Unique Boutique, Keith Muramoto, Anne DeGraf and the late Elmer DeGraf.

Chapter One

On the east side of San Francisco's Twin Peaks, an electric trolley exited from a two-mile long tunnel onto Market Street, dragging sparks from the overhead wires. Anne Klausen disembarked and crossed three lanes of traffic against the light. A spanking new '41 Hudson yelped and smoked to a halt. Its horn tooted as the driver hurled dissents out the window. A stack of civilians on the far sidewalk yelled at the young woman to go back. With eyes fixed to the ground, Anne didn't hear the demands as she mumbled out a stream of chatter to the white line underfoot.

"On the bottom end of the food chain, huh? I'll show him. Who does he think he is? Well, I'll tell you who he is. He's a big ugly Kraut with bad breath and sunspots, that's who he is," and she reached the other side of Market and jaywalked across Castro Street.

More beeps. More warnings.

"Why, he's nothing more than a booze hounding, whore mongering slimeball."

She approached a nearby Art Deco building where neon letters read: THE CASTRO. Arched windows, interlocking clay pantiles, and green and blue sconces conveyed a Hollywood-like elegance. The marquee heralded the feature attraction, *The*

Maltese Falcon. However, the images of Humphrey Bogart and Mary Astor did little to quash the gnashing inside her head.

Anne plodded into the lobby and passed a pair of high-back purple velvet chairs under a grand chandelier, feeling insignificant. She hurried through the concession line and ordered treats from a cashier, saying, "Just because a father sermonizes atop a bar stool, doesn't make him more meaningful. Hell, it doesn't even make him necessary, right?"

"Okay," the young employee said.

Anne left puzzled glimpses behind and strutted up a carpeted staircase, ranting to the image that followed her from the floor-to-ceiling mirrors. She reached the loges and flopped into a cushioned seat and started to tilt a box of popcorn toward her mouth when a pain cried out. With a groan she unlaced her saddle shoes and eased them aside. Beneath her bobby sox, arthritic toes struggled to straighten. While massaging her abused feet, her vision wandered along an aimless path of walled murals. Decorative vases and pots displayed painted figurines, which portrayed different members of ancient court life. A retinue of concubines, erotic dancers and female serfs attended a king who sat upon his throne.

Need to shake things up, she thought. It's time women took their rightful place. Let the men do the indentured-servant thing for a while. Do them some good. At that moment a sharp discomfort began to rise from her gallbladder, conspiring with the ache in her head and feet. While the blitheness and tautness of her frame befitted her teenage status, a decade of ballet had taken its toll.

"He'd love to see me now," she said with a huff and threw the empty popcorn box to the floor and snatched a black rope of licorice from its container. Slumped further back into her seat, she bit into the sweet, waiting for the aromatic chew to flatten the edges of her frantic mind. A few minutes later, music catapulted from speakers as if to assist her efforts. Maroon drapes separated. The houselights dimmed as human profiles stepped across the silver screen.

Sam Spade whirled his lover around and said in heated passion, "I don't care who loves who. I won't play the sap for you anymore."

"I've been bad," his beloved answered. "Worse than you can know."

"You tell him, girl," Anne called out.

Hearty "shhhs" sounded from all sides. She thought about returning her own salutation and turned halfway around to do so but realized that these strangers were not the cause of her gloom. Hopeful for a quick elixir, Anne returned her gaze forward, but not even the premier of John Houston's film could erase the snapshot of a nagging father. Without explanation, Bogie whined to a stop. A glare showed itself like an uninvited guest. Owning a triple chin, a Hitchcock-looking fellow manned the stage and held up his hands to solicit quiet.

"Ladies and gentlemen, may I have your attention, please."

Irritation laced the audience's murmur. Heads skittered here and there.

"By order of Lieutenant General John L. Wright, head of the Western Command, all citizens are to return to their homes this instant."

Questions shot back, but the dour man provided few answers, offering refunds as a poor substitute. He sauntered off and left the task of herding out the throng to his subordinates.

Outside, the drone of sirens roller-coastered across the city. Merchants hung "Closed" signs and lowered chain-link gates over storefronts, not with the lazy touch of a day's end but with the frantic stroke of an emergency. Cars scurried from parking spaces. Pedestrians' puzzled expressions, twin to Anne's, passed her in the opposite direction. Older folks darted one-way and then another while mothers herded their young indoors.

Anne sprinted down Eighteenth. At the corner of Sanchez, she turned right, away from her Mission High School, and raced alongside a streetcar through Dolores Park. A young boy, pressed against the transport's window, followed her with his empty cast.

She arrived two blocks later at the foot of Liberty Street. Air escaped in quick spurts as she gaped at the escarpment. Resolute, Anne tackled the hill when from behind she heard the skidding and clashing of automobiles. Her vision remained steadfast upon the climb, ignoring the angry voices from below. The peak of Dolores Heights and a tired bungalow soon came into view. She leapfrogged the rickety porch steps to the entrance where her key fumbled within her twitching hand. Damn. She found the lock, flung open the door and sprinted inside and flipped on the radio. The gargled hum of cold vacuum tubes amped up her anxiety. Come on. Come on. Her shoe drummed against the oval carpet until a minute later a familiar voice poured into the living room.

> "At eight A.M. on this day of December seventh, nineteen hundred and forty-one, a date which will live in infamy, the United States government was suddenly and deliberately attacked by Japan." Franklin Delano Roosevelt further detailed the bombing of Pearl Harbor as well as the duplicitous actions of the Japanese ambassador, Kichisaburo Nomura, and Emperor Hirohito himself. In conclusion the President said, "With congressional approval, I do hereby declare war on the Empire of Japan and all her allies."

Anne's thoughts sank under the Philco's chatter. She feared that all that had been would be no more. Past innocence sprang forth: ice-skating at Winterland; potato-sack racing at the Fun House; swimming at Sutro Baths. Other images of things to come flashed before her as well: the Ballet Russe de Monte Carlo; the San Francisco Opera. All lost. She made her way to the kitchen and plucked the telephone from its cradle. The receiver quaked within her grasp as she dialed a memorized number. A broken beep greeted her. Damn. She crumpled to the linoleum floor and stared at the phone swaying by its cord.

*   *   *

Platinum blonde was this month's hair color while cherry-red decorated her lips. Rose McNally fondled the microphone, flashed a leg from the slit of her sequined dress and said, "Howdy, boys. How's God treatin' ya this fine afternoon?"

Her trademark greeting seemed fitting for a Sunday. In fact many were of the opinion that the striptease artist had a special covenant with the Man upstairs. The way she put it, "God works harder for sinners." There was enough unemployment going around, what with the New Deal faltering and all. No reason to put the Lord out of a job as well. The burlesque owner would do her best to keep Him busy.

"In honor of the fiftieth anniversary of those no-good lowlifes who call themselves the Republican Grays, I give you the Music Box Dancers."

The Republican Grays were a bunch of civilians who formed a militia group back in 1890. They adopted the natty uniform of West Point to pretty up their image. But it was too late.

A line of young damsels bounced from behind a curtain and high-kicked to the saucy tune of the "Can-Can" from a vinyl 78. With the fall and rise of petticoats, Grays whistled and yelled.

Rose retreated from the podium and sat atop Elmer Klausen's lap, stroking the sergeant's flabby arm. Plenty of flesh hung from other parts of his frame as well, which contributed to his general lack of form. He owned an East European bust with puffy cheeks, bushy eyebrows and a honker of a nose that served as a perch for his wire-rimmed moon glasses. For a final affront, a chain of sunspots claimed the space atop his balding head.

"Wanna come by later for a meal?" Rose said.

"Can't," Elmer said, raising his voice over the music. "Gotta talk some sense into that child of mine."

Unable to decipher his words, she leaned into him and said, "Bring her over to the club. I'll fix something for everyone."

"Uh, don't think that's gonna work."

"What?" Rose bent closer, the RCA trying to override the sound of some crisis forming outside.

"Let's keep it simple."

"By *simple* you mean keep this…whatever this is between you and me… behind closed doors. Have I got that right?"

"Can't hear," and he cupped an ear with his hand.

Her fingers fell from him and she caught up her dress to rise. Before she could get to her feet, however, a phalanx of State Reserve soldiers stormed in and she reseated herself.

A baby-face officer yanked a cord from its socket to silence the music. Frilly dresses froze within the folds of their owners' grips.

"What is the meaning of this intrusion?" demanded Major Mikael Fredericks in a loud tone. Short of stature, the Republican Gray's leader often resorted to bluster to make up for his five-foot, six-inch frame.

"Your outfit is being placed under my authority for the time being. You and your men are to rally at the south end of the Golden Gate Bridge to await further orders."

"I'm afraid that is quite impossible," Fredericks said, "as these charming ladies," and he motioned with his hand to the dancers on stage, "charge by the…"

"The Japs have invaded Pearl for chrissakes."

Grays washed down their drinks and scurried past Fredericks as he continued his protests. "But there is no refund."

Elmer shot up and dropped Rose to the hardwood. With her undergarments resting upside down over her head, the madam struggled before calling out his name.

"Mister Klausen, you're forty-five years old. Government don't want ancient relics shooting at shadows from the past. Now get your decrepit buttocks back here and help a lady to her feet."

"My *buttocks* are as good as the next man's. No reason to apologize. Even the best of persons have 'em," and he left her on the floor and pushed his way through the exit with the rest of the pack.

"Men," she said as she flattened out the pleats in her dress, "shoulda been a lesbian."

Outside, an argument ensued between different factions.

"Colonel," Baby-Face said to Fredericks, "your men will switch out those copy-cat West Point uniforms for that of the California State Military Reserve as soon as such becomes available."

"I'm afraid you are under some sort of miscomprehension."

"Excuse me?"

"It's *Major* Fredericks, thank you very much."

"Hard to believe," the officer said before making his way back to the motorcade.

Even though the roar of the seven-ton cargo trucks swallowed up his ranting, Fredericks challenged Baby-Face's authority. "And what distinction would you be in possession of regarding real soldiering?"

The motorcade began to roll down Polk Strasse. Its rumble faded to nothing as it turned onto O'Farrell and headed west.

Fredericks corralled the disbelief of his boys, saying, "That misguided soul was somebody's wet dream when we were clearing the Barbary Coast of degenerates and undesirables back in fifteen."

All voiced their agreement. They were left with the dirty work in prepping the city for the World Exposition, rousting the charlatans from Pacific and Broadway streets, escorting pimps, prostitutes, gamblers and junkies aboard ferries to wallow across the bay in the broken down city of Oakland.

"And let us not forget those of us who did battle in World War I and later in the thirties while garrisoning the docks from..."

Rose stood in the entranceway and listened to Fredericks rally his troops. She turned around to her girls and said, "Better grab some shuteye. Looks like we're gonna be busy."

The ladies twirled boas in giddy laughter as if nothing could be better than a good war. God bless the sinner.

Chapter Two

Three chevron stripes decorated Elmer Klausen's right shoulder while stitched upon the other was a golden bear. The lanky vet lumbered from a tollbooth toward a knot of militiamen. In full-length wool overcoats, the soldiers clicked up their heels to attention.

One, a young buck of a Republican Gray, raised a stiff hand to his forehead but Sergeant Klausen was quick to correct, saying, "I'm no officer, son. Now put away that salute."

The kid forced the gesture to his side, ready to answer with a "sir" but guessed that such would be rebuffed as well and stood edgy with the unknowing of what to do next.

"Relax," the old man said as he put a hand on the boy's rifle to steady him. "Let's take a peek at that hardware of yours."

The unit presented their Springfields for the morning inspection. The sergeant examined each in turn, checking the bolt action before putting an eye down the barrel.

"Remember, men," he said in a mentor's voice, "never shoot from the same spot twice." He reminded the recruits how the white smoke of these ancient weapons betrayed a warrior's position. Klausen swerved into politics, admonishing the State Reserve for not furnishing them with the more modern M-1 gas-operated rifles. Without further delay, he posted half a dozen Grays at the north and south ends of the Golden Gate Bridge alongside six-inch cannons.

"Private Ponti," the sergeant said, "you'll assist the Reservist at the inspection depot."

"I don't think I gonna like this duty," the Italian said with an accent.

"Wasn't meant to be a popularity contest."

"*Mamma mía*, you got something right there," and added in a kidding voice, "*Sir*."

Elmer Klausen shot his childhood friend a playful smile, saying, "Don't start."

The pair had terrorized North Beach and the Mission District together during their younger years. They stood in marked contrast to one another. Elmer was a good six inches taller and at least seventy pounds heavier, but Tony was the more outgoing, often paving a smooth path to the girls with his slick Sicilian charm.

A sedan rolled to a stop at the roadblock. With mirror in hand, Private Ponti scanned the undercarriage. A Reservist approached to verify that the driver was Oriental and reminded the Gray to search the engine compartment as well.

"Sonny, I know you no want get hands dirty. So back off, *capisce?*"

"Get to it," the Reservist said as he pointed with his weapon to the hood of the car.

Frustrated civilians maneuvered a one-eighty and returned the way they came. Taillights sparkled from the span like columns of red candles in a Chinese parade.

Tendrils of fog moved through Sergeant Klausen's bones. Whips of air snapped at him. He pinched up his collar and started toward the warmth of indoors when a raspy bellow pierced the day from the seaward side. He peered through his binoculars and then picked a walkie-talkie from amongst the lint of his front pocket.

"U.S.S. *Lexington* inbound, a quarter mile west. Over."

"Copy that," responded a captain from a naval trawler below. "Sighting confirmed. We'll take it from here. Over and out."

The vessel motored in a wide arc from the bridge's mid-point to the San Francisco shoreline, dragging a steel net and its 25-ton anchor toward the winch house. Searchlights poured upon the scene from nearby Fort Point. Completed in 1861 to protect the federal government's gold supply from the Confederacy, the citadel was recalled into service to oversee the operation of the newly installed anti-submarine barrier.

A quartet of tugs arrived to guide the aircraft carrier through the narrow channel to the Hunters Point Shipyard. Satisfied all was well, Sergeant Elmer Klausen wheeled around to his earlier intent when he bumped into the hooded frame of another. His weapon jerked up.

The girl guided the gun to the side, saying, "Put that thing away before you hurt somebody."

"Could've warned me with a 'hello' or somethin'," Elmer said to his daughter.

"Quit your fussing."

"If we could bottle that sarcasm of yours and drop it on the Japs, this war'd be over by daybreak."

"Here, brought you coffee, plenty of sugar," and Anne handed a thermos to him.

A cliché entered the father's mind, swirling around a cloudy theme of sweetness and disposition, but the numbness in his cheeks reset his priorities and he wrapped his ropey hands around the mug. "A few of the boys are bivouacked down in the old money room, down the concrete tunnel below the toll plaza," he said. "Why don't ya see if anyone needs some of this goop ya call coffee? We'll meet up after my shift, ride home together."

"What if I want to leave now?"

"Could kill your mother for dyin' so young. Now get."

The wind's bite sharpened with the departure of his child's insolent tongue. She walked away in a haughty posture, her chin turned upward.

Words pushed through his walkie-talkie. Distracted, the sergeant couldn't comprehend the message. "Repeat. Over."

"Net remains open. *Bunting* outbound. Over."

"Ten-four. Out." Klausen returned the radio to his pocket and lifted his glasses. The seventy-foot minesweeper came into focus. He combed the surrounding area. No unauthorized crafts showed themselves, all safe. Nearby, a collection of Grays milled around a drum's fire. The sergeant strolled over and rubbed his palms over the flame.

"Nicola and the girls, everyone good?" Klausen asked Tony Ponti.

"Five daughters," and he shook his head. "You think one boy roll out, but no. What are odds to this?" He finished off with another *mamma mía* before asking, "How your little Annie?"

"Not so little anymore, 'cept between the ears. Wants to run off to L.A. and dance with the stars. Go figure."

"Not one of my girls permitted out of house until thirty," Tony said with a smile, a smile he had owned forever.

"Extinguish that beacon," ordered an authoritative voice from behind, "unless you are of the intent to escort the Japanese to a front row seat?"

"It colder than my Aunt Marcella's bottom," retorted Ponti. "'Sides, no enemy here for week or two."

"Private, did you not grasp the order?" Fredericks said as he stepped into the light.

"*Sí, Sí*, I grasp plenty." He suffocated the blaze with the recapping of the drum's lid and dispersed to his post.

Klausen did not appreciate Fredericks's interference. It was a minor incident, which he felt capable of handling on his own.

"Perhaps you're of the opinion that I was too onerous with the man?" Fredericks said.

"Maybe."

"Maybe you possess a predilection for Ponti. Perhaps that would be the only *maybe* in this affair," Fredericks insisted. "*Maybe* you are two of a…"

"Just friends from the old days is all."

"If you say so." Fredericks sauntered away leaving no space for rebuttal.

Scattered thoughts careened off each other like bumper cars. Elmer took his vexation across the lanes, dodging traffic. His frown fell over the railing to the churning water below, his mind ebbing with the Potato Patch, a mile section of hellish water that spilled off the San Andreas Fault. He raised his binocs and gathered in the *Bunting*, its bow splitting the stubborn confluence of Pacific Ocean and Sacramento River. The civilian ship powered toward the northern tip of the Marin Headlands where twenty or so mysterious metal canisters rolled about. Then an angular shape, stitched on the front edge of a fog bank, materialized. The torpedo boat bobbed in and out of the rolling mist. Klausen's fingers rolled over a knob, reeling in his fear. Figures dashed from one lens to the other, limbs swayed puppet-like before him. He grabbed his radio.

"Ensign, *Bunting* on collision course. Over."

"Say again. Over."

Jesus, Son of Joseph.

The sound of distant horns told him he was too late. The jagged discord of twisting steel competed with the piercing of mechanical alarms. Screams were lost on the wind.

Drivers and passengers scrambled from cars and rushed forward. The sergeant motioned for a group of nearby Grays. They intercepted the block of civilians, urging everyone to return to their vehicles. Curiosity won over, however, and they pushed through, thirsty for a first-hand view of the war.

A silver-haired woman, with a flower printed bandana around her head, sighted the tangled wreck and gasped, "Oh, my goodness."

Fredericks marched over and took charge. "Lady, you must remove yourself."

"I never thought this day would come. Isn't it terrible?"

"The elucidation of *terrible* would be that semblance wrapped inside your scarf. Now move along."

"Well, I never."

The Gray's commander turned to Klausen and said in a condescending way, "I hate to inconvenience you, sergeant, but kindly tend to your duties and extract these people from the area."

*   *   *

The Chevy's hooded headlights strained to show the path through the Presidio where streetlamps now rested dead. A full moon's incandescence aided their journey, washing over a grove of eucalyptus trees, a row of barracks and a trio of aluminum hangars. Father and daughter passed cavalry stables and Crissy Airfield where the boys of Battery E tented themselves on a rare speck of available space. Nearby, a squadron of bulldozers shoveled a beach into the box-beds of dump trucks. Further down Pershing Boulevard, sandbags sealed the bays of administrative buildings to entomb the structures for the duration of the war.

They soon came to a turnstile at the east exit. Elmer adjusted his rearview mirror to study an MP stepping the length of his '39 Chevy. The young soldier's hand brushed alongside a pair of suicide doors until coming to the driver's window. He tapped on the glass with a pair of knuckles.

"I.D."

"Pretty nifty, huh?" Klausen said. The 4-door Master Deluxe cost him every penny he owned at the time, over seven hundred dollars. He pampered the dark-blue sedan with a weekly wash and wax, causing his daughter to wonder which was his favorite girl.

The private examined the old man's license and then noticed the uniform. "Didn't know you Grays were allowed to roam the countryside willy-nilly during time of war."

"War? There's a war goin' on?" Elmer said before turning sideways. "Can you imagine that, daughter?"

The sentry handed back the wallet. "Get a move on."

A shitty grin sliced across Klausen as he cruised onto Lombard Street. Reflectors from the four-lane boulevard popped up like runway lights. At Fillmore Street they took a right. The

13

Marina District disappeared behind them as they crawled south through Cow Hollow. Restaurants, taverns and inns stood empty. A few solitary stragglers peered up and down the block with their befuddlement.

The eight-cylinder growled as it climbed Pacific Heights. The rock and brick mansions of the city's wealthiest clung to the hillside. Blackout shades, drawn behind leaded windows, hid any signs of life. Shadows of Edwardians, Victorians and Mission Revivals melded with the night as clouds roamed past the moon.

Anne fell silent as if the pervasive stillness had put a spell on her. Even the stone-cold structures seemed to be mourning the day's events. The *Bunting* catastrophe had announced that the unknown was here. The quiet agreed, seeping through the avenues, sucking the lifeblood out of her San Francisco. So full of vim just a few days previous, citizens referred to their beloved home simply as the "City". No other urban area deserved such notoriety, but this scene before her stood as a stranger.

The Chevy lumbered down the south side of Pacific Heights and across Pine Street to the flat that contained Japantown. A sign lulled past announcing Zone 22. Zone 22? As if the district contained such abhorrence, such inflamed disgust, that its mere utterance might transmit an unfathomable contagion.

The military had taken up positions at every other avenue. Guard shacks and rifle-toting MPs blanketed the area. How did things get to such a point? Anne pondered. One day you're watching Bogie spin his magic, the next you're in the middle of brimstone and damnation. The martial law atmosphere, however, inferred something different to her father.

"Gonna continue with that ballet instructor of yours?" Elmer said, breaking the dead silence between them.

Entangled within the unfamiliarity around her, she didn't hear her father's question and asked that he repeat it.

"Merichino Scitzo or whatever his name is."

"Merishio Ito," corrected Anne. "And, yes, I intend to continue."

"He's a Jap, ya know. Works down in Japantown."

"You've been paying for my dance lessons these past ten years. I would like to believe that you know where his studio is."

"Should've sent your fanny to boarding school instead. Teach ya some manners, dial down that attitude of yours."

"At least Mr. Ito doesn't hide behind the pretense of being someone he is not."

"Don't use that tone with me," he said, knowing full well the intent behind her jab. He released the tension from the steering wheel. "No need goin' 'round askin' for trouble. Until the war is over, we're Dutch, not Deutsch, got it?"

"Whatever you..."

"Those were tough times back in seventeen," he interrupted, "when President Wilson organized the Enemy Alien Registration Section. Some twenty-three-year-old snot named J. Edgar Hoover interrogated thousands of Germans, sent many to prison. What hurt most was the humiliation your mother and I suffered at the hands of neighbors and so called 'friends'. Decided to make a shift in the family name, added an 'n' to *Klause*."

"Moving around the alphabet doesn't change who you are."

No response.

"I don't see any of your militia buddies altering their identities," she persisted.

"That's 'cause they're fools."

"*Afraid a fool will scorn the wisdom of your words?*"

"What?"

"Proverbs 23:9," Anne said.

"Got too much religion in ya."

"I could spare some."

"Wouldn't know where to put it."

Mission High School and Dolores Park drifted behind them as they approached the foot of Liberty Street. Within closed circles the blacktop held the honor of the City's steepest lane. The Chamber of Commerce, however, awarded this tag upon Filbert Street near Telegraph Hill where tourists of yesterday felt safer, where homes had announced themselves with greater dignity and grace. This was fine with the Klausens as such attention might be a poor fit for them anyway.

The father down-clutched. The Chevy sputtered forward in a low grind of gears. At the top of the hill, Elmer steered the car into the driveway, pulled on the handbrake and turned off the engine. The bungalow rested between homes of chipped paint and haggard rows of shrubs. The neighborhood once stood as a monument of things to come, of suburbia to be, a short buggy ride to last century's financial district. Now it was nothing more than a tattered picture of its former self, forgotten.

Cypress trees hid many of the homes from view, pushing them deeper into the night. Not a glimmer shown anywhere with the exception of one. **425** lit up like a Fourth of July sale at Macy's. Talk was not necessary. The father's rigid demeanor alerted his daughter.

"It was before sunrise when I left to bring you a snack," Anne offered as an excuse. "You do remember the snack, don't you, daddy dearest?"

"Gotta get your head out of the clouds and quit prancin' around in swan costumes, doin' the hoochie coochie. There are more important things," he said as he exited the sedan.

"Excuse me," interrupted a voice from the curb.

Elmer turned around and glowered at the sudden appearance of the neighborhood reject. Dressed in khaki with a shock of frizzled hair squirting out from under a white helmet, he looked more like a deranged zookeeper than a Block Warden.

"Hello, Curly."

"It's Sean, Sean McGinnis," the young man said with demand in his voice.

Klausen, hearing a suggestion of disrespect, said in slow fashion, "C-u-r-l-y, whaddya want?"

The boy threw out his chest in protest and stuck to business. "You're in violation of ordinance three dash fifteen of the Civil Defense Code, which states, and I quote: 'Until further notification private and commercial residences are hereby required to obey all blackout procedures including the use of…'"

"Go piss on someone else's yard. I've had a long day," and the old man showed his back to the irritant and lumbered over the crabgrass to the porch.

"Better knock some sense into him," the Block Warden said to Anne after her dad had disappeared inside.

"He never made any sense before, why should he now?"

Her mouth turned upward as if to say that such effort would be wasted, but Curly interpreted it as something else, as a smile meant for him. Very interesting, he thought, and responded with a grin of his own.

Chapter Three

Building No. 35 buzzed with life. Operators spoke into headsets, hands whirling. Cords slid in and out of jacks. Young men, not old enough to vote, hurried to scoop up messages from one basket and place them in another. Secretaries came and went from the war-room where the Fourth Army's top brass struggled with the news.

Lieutenant General John L. Wright turned around from a wall map of the Pacific Coast and said to all, "Where in the good name of Moses is the Japanese fleet?" Pearl Harbor was history, no time for "what ifs". His glare darted from one officer to the next.

"Reports of attacks on U.S. maritime ships," said a graying man with two silver stars on each shoulder, "put the enemy somewhere northeast of Hawaii."

"The entire fleet? How fast are they moving? What direction? Heading toward Alaska? Washington? California?"

The rapid-fired questions silenced the room for a moment. The Western Theater of Operations knew no more concerning the Japanese Imperial Navy's whereabouts now than it did before December seventh.

"Our latest intelligence lists San Diego as the most likely target. The Sixth Naval Division is…"

"I don't want suppositions," the lieutenant general barked. He circled the conference table, brushing the backs of the leather chairs. "We need hard data."

He left the murmurs behind and walked to the glass entry and studied the frenzy of activity in the adjoining room. Behind the tapping of typewriter keys, behind the clicking of heels, the cold stare of fear took hold. Without leaving the scene, he said, "Make no mistake, gentlemen, the fight is waiting outside our front door."

*   *   *

From the captain, orders were given in Japanese: "Prepare to surface. Answer bells on all engines."

From the second-in-command: "Preparing to surface. Securing ventilation. Shorting bulkhead flappers. Ready in all respects."

From the captain: "Surface."

Instead of rising on an even keel, the submarine aircraft carrier heeled over to starboard, acting heavy. The engineer sped to the port tank and shut it down, but she continued to roll. With luck the sailor spied a can of tuna jamming open a ballast vent, allowing seawater to continue to enter. He removed the obstacle with a wheel spanner. Air filled the trimming tank and the I-25 came up.

"Open the hatch," Commander Meiji Minoru ordered. "Open main induction. Lookouts to the bridge."

Once the diesels were turned on to charge batteries and provide running power, the command was given to redistribute all provisions along gangways as well as engine and control rooms. At the same moment a rush of sailors formed a human chain across the foredeck. Pontoons and struts rode the cradle of arms while a fuselage and its folded wings rolled along a catapult's track.

A team assembled the E14Y floatplane with expediency, but past failures worked on their collective psyche. Eight days prior the crew gazed with a helpless feeling as a parade of three hundred and fifty Zeros slung across the sky like arrows.

Whether it was mechanical or human error that forced the grounding of the sub's reconnaissance craft during the attack on Pearl, no one knew for sure. No matter, the damage had been done. Reports were filed and reprimands made, but new orders had arrived. The I-25 must not fail again.

Lieutenant Commander Minoru paced across the bridge. He glanced at his watch and yelled down, speaking in Japanese, "Airman, sunrise fast approaches."

Third Classman Nobuo Akita lurched up from the plane's engine and banged his head against the hood. "*Hai*, sir," and massaged his scalp before returning to his task. Amidst the tangle of wires and plugs and rods he cursed his fate as busy voices streamed behind him.

The commander spun around to the radio operator at his side. "Ensign, does radar report any American activity in the area?"

"None, sir."

"Keep me informed."

In his hurry to affix the stubborn propeller, the pilot sheared off a pushrod's bolt. "*Bonkura!*" His complaint disappeared beneath the pounding waves.

More requests rained down upon Nobuo. "An update on the repairs."

The grease-spotted head rose for a second time. He glared at the bridge, restraining his frustration as best he could, and called out, "The cam plate has come apart. In a monoplane's radial engine, sir, the pistons are connected to the crankshaft with a...."

"Inform the bridge," the commander interrupted in stilted voice, "as soon as the thing is fixed."

"Well, sir, technically it's not a *thing* but a seaplane or commonly referred to as a..."

"Airman, your craft awaits your attention."

"*Hai*, sir." The response was the best that could be offered. He bent over to retrieve the plate when a rogue wave slammed him to the deck. The engine part flew from his grasp, skittered across the platform and out of sight.

"Get back to work," a demand sounded.

"*Bonkura!*" With wrench in hand, Nobuo marched toward the conning tower, rambling in heated words along the way. His shoulders tilted backwards in such a way as to thrust his soft belly outward, a figure more suited for that of an accountant than a warring pilot.

Another's hand reached out to him. "You must bring your thoughts under submission."

Nobuo wrestled the sailor's arm away and ascended the ladder with his rage. Others ceased their activity, putting the conflict on hold, surprised by the barbarism that occupied this placid man. He drew within close quarters of his skipper, ready to fill the air between them with hellfire, when a cadet produced the missing cam plate.

"You have something you wish to say, Mister Akita?" Minoru asked as he viewed the engine part before him.

Nobuo fell quiet and excused himself with a salute as judgment followed him the entire length of his retreat.

"Like giving money to a cat." With little confidence that the recon mission would start on schedule, the captain descended the bridge and retired to his quarters. There he found the fixed presence of Admiral Yamamoto hanging on a wall.

"You have surrounded me with idiots and fools, but you do not deceive me. I will not be tossed about at your leisure within this menagerie of clowns. Our foe is plentiful, more than enough to share. Buddha will show the way."

*   *   *

The submarine came into the wind at twenty-four knots. A towbar from the nose of the floatplane hooked onto the track's shuttle. The engine roared to life. Nobuo strapped on his canvas-wool hat. The fuselage vibrated. The control panel shook, rpm's were at 4400, 4600, 5000. Nobuo, seeing trails of steam below, knew his fate waited but fifty meters away. Doubt filled his goggles as he brought to mind the uncertainty of his repairs. I must do this, he thought, and gave a thumbs-up. Holdbacks under the rear wheels slid away. Freed, the plane screamed down the rail. At the end of the runway, the E14Y dipped from view. The crew drew in sharp breaths until the plane reappeared above the deck line. All yelled a relief, cutting the stiff breeze with their fists.

Nobuo banked left and headed for Attu Island, the western most point of territorial America. He came to the mouth of a small inlet as a rising orange ball pushed the night aside. The tips of firs and pines began to glow as the new day expanded across the terrain.

He flipped on the switch to a mounted camera (a Doris 3x4), lowered his air speed and cruised over the harbor at Attu Station. Moored behind an earthen seawall, tidy rows of trawlers started to awaken with activity. Fishermen sorted out crab pots while others sat on slabs of stone with oil lanterns, mending nets sprawled before them.

Nobuo circled around, filming, searching for any hint of military presence. A thick mat of trees smothered a nearby ridge. Might conceal enemy fortifications, he thought, and crisscrossed the land, using the gray light to put a spot on possible roads or netted camouflage or artillery that might show themselves. None did and he proceeded toward Kiska. The morning went without event, flying from one end of the Aleutians to the other, until two hours later he started the return trip. At a speed of seventy knots, he climbed to eight thousand feet to avoid detection. Things appeared normal until he noticed a heaviness to the yoke. The wheel fought his steering. Ice covered the tips of both wings, and he slid his scrutiny to the temperature gauge.

"Fourteen degrees?" He checked the instrument panel and the artificial horizon indicator. "*Bonkura!*" Disoriented by banks of thunderheads, he had continued on a two-degree upward angle, confirming such with the vertical speed gauge and the altimeter. The E14Y was at nine thousand feet and rising. With both hands he muscled the yoke forward. The nose overreacted and went into a dive. The distant horizon spun clockwise. The ocean became indistinguishable from the sky. G-forces pinned his body against the seat. Cheeks flapped in the updraft's vortex. White caps came and went until the elevators responded and the aircraft leveled out, gliding no more than ten meters above the sea. One more revolution and he would've been fish-food.

Droplets formed on the raised pores of his skin. He leaned his head back and thanked the gods while his heart raced in rhythm with his beating breath. In a reflex move, after confirming that he had not departed for the Yasukuni Shrine, his hand stretched out to the dashboard. He felt around, but the photo of his Aiko was not there. *Where are you, my flower?*

The E14Y sat down upon the calm sea at the rendezvous point. The I-25 emerged from the depths and pulled alongside. Nobuo, after the ship's crane had hoisted him and his craft to the deck, directed the monoplane's dismantling. The sun glinted off different parts in a disquieting withdraw to the waterproof hangar. With a sense of desperation, the pilot rushed past Commander Minoru and went below.

The curious behavior caused the captain to move his head from side to side. "Only death can cure an idiot."

In his cabin Nobuo found the framed pic of his daughter, brought her close and said, "I will never leave you behind again." And he gaped upward, past the steel ribs, past the hull to the heavens. "Hachiman-shin, keeper of the majestic blue heron, I pray that you do not separate father and child." For he knew that such punishment would be the heaviest of burdens to bear. This worry had fastened itself due to a past indiscretion. Born out of wedlock, disgrace would consume his seven-year-old forever unless some rich discovery could be found.

He thought of the events of that morning, of his mission to film the Alaskan archipelago. His camera might be of value in his country's plans to invade the islands, a grand invasion to be certain. Airstrips would be built. Squadrons of Zeros would descend upon the lower forty-eight with their fury. Then his thoughts returned to the truth of the matter that today, albeit a day consumed with courage, was not sufficient in the least to honor his offspring.

His vision slid from the black-and-white to a four-hundred-year-old sword. Dragon fittings decorated its casing. He unsheathed the blade to admire its craftsmanship. The curved steel was flat to the middle ridge before tapering in a wavy, grainy pattern to a sharpened edge.

"What do you have to say for yourself? Does my child's fortune lie at your tip?" He thought of a second alternative and said, "Or perhaps it rests within the mystery of your inscription?"

Characters were embossed on the handle, reading: SEN ZORI. He pondered its meaning—*a thousand sandals*—as he had done many times before, but its significance escaped him.

Chapter Four

Anne boarded the #24 bus and dropped a nickel into the farebox. The driver cranked a handle and the coin clanged down a metal chute. Groggy from the early hour, the teenager ignored the civil servant's "thank you" and shuffled on, weaving her way between standing passengers until clamping onto an overhead rail. Her movements matched those of others who bobbed and bounced with the transit as it rocked along the uneven blacktop.

She surveyed the cargo, statues cemented to the 5:00 A.M. hour, pancaked in a lifeless heap. Many faces seemed familiar but they remained as strangers. Toward the rear a disheveled person sipped from a half pint of whiskey. A few rows closer, a trio of Japanese men sat with their lunch pails. Across the aisle a young couple leaned on each other. Anne pictured herself in the girl's spot, cuddling up to a boyfriend, and then shook the notion from her head. Don't go there, she thought. Don't torture yourself, and she slid her vision toward the front. Partially hidden behind a teamster-looking guy, sat a familiar figure with tobacco stains on his wrinkled white shirt. His milky pupils stared at the advertisements above, a place to put his vision as the blind often did. Still, she did not recognize the paunchy man until a black lab, sitting at his side, crept into her examination. Harry Mitchum was her parish's curator and a very accomplished man, as was his dog, Gaspar, according to available rumors. To see the pair at this time of the day struck her as odd, even more so was Mr. Mitchum's nonstop conversation with the bus driver, an overweight Negro who divided his time between road and companion.

The two debated many topics. Their talk drifted down the aisle disrupting the quiet. Riders stirred from their slumber and grumbled. As if to abate the storm, Mr. Mitchum unearthed a violin from a leather case. He tuned it and played Verdi's "La doma è Mobile" from Rigoletto. The melodic sound reminded Anne of the music with which he filled Mission Dolores Church on Sundays. Two elderly women in matching blue overalls surrendered an approval with a single clap while others drifted back into their sleep.

On the southern boundary of San Francisco's Japantown, they stopped at the request of a soldier who waved a flashlight in the middle of Geary Boulevard. Anne flexed over a lump of a person sitting beneath her and peered out the window to witness a helmet with the inscription MP. The same initials were visible on his armband.

With baton holstered, the trooper boarded and said, "Routine inspection, folks. No reason to be alarmed."

"*Routine?*" Anne said to the lump. "Men in military garb galloping around holding up traffic is not routine." A cynical laugh spilled from her lips onto the glassy-eyed commuter. "Unbelievable, as if we were living in some war-torn country."

The man adjusted a sweatshirt he used as a pillow, rolled away from the babbling and scrunched up in the fetal position. And then the obvious hit her—that *her* country, *her* city, was indeed at war. She hiked up her expression in an apology but found the lump's backside instead.

The MP examined her frame with thoroughness. Anne returned a glare as if a single gesture could resolve all the problems in the world. Embarrassment occupied him and he moved on. Midway down the aisle, the soldier came to a gray-haired Oriental who hugged a bundle wrapped in butcher paper.

"What's in the package?"

She fumbled out something in a foreign tongue as she brought her possession close to her chest.

"Let's see what you have there," the MP said.

"No see," and she crouched over her parcel.

The military policeman reached out. A tug-of-war ensued. The Oriental's protests achieved a higher octave as the struggle advanced. Not knowing why, Anne scurried to her aid.

"She's not the enemy," Anne said, but he wouldn't release his grip.

With a final pull, the MP wrestled the object away and began to peel at the layers of brown paper. In a rush he extracted the first item that met his touch. To his surprise a pair of woman's undies hung suspended between his pinching fingers. Behind a cackle of laughs, he returned the laundry to its owner.

"All right, all right," and he pressed down the air before him for the return of order.

He backpedaled in clumsy fashion and tripped over a sneaker. Halfway to the floor, he caught the chrome grip of a seat. An unsettled smile began to grow as he rose, dismissing the mishap with a throaty cough. He thanked everyone for their cooperation and dismounted in a hurry from the public transport.

The Oriental turned to her rescuer as the bus rolled forward. "Most grateful."

"You're welcome," Anne said while rebinding the package. "Who do they think they are? Why I've got a good mind to..." and halted herself at the presentation of a smile from the Japanese lady. "What?"

"You funny girl."

"Sounds like something my father would say. Just the other day he..."

"That good enough."

"Sorry, my mouth tends to go its own way sometimes. Please forgive my..."

"That good enough."

Silence accompanied them to the intersection of Fillmore and Bush where they started to disembark together when the driver said, "I apologize for the inconvenience, ladies."

"Wasn't your fault," Anne interjected.

"That voice…sounds familiar," Harry Mitchum said.

"It's Anne Klausen. I'm a fellow parishioner."

"Ah, of course, Elmer's daughter."

"Unfortunately."

"Well, it's certainly a pleasure to meet your acquaintance after all this time," the blindman said as he collected his black lab.

"I better go," Anne said.

"Stop by the church. I've heard favorable reviews regarding your dancing. You can find me out back by the cemetery."

"Sure," Anne said, sounding sincere. "Well, until then," and she nodded a goodbye before guiding the old lady down the steps.

On the sidewalk the woman bowed and said in broken English, "Nice to see you again," and muddled away in her sandals.

Anne studied the fading Oriental but no recollection of a previous encounter came to her. Accompanied by this curiosity, she departed down Bush toward her dance studio.

The main thoroughfare appeared deserted with the exception of those trudging home from the midnight shift at the S & H Sugar Refinery or the assembly line at Levi Strauss or perhaps from the monoliths along financial row. She passed others who walked with a fresher pace—an army of workers sent to the Capitalistic Front to clean windows, sew jeans and wash laundry of complete unknowns.

She turned onto Buchanan Street, the commercial heart of Japantown, or "Little Tokyo" as the locals referred to the neighborhood. This northern end of the Western Addition started to pulse with life. A diminutive man threw a bucket of water and started to mop the pavement behind her. Steam rose from vents. Smells of bean paste and melon-flavored pastries greeted her. Cream puffs, orange sponge cakes and sweet potato candies summoned, but she resisted the seduction and continued on past a series of sushi bars. Red, gold and green exteriors boasted imported sounding names such as Mikado and Massei-an and Kimigayo. Next, the Kinmon Press, the Nagaya Hotel, the Nippon Hospital, and the Soko Fish and Tackle Shop came and went.

Anne slowed in front of a news rack to speed-read the headlines: "U.S. Pacific Fleet Heavily Damaged"; "Eight Battleships Destroyed, 2400 Americans Killed". A shiver ran through her. Can't be, she told herself. The scent of all things sweet and delectable began to waver, but she would not let the truth of the day deter her.

She entered a brick two-story building and flew up a flight of stairs toward an office. A frosted glass entry framed the silhouettes of more than one man behind it. Anne leaned into the gold leaf lettering—MR. MERISHIO ITO / DANCE INSTRUCTOR—and listened for an explanation. Her body's weight eased-open the unlatched door.

The busyness halted with the sound of a brassy moan. At the sudden appearance of the teenager, several hands rushed to gather up maps, documents and other papers. Another man, dressed in a black pullover, threw a tarp over a piece of machinery with knobs and buttons and switches.

Instructor Ito hurried to escort Anne back out into the hall and said, "May I help you, my dear?"

"Well, yes." Anne hesitated, uncertain what meaning to attach to his abbreviated behavior. "Is my letter of recommendation ready? I need to postmark the application by Friday."

"Scholarship to Ballet Russe de Monte Carlo, correct? In Los Angeles?" he said. "Very busy right now. You come back other time."

"But I…"

And he disappeared behind his title.

Frustrated, Anne retreated down the staircase to the exit. She found herself shuffling forward, kicking a discarded soda can, when a jumble of noise puffed up from where she had just left.

The person in black appeared from the studio's entrance with cardboard boxes in his arms. Others followed with similar freight as they hastened toward the rear of a delivery truck. Anne slipped to the cover of a nearby alley.

The men, probably eight in all, rushed about, casting quick glances here and there. With finality, the doors of the truck and two sedans slammed shut in a chorus of metal thuds. Anne hid within the shadows until the caravan vanished down Post.

She stepped from the passageway and retraced her path to the brick edifice. A sign hung on a window—"Closed Until Further Notice". Anne poked at the doorbell, yelled, but no one answered. She slapped at the bolted entry, waited and banged some more. Confused, she trudged away.

At a nearby bakery, a rare treat of hot chocolate and pastry were lost on her as she gawked out the window at wiggly washes of reflected light upon the fog-dampened street. Gobbledygook crowded her mind as if she required some sort of activity to set a proper pace to the day. With a pressing migraine, she left and made her way to a bus and boarded.

Thirty minutes later she landed at her usual stop in the Mission District and walked without purpose up Sixteenth past Guerrero Street where frenzied activity punctuated the emerging morning. Children and adults, walking at different paces, carried various objects to the patio area of the Columbia Park Boys Club. Books, tires, camp stoves, hot-water bottles, magazines, splints, cots and jarred jams/jellies jostled from one volunteer to the next. Absorbed by the uncertainty of Mr. Ito's availability, by the scholarship's deadline, Anne felt disengaged from the patriotic scene before her and moved on.

She made it to her high school an hour early, surprised to see a neat line of Oriental students forming at the east entrance to the girls' gym. Anne spotted a familiar face or so she thought. The girl stood five-foot-six, towering above the rest, and wore raven hair, a white cotton blouse and a plaid skirt. Where had Anne seen her before? She didn't share any classes with her.

Perhaps away from the campus, perhaps in Little Tokyo.   Not
satisfied with the answer, Anne approached.

"Hi, my name is Anne Klausen. Haven't I seen you down
in…"

"I know who you are," the raven-head interrupted. There
was no trace of an accent, her English as pure as Anne's.

"You know me?" Anne said and thought of her run-in just
over an hour previous with another who spouted more or less the
same. This coincidence pushed her to want to know more, but the
arrival of the vice principal halted the conversation.

Miss Threadgood, an old biddy of an administrator, put up
a wall of authority. "You have no business here, Miss
Klausen. This is a restricted area." With a Cheshire-cat-smile,
the V.P. hurried the senior elsewhere before swiveling around to
utter a series of commands to the string of Orientals.

"Everyone move along into the gym.   Chop, chop,"
clapping with a drill sergeant's beat.

*   *   *

A uniformed young man entered the last period government
class and said to the instructor, "Whaddya got to say for yourself,
Mr. Piner?"

Mr. Piner was a gentleman in his late sixties with a
scholarly presence, sporting a burgundy bowtie, a woolen double-
breasted waistcoat with pocket watch, and wiry untamed silver
hair. "Ah, hello." Unable to place the person, he said, "I'm sorry,
who are you?"

"Sean McGinnis. You gotta remember me—good with the
ladies, class of thirty-eight."

Not the brightest of pupils as the teacher recalled, quite
forgettable in fact with the exception of his red mop of hair, and
pointed with recognition, saying, "Curly, right?"

"Not right." Irritation laced the visitor's voice. "Sean
McGinnis, like I said before."

"Well, thank you for that, I suppose," Mr. Piner said and then remembered. "Miss Threadgood did say that a civil servant would be dropping by today to speak to the class."

"Bingo," and without waiting for an introduction, the Block Warden addressed the students. "Here's your I.D. from Civil Defense," and he held up a two-inch square laminated sample. "If an invasion's comin', you wouldn't wanna be confused with all these Nips runnin' around."

He handed a batch of the tags to Mr. Piner before returning to the seniors with another command. "Post these flyers around the neighborhood." He began to pass out leaflets to the first person in each row, saying, "Gotta know your air raid procedures."

Yellow handbills made their way toward the back. A hum filtered from one seat to the next. Heads whirled right, left.

Mr. Piner, after seeing the concern, left his desk. He viewed one of the circulars and said in a mild fashion, "Actually, students, these suggestions make perfectly good sense— *stay home, put out lights, lie down, stay away from windows, and don't use the telephone*." His professorial style intellectualized the subject in an attempt to collect any runaway emotions. "There is no need for panic at this juncture. Isn't that true, Mr...," and he turned around to see an oval mound of freckles hiding behind a gas mask.

The Block Warden appeared as some giant insect with compound eyes. He swirled a clacker by its handle. Loud clicks filled the room.

"If you hear this sound," he said between clumps of oxygen, "go to a high ...and crouch. Cover your ... with a wet towel. If tap water isn't ..., use urine."

The seniors looked to their teacher for translation. He stared at the oddity and said, "Mr. McGinnis, take off that silly thing," and circled his fingers at the redhead to hurry him up.

The guest speaker did as he was told while motioning toward his former instructor as if to include him in his next segment. "Mr. Piner here was in the last war. Used to talk about his experiences over in France."

"Well, I've always felt that personal events help to enliven the…"

"Told of those nasty gas attacks, too. Ain't that right?"

"As a matter of fact, I do remember the Argonne Forest where…"

"*Where green clouds swallowed one whole,*" the Block Warden interrupted, finishing the teacher's thought. "Think that's how you put it."

"My memory is vague but…"

"*Breathing in the poison as you tried to run, only to stir up the deadly chemicals even more.*" His hands twitched, as might a storyteller's.

"I don't think we need to…"

"*The stomach erupted, pushing up intestines, bile, and all matter of foul stuff.*"

Winces and grimaces showed while squeals erupted from different corners of the room.

"Mr. McGinnis, that will be quite enough."

"*The victim gasped for his last bit of air before…*"

"Curly!" Mr. Piner's palm slapped flat upon his desk before he stepped forward to show the exit.

"World is coming to an end," the Block Warden shouted back over an ushering arm.

The instructor, after shutting the door, felt compelled to address the ugly truth. "War is abominable, boys and girls. There is no denying. However, there is no sense in promoting exaggeration for its own sake. No good can come from such…"

A raised hand beckoned him. Somewhat annoyed, he ceased his lecture and said, "Yes, Miss Klausen."

The pupil slid out from under her desk to a standing position. "Why have the Japanese students been restricted to the east gym?"

"You are no longer permitted to mingle with them. Anyone found doing so will answer to Miss Threadgood directly. Is that understood?"

"Sir," Anne said, "that's not an answer."

"That will be quite enough. Sit down," and he went on to other matters, reminding all that the military would be taking over the auto and wood shops from three P.M. until dawn, that such areas would be off-limits as well.

He further stated that time was short, that their services would soon be requested, some as volunteers, others as soldiers. His voice was cheerless and sober, suggesting a suppressed urgency. He switched to his teacher's voice and told everyone to open their texts, but the focus of the seniors remained scattered. Questions skittered about; order began to leave the room.

Anne stepped to the second floor window and was stuck there for several minutes, her stare following the wind-dance of palm trees along the Dolores Street divider. A group of Orientals appeared below, walking two abreast down the sidewalk. Miss Threadgood with her Cheshire-cat-smile led the procession while a black-and-white followed at a discreet distance. The girl from that morning shuffled along in the middle of the pack, her head bowed in obedience. The melancholy scene unsettled Anne as she watched the bunch steer down Seventeenth.

"Miss Klausen, return to your seat. Miss Klausen?"

Chapter Five

Anne glanced at the clock on the nightstand and rolled back over. Entangled in sheets, she squirmed and tossed and kicked, dragging the covers with her. Wired tight, she sat up and threw her legs over the side of the bed. She found a lamp's chain and made her way past fuzzy fixtures to the bathroom. Matted hair and dark circles goggled back from a walled mirror. Frothy curls of toothpaste soon framed her mouth. No pronouncement pushed forth to describe the image before her, nor did she seek any as she carried on with her morning ritual.

At around 4:00 A.M. Anne met the newspaper boy at the top of Dolores Heights. The Schwinn's handlebars held onto two canvas bags. On the outside of each was inscribed SAN FRANCISCO CHRONICLE. Billy was thirteen, she guessed, with an outsized smile that was easy to accept, a nice way to start the day. But as she walked closer, his drained features drew in her concern.

"What is it, Billy?"

Embarrassed, the youth straightened up and attempted to put on a cheerier arrangement but failed.

"Nothing so sacred you can't tell me," Anne said. "After all, I'm your best customer, right?"

Billy came back around. "Couple of the guys…and I volunteer as messengers for Western Union…part of the…War Production Training Program." His speech cracked under the weight of the thought to come, but he fought off the fright inside and continued: "You know Mr. Jones, lives down on Eighteenth?"

"Sure. Hank Jones. He's one of my dad's militia buddies. Well, not really a buddy. In fact he and my dad are kind of..."

"The return address on the telegram was from the War Department. Only one kind of news comes from there, and it isn't the good kind. Anyways, Mr. Jones answered the door, eyed my uniform and went back inside. Never even bothered to ask what was in the letter. Must've known, though. I slipped the telegram into the mail slot and left. Felt like I was death's delivery boy. It's been almost a week. Can't sleep." His hands moved back and forth over the handlebars.

Anne paused for a moment before saying, "Maybe a cup of hot cocoa would taste good. Come inside?" and pointed back toward the house.

"Thanks, but I'm running late."

"Are you positive?"

He slid his head up and down as if that was all the energy he could spare.

An alternative popped into Anne. "Don't go anywhere, wait right here," and she quick-stepped back along the driveway to the trunk of the Chevy.

A moment later, Anne returned, saying, "Take it," and handed him a walkie-talkie. "My dad won't miss it. Besides, this way we can keep in touch."

"Thanks."

"Radio me anytime. I'll keep the other one in my duffle bag."

He repeated his appreciation and pedaled off.

Anne didn't think it right that someone Billy's age should be exposed to war's raw side. Her thoughts kept her there until the Schwinn disappeared around the corner.

Back inside, the coffeemaker flashed a red light. She poured herself a cup and walked to the Formica table with the *Chronicle*. In the background the pot hissed as she inspected the obituary column, which listed sailors aboard the U.S.S. *San Francisco* who had perished at Pearl. An index finger ran down the Joneses—eight. To her surprise, the names of others continued onto the next page. Can't be. Her disbelief fell from the periodical and followed a beam of light, which had found its way through the divided curtains. It took her emptiness across the linoleum to the entryway where a muted scraping noise traveled down the hallway.

Her father scuffled into the kitchen, selected a section of the daily and dropped into a wooden chair. He nudged his wire rims up the bridge of his nose. Pasty lips smacked as he leafed through the comics, oblivious to his daughter's presence.

"And good morning to you," Anne said.

He responded with a grunt.

"Did Hank Jones have a son in the war?"

"Arnold, I believe. An only child." The paper crinkled as he creased it in half to better focus on his favorite cartoon strip.

Anne didn't think the name *Arnold* Jones was amongst the listed casualties. Maybe he met his demise elsewhere, she thought, and said in a spurt, "I think he was killed."

He lowered the comics.

"Billy delivered a telegram to Mr. Jones's house the other day from the War Department," she said.

"Could be something else."

"Billy didn't think so."

"Billy's just half grown," and he lifted the periodical back up.

"Blondie" coaxed a grin from his countenance. Anne thought it outrageous that a cartoon character should capture a place of higher priority than the death of a fellow Gray's child.

"I thought you might show at least a smidgen of humanity."

"For Jones?" he said behind the paper. "Not worth it."

"What's that suppose to mean?"

He lowered the comics. "You were too young to remember, but Hank Jones never went to your mother's funeral, never even paid his respects."

"Why do grown men hang onto the useless fodder of the past? Let it go."

"Like those childhood fantasies you drag around with you?"

"You've got some nerve judging me when your own life is out of whack."

"Never pretended it wasn't." After putting some thought into her statement, he peeked above the rim of his glasses and said, "What're you referrin' to?"

"I intercepted a letter from your employers yesterday."

"No one gave ya the right to open my..."

"There was a severance check inside," and she waved the document before him.

"Keep it. Not worth much," and he snapped "Blondie" back to his attention.

"You said that you quit Acme Brewery to join the war effort, to help with the cause. What a sanctimonious fraud."

"Thought the first part made for a better story," he said with disinterest.

"You were probably caught drinking the company profits. That would be my guess."

No response.

"Now who's going to pay the bills?"

"There're jobs to be had down at Bethlehem Steel. You could work there," he suggested, alternating between flat speech and reading, pupils sliding up and down. "The textile factories always need people. Maybe ya could learn how to sew."

She exhaled her frustration, snatched up the comics from his grasp and stormed out of the kitchen.

"Hey."

Within the stillness that followed, he thought that perhaps she was right regarding Jones's son. Decent sort, from what he could remember of the kid. Have to stop calling them *kids*, he told himself. *Kids* don't sail off to lay down their lives for freedom. Only *men* could bring life to such clichés. He started a silent prayer but surmised that such wouldn't count for much coming from the mouth of an atheist, and he picked up the sports section.

*　　*　　*

Distracted, Anne collapsed onto her bed. She traced the cracks along the ceiling when a crunching noise sounded beneath her. With some effort she freed the newspaper. A thinly clad Blondie grabbed onto her curiosity. The character, after Anne had flattened out the comics, appeared as a flapper girl. Typical, she thought, liquor and cheap women, all he's ever known.

"What a minute," and she studied the cartoon closer. "*Liquor and cheap women*. Of course," and bolted up with a promising idea.

*　　*　　*

The ring of the doorbell brought Elmer out of his seat. He glanced at his watch—5:00 A.M.—and went to investigate. Through the peephole he spotted a familiar burgundy panel truck in the driveway.

"This a social call?" Elmer asked after opening the front door. "Got no booze in the house."

"I don't require such at this early hour," Fredericks said. "We are present on the government's time," and he gestured with his raised thumb back toward a black nondescript sedan. "The Fed wishes an audience with you and the little one."

Lieutenant Hank Jones stepped to the entrance and ran through a prelude of sorts, meticulous in every gesture as if rehearsed a thousand times. He fingered a brass button of his militia uniform and straightened his lapels before saying, "Yeah, ask…ask some questions."

The Gray's torchbearer turned to his subordinate. "Did I not just say that?"

"Not directly. Mou-mouthed something about an audience."

"Oh, for the glory of God."

Elmer thought to inquire regarding Jones's son, but the disharmony before him promoted an awkwardness that might be

39

difficult to navigate. An official looking person approached, owning salt-and-pepper hair, cropped tight under a narrow brimmed fedora. He wore a Sears and Roebuck suit with a button-down white shirt and black tie.

"I'm Agent Harris," and he showed his badge. "Mind if we continue this discussion inside?"

Elmer showed all to the living room where he scooped up beer bottles, cigar butts and candy wrappers. "Sorry 'bout the mess. Must be the maid's day off," he said without a chuckle.

"Is your daughter home?" the agent asked.

"Where else would she be at five in the mornin'?"

"I'd like to speak with her."

The teenager overheard the request from her bedroom and came down the hall and sat on the ottoman in front of the chair that occupied her dad. She scanned the federal man to size him up. He had a long face, rich in seams as though carved from an ancient rock. His frame barely filled out his cheap wardrobe. There was no waste of body fat, lean and fit for his length.

"Ma'am, did you know a Merishio Ito?" Harris asked, his eyes stone still.

His straightforward approach caught her by surprise. Under his no nonsense stare, her throat constricted, her voice began to buckle.

"I did. I mean, I do. Why?"

"Did Mr. Ito run an establishment, a dance studio to be more precise, at 1211 Buchanan Street down in Japantown?"

"Yes, he still does, but what..."

"And did he work there for the last ten years?"

"Now just a minute," interrupted the father. "Is my daughter in some kind of trouble?"

"Just following up on a few inquiries."

The father, however, had a different bent on how things were progressing and left his chair and stood beside his daughter. "What's going on here?"

"We have reason to believe that your child's instructor is working with the Black Dragon Society." The agent paused before saying, "He's a spy."

Anne blanched. The animated frames of *Blue Bolt Comics* flashed up before her with heroes battling atomic cyclotrons and espionage rings. But this was the real world, as her dad was fond of reminding her, and she said in surprise, "That's not possible. He's a professional. He was gathering this consortium in support of the arts." With a stunned expression, she added, "They were going to sponsor me for a scholarship."

The Fed handed over his card in case Mr. Ito should try to contact either of them before turning to the two Grays. "Thanks for your help."

"At your favor, sir," Fredericks responded with a patronizing grin. "I can assure you that the Republican Grays are willing to accommodate any..."

Agent Harris halted the rambling with a goodbye, tapped his fedora and exited. Fredericks squawked at the space where the FBI once stood, plucked a walnut from a nearby decorative dish and addressed his sergeant.

"Mister Klausen," the militia chief said while peeling the shell, "one might debate your loyalties under such circumstances."

"Yeah, where are your loy-loyalties?" Jones mimicked.

"May I continue?"

"Well, ge-get on with it."

Fredericks faltered. "Where was I?"

"*One might debate,*" Jones interjected with delight.

"It was a rhetorical question. You are familiar with the term, aren't you?"

"All right, enough," Elmer said. "Outta my house."

Upon crossing the threshold, the major turned around and said, "Careful, Klausen. Your tone smacks of insubor...," and the door slammed shut.

Elmer flung his fury here and there, all around the living room. "Shit for brains...Cow pie inhaling twits..."

"I never cared for those two either," Anne contributed. "There's something not right in their heads."

He studied her attempt at forming some sort of alliance and then remembered the FBI's accusation regarding her instructor and said, "You're never to set foot on another stage while livin' under this roof, understood?"

"I can find another roof easy enough," and she tramped down the hallway.

"Time ya grew up," he called out to her, "and tossed out those dancing slippers and fufus."

"They're *tutus*," she yelled without turning back around.

The hormonal shifts of a teenager had forever eluded his understanding. With his specs removed, the father lowered his head to his fingers and massaged a dull pain. He'd encountered Germans hand-to-hand, worked a sixty-hour week, and dealt with pickax-wielding strikebreakers but never experienced a greater challenge than the raising of a daughter. His contemplation shifted to the heavens above, and he ordered, in no uncertain terms, for his wife to return.

*   *   *

On her way to catch a bus, Anne came across Billy hanging around with three other newspaper boys at the corner of Eighteenth and Church. She sang out a hello as she swung past the collection, but no greeting was returned when she spotted the source of their absorption. Above the street sign perched a special moniker with the name ARNOLD B. JONES. Anne had seen other such plaques before as part of the "Gold Star Marker" program to honor the City's bravest. She strode off thinking that the conflict had stolen another life and made a mental note to express her sympathies at some later juncture. Yet the *when* of such a consideration might prove difficult considering the delicacy of her father's relationship with the elder Jones.

She continued her walk and noticed, perhaps for the first time, the number of flags that hung from neighboring windows—

foot-long rectangular silk banners of white, framed in a red band with a star stitched to its middle. The Sullivan's place honored such a tradition, flying a standard with three Blue Stars (number of household members in armed services). The Cunningham's showed a lone Gold Star (household member killed in action), as did Jones's.

In a daze she lumbered past her bus stop and continued until the hectic comings and goings of Market Street snapped her back. She boarded a streetcar, but the sadness of that morning soon reappeared. She was sitting there with her wanderings when the seam of her duffle bag rubbed against her leg. With a remembrance, Anne snatched it up. She fingered through the pack and lifted a black rectangular instrument to her mouth and pressed down on a button.

"Billy, this is your best customer. Come in."

Static was the lone response. She tried again with no luck and let the radio fall into her lap.

"Excuse me," a young woman said from the aisle.

With her engrossment on the walkie-talkie, Anne didn't answer.

"Excuse me," the lady repeated, tapping Anne on the shoulder. "I hate to bother you but I left my purse here somewhere," and she searched with her roaming eyes.

Anne slid her weight forward and pivoted backwards on one arm, extending the other along the divide of the seat. "Here it is."

"Thank you."

The female's youthful impression, champagne hair and generous application of makeup caused Anne to blink. It's Blondie, the cartoon character. Aware of her day's purpose, she pulled on the cord.

Chapter Six

There were many stories as to how the area known as the Tenderloin received its name. One version referred to the district as the "soft-underbelly" of the City, with allusions to vice, corruption and graft. Another relayed the rumor that cops received "hazard pay" for working these streets, thus able to afford a good cut of meat. And yet a third noted that the name held connotations to specific body parts of a prostitute. Whichever story one preferred, the neighborhood's rough and tumble reputation could not be denied.

*   *   *

Buildings butted up against one another in a running canyon of brick. Laundry of different shapes and colors decorated outdoor railings, swaying in the breeze like flags of state. Anne adjusted her bag and advanced up O'Farrell. She passed the Blue Duck Hotel where a sign dangled between sunburnt curtains— "For men only / Transients welcomed". In the lobby soldiers slept on cots and tattered couches. Feet crossed each other, propped up on a windowsill or a coffee table. Most hotels ascribed to Mayor Rossi's request to provide additional sleeping space for the boys in uniform. Even the yawning Cow Palace housed men in the main arena where bovine had once been quartered. Now two troopers per stall was the order. No quota regarding the number of fleas.

Three buildings down, more drifters than players crowded Al's Billiards. A couple of gents sat on stools within the hanging smoke. Next door a billboard advertised games of a different sort: TEXAS HOLD'EM, OMAHA HOLD'EM, STUD AND DRAW POKER. A bare bulb illuminated its entrance where a water-stained wall hid the activity that lurked behind. Further up the lane, Anne peered inside a five-cent beer hall. Customers showed little emotion while babying their drinks. Within another doorway, she caught the slant of a slinky dressed figure. A blouse dipped halfway down ample cleavage while black hosiery decorated meaty legs. With red spilling over the outline of her lips, the woman sent a soft greeting to Anne.

At the Larkin Street intersection, the sun made an appearance to provide a respite from the rolling shadows. Bundles of blankets and debris snagged onto Anne's peripherals, and she peeked sideways to the concave entrance of a closed factory. An untied pink sneaker slipped out from under a moving mound of discarded nothings. Did the war sculpt such tragedy or was the normal chaos of the everyday world the culprit? Before an answer could arrive, the shoe withdrew like a recoiling serpent.

Anne passed an all-night diner and proceeded to the grandest structure in the Tenderloin. Blanco's had been an infamous brothel dating back to the Barbary Coast days until Rose McNally acquired the property five years ago. Of the dozen or so burlesque theaters in the City, the Music Box was by far the most popular.

The teenager entered, placed her carryall upon the foyer's marble floor and approached a display case. A photo of movie producer Cecil B. DeMille enticed Anne's inspection. She remembered her father's story of how the tinsel-town icon had given Rose her stage name, inspired by the Rand McNally Atlas. Probably got the label, Anne thought, because of all the miles she's put on her back. Slut. The term sounded bitter even to her. Nevertheless, what was she to think now that the striptease artist's latest conquest was her father?

She sidestepped to a poster, which advertised the 1934 film, *Bolero*, starring George Raft, Carol Lombard and a svelte Rose McNally. Next, she regarded a newspaper clipping of the dancer riding nude on a white horse down a crowded street during the Chicago World's Fair. She read aloud the headline: "The Trotting Trollop," and then she added, "Seems about right."

"Right indeed," a voice repeated from near the entrance. "Unfortunately, the judge dismissed the charges for indecent exposure."

Startled, Anne spun around. "Miss McNally, I didn't know anyone else was here," and she remembered pouring over the risqué pictures. "Just curious."

"Perfectly all right, dear." The wrinkled folds of her dress and her tattered appearance spoke of someone who had just concluded the last leg of an all-nighter. "If it wasn't for curiosity, I'd have been out on the streets a long time ago."

From the woman's sagging shoulders, a fox hung with its glass pupils in a fixed stare. A leopard print evening dress belled out from nylon-veiled calves while a peacock-feathered hat held down a mass of untamed curls. Bears more resemblance to a stampede at a circus than a movie star, Anne thought.

An earlier part of the conversation resurfaced and Anne asked, "You were *sorry* that the charges for indecent exposure were dropped?"

"You bet. The tabloids robbed me of my destiny. I was to ride the rags of gossip right to the top of the burlesque heap. Pleaded my guilt before the honorable Arthur Williamson the Third. I suspect he desired an abrupt ending of the scandal before any unwanted publicity came knockin' on his own door. Never did resume my courtship with the judge after that. We're still acquaintances, though. Never know when a girl's gonna need a favor," she said with a smile.

"Haven't heard of anyone trying to break *into* jail."

"Sweetheart, nothin' translates faster into cash like good old fashion smut." Miss McNally peered into her reflection upon the glass case. "Oh my," and started to pin back her sagging ringlets. "Heard from my sources that your dance studio folded."

"Another casualty of the times, I'm afraid," Anne said. "My dad's been incorrigible, gloating over the prospect that he won't have to support such *silliness* any longer, as he likes to put it."

"Listen," the owner said, her eyes shifting to Anne's image next to hers on the glass, "we girls gotta stick together. Otherwise, these men will get the notion that *silliness* has no place in this world."

"Well, that's kind of why I came," Anne said in a meek voice.

In anticipation of more to come and exasperated with her cleanup efforts, Miss McNally turned back around and said, "What can I do for ya?"

*   *   *

Tables dotted the main floor in cabaret style while more intimate seating lined the horseshoe balcony. Workers poured from the kitchen with white linen and candles in hand. Performers, arriving late, received the usual scolding from their boss before scurrying to various changing rooms. Musicians lugged equipment and odd shaped cases and began setting up while a single patron took his customary seat, coming early to parlay with the ladies.

"Got these Nips running all over like they own the place," Lieutenant General Wright said to Rose.

The owner tipped an aperitif to her painted lips, leaving her imprint upon the flute. "Ya get a little crotchety when you're runnin' on empty. Have some food. Got an excellent chef. He'll cook you somethin' straightaway."

The offering went unnoticed, his mind abuzz. "Damn Japs. Can't tell 'em apart. Good guys, bad guys—all look the same. What's worse is Washington's got my hands hogtied. If I had it my way, I'd clear out Little Tokyo and send those mongrels packing." His bourbon sat suspended in mid space as if his thought had stalled. "Damn Japs."

A middle-aged woman, with a tight mouth and a hawkish stare, overheard the indignity and stole the last sip from his grasp.

"What the…? Can't a guy finish his drink around here?"

Rose peered up at the waitress, not paying any attention to the lieutenant general's complaint, and said, "Number Two, use the wildflower bouquets instead of the violets." Then another detail came to her. "And go backstage and tell the girls it's time for rehearsal."

For simplicity's sake, a numerical digit designated each alien employee. Numbers One, Two and Three were Japanese. Numbers Four and Five were Chinese. Rose waited until Number Two had stepped to a discreet distance away and punched Wright's shoulder.

"What's that for?"

"Most of my Orientals are genuine U.S. citizens. I'll not have you disrespectin' them with your *Japs this* and *Japs that*. Got it, soldier boy?"

Wright searched for his hat as if to leave when a spotlight captured a sexy Miss Dirty Martini on stage. A sequined gown hugged her curves while two ostrich fans tagged along. Intrigued, the lieutenant general calmed himself as Glen Miller's "I'm in the Mood" ascended from the orchestra pit. Three-foot-long feathers crisscrossed the dancer's carriage as she traipsed across the platform, but her uneven gait caused Rose to rise to her feet.

"No, no, no. The fans, darlin', move 'em as if they are one with the music." The owner instructed the band to restart with a four-four beat and demonstrated her intentions, moving with a fluidness that belied her forty-year-old frame.

Dirty Martini asked a few more questions in order to get it right. Why wouldn't she? Immortalized by her employer, the fan dance had to be done with perfection. Anything less would be disrespectful to Miss McNally's legacy, to the Music Box's.

"Start from the top," Rose demanded.

Partway through the session, the performer slipped behind a translucent screen. Her black silhouette danced upon the see-through curtain. Articles of clothing flew from her body. She slid to the front as ostrich feathers fanned over her in seduction. Wright stole a fleeting glimpse of a hip, a breast and, as the entertainer swiveled around, a pair of melon-shaped cheeks.

Rose noticed the commander's sappy demeanor and said, "Close your mouth before ya let the flies in."

He gave her that give-me-a-little-respect glare. She rebutted with a snicker, as if she could care less and left to tend to other business.

*   *   *

Rose marched into the kitchen and called out, "Number One?" A ball of activity smothered her request. With fingers forming a reed to her mouth, she whistled like a teamster to a cluster of employees. "Anyone seen Number One?"

"No see," replied Number Four. Reports of the Japanese massacre upon his native Nanking were hard to let go—the killing of 300,000 fellow Chinese, the rape of 80,000 women. "No care for Number One."

Over the popping of grease and the rattling of pots, the boss said, "Customers are waitin' on their orders. Got no time for settlin' international disputes, savvy?"

"Savvy, but no need Number One." Number Four turned away and sputtered something in Cantonese to Number Five when someone entered through the swinging door.

"Number One," Rose said, "where ya been?"

Number Four interrupted before One could reply, saying, "He no in kitchen, that for sure."

"Then how anything get done in here?" Number One retorted. "Chinese give little. Everyone know that."

Four picked up a ladle. "I give you this," and stuck the utensil against the nose of One.

"All right," Rose said, "enough already. No reason to bring the fight indoors." She separated the different Oriental factions, but Number One didn't possess the patience to put up with any further nonsense and fled.

"Get back here," Rose called out, but he was gone. She turned around, glared at Four and put her hands on her hips. "See what ya did?"

"I cook for you," he said with a broad smile, the ladle still stuck in the air.

"That spoon ain't gonna do much good up there."

A quizzical look crinkled his brow until he widened with recognition and said, "I understand," and lowered the ladle along with a bow.

In the hallway, foreign sounding words were tossed all about. Anne left her cubicle to investigate and discovered that one of the persons was the Japanese girl from school. The two teens stared at each other, startled by the other's presence in such a place until Anne said hello.

No response.

"You never told me your name," Anne continued.

An older woman, standing behind the silence, encouraged the adolescent forward with a nudge.

A protest and, "My name is Mishi."

"I didn't expect to see you here," Anne said.

"No, I suppose not."

Another poke came from the rear. Mishi pivoted around to the annoyance and whispered something in a harsh way before returning to Anne. "This is my mother, Sato Ishigawa."

"Haven't we met before?" Anne asked.

"You help on bus."

"Right," responded Anne. "It's nice to meet you again, for the first time." Another thought came to her. "You implied that you knew me before but when?"

"See you in here short time ago…with Mr. Klausen when he…when he…"

"When he was fooling around with Miss McNally?" Anne offered. "Not to worry, his reputation travels with him wherever he goes."

A third nudge came to Mishi, but this time from her right. "And this is my father, Hajime Ishigawa."

With hands stiff at his side, he was full of deportment. "Correction. I am Number One, head chef. Wife is Number Two. Daughter is Number Three. You no talk to Numbers Four and Five. They Chinese. Thank you very much."

"Daddy, we go to school together," and the daughter flashed these big eyes as if he wasn't fooling anyone.

Anne didn't understand the need for the Ishigawas to hide behind numbers, admitting that it might take time to adjust to the new order of things.

"We proud to be under employment of Miss McNally," One countered with a knowing. "She very wise person. Numbers have purpose."

His broken English betrayed his status. He and his wife were nationals or "Isseis", immigrants born in Japan and ineligible for U.S. citizenship. The daughter was a "Nisei" or American born and a legal citizen.

"We might be working together," Anne said to all. "At least I hope so. I'm auditioning today."

"You dancer?" Sato asked with a suspicious glare.

"I am a ballerina, or was. It's a long story."

"Ballerina honorable job," Hajime said before his wife could offer an objection and led her away to let the girls get acquainted.

And they did. Mishi asked questions pertaining to ballet; Anne about the Orientals' restriction to the east gym at school. They discussed trivial matters as well, sharing their favorite pop chart hits. Billie Holliday's "God Bless the Child" spilled from lips within the same breath.

They pranced past a makeshift row of cubicles until coming to one with the letter ᴅ posted above a curtained entrance. A single vanity with a couple of chairs and a coat locker was all the furniture the dressing room could accommodate.

"How did you come by the audition?" Mishi asked.

"Evidently, a performer by the name of Alexis sustained a serious injury, opening up a slot."

"That's not the whole of it."

"What do you mean?"

"Well, according to my reliable sources," Mishi said, smiling, loosening up, "Alexis violated one of the establishment's most sacred tenets." She fell silent to squeeze out as much drama as possible.

"Yes?" Anne said with a prying gesture, impatient.

"I don't know if I should say anymore."

"You tease, you're awful."

"Well, all right, but you have to promise not to tell anyone."

"For heaven's sake."

Mishi folded her arms and shot a stare.

"I promise. Satisfied?"

Mishi made sure that the curtain was drawn and then whispered, "Alexis dated a couple of the regulars."

"Customers?"

"Well, not just any customers—the lieutenant general and the chief of police."

"Commander Wright? Chief Delaney?" Anne said with shock.

"Shhh." Mishi peered back as if expecting the local constable to march in. "Keep your voice lowered."

Anne signaled her agreement before exchanging a playful laugh as if they had been friends forever. Mishi chewed on an offering of black licorice while Anne struggled with her bobby socks. The cotton fabric slid off of tender feet. Purple and mustard colored contusions appeared alongside knobby toes, which swelled up red like raw meat.

"That's some kind of ugly," Mishi said as she pointed with her ropy treat to the discolored hoofs.

"Could be worse, I suppose. They could be attached to my rear-end. I guess that's something."

"How can you dance on those things?"

"Only feet I've got. They'll have to do."

"So you're in denial."

"Denial isn't so bad, helps wiggle the truth into alignment," Anne said as she wrapped white, medical tape in a figure-eight pattern from the ball of her foot to above the ankle. She laced up her slippers and hiked onto her toes for a test.

Mishi took on an admiration. Couldn't do that, she surmised, and said, "You are one tough broad."

Anne returned a soft smile before kneeling to her bag in search of sheet music, something to offer the musicians, when she remembered leaving her favorite piece on the kitchen table at home. Damn.

*   *   *

Lights dimmed to cast the performer in a hazy outline. Tchaikovsky's *Swan Lake* had become part of her, as natural as riding a two-wheeler. Without musical accompaniment, she floated across the stage, hovering a breath above the hardwood. Imprinted on the scales of her mind, melodic notes took her on a journey.

The languid entertainer broke into a *pas de chats*. Rose nodded her approval, but the lieutenant general couldn't see the point of having such highbrow entertainment at the joint. Not what the men wanted, he said. Rose, entranced by the artistry before her, hushed him, told him to have another drink.

"The boys'll boo her and your precious strip club right out of town."

"This ain't no strip club. This here's a bona fide theater of burlesque."

He waved off the notion, got up and sauntered toward the exit.

Anne, after the completion of her audition, bounded down and hurried over to the vacated seat and said to Rose, "What did you think?"

"Very classy. Reminds me of myself when I was your age. Studied ballet back in Kansas City. Never was as good as you, but the training helped me land a job as an acrobat with Ringling Brothers."

Anne smiled, waiting.

"However, my irked friend might have a point. Servicemen want more...," and she fluttered her hands like a wizard in search of the right word, "...*skin*." She cocked her head at the truth of the matter as if there was nothing that could be done, that the peculiar desires of the male species had been established long ago.

Desperate to secure a job to help pay the bills at home, Anne offered in haste, "I can bare a limb or two."

"May not be enough."

Chapter Seven

Ribbons of cables extended from the bridge and disappeared into the misty heavens. Elmer liked to think of them as lifelines to his dearly departed wife. The image soothed his weary mind, a brief escape from reality. At the end of the day, however, truth won over and he tried to shake off the cold.

Below the Gate, a trawler hauled back the anti-submarine net. The outbound U.S.S. *Hornet* and an escort of three destroyers soon arrived. While the distance from the span to the water varied, pilots of large ships sailed at low tide to insure safe passage. Sergeant Klausen leaned over as if to touch the antenna from the monolith's signal bridge. His vision squinted along the carrier's deck as he began to count in his head. He reached to sixteen before the *Hornet*'s cargo of B-25s slipped from sight. Must be headed for Hawaii, he thought, and trained his binoculars to the water's surface aft of the ship. No trails of bubbles or periscopes or upside down V patterns. Good.

Klausen folded his arms across his chest for warmth. His legs buckled against the onshore gust as he started to head indoors when one hundred yards further down the restricted walkway, a figure slipped in and out of the soup.

"Who goes there?" yelled Klausen.

The echo of gunshot came to him. In reflex the sergeant went to one knee. With the crook of his finger, he slid the Springfield from his shoulder and took aim. He studied the highway. Nothing unusual. A second bang came from further away. He sprinted in the direction of the disturbance, his weapon at the ready. Drivers, not knowing the nature of the alarm, lurched to a stop.

Upon reaching the north tower, Klausen paused to gain his breath. He stilled himself to better detect any peculiarity. The broken outline of a man approached. From the distance, bits and pieces aboard a person's frame punched their way through the fog until their collective parts stood before him as a whole.

"Cou-couldn't catch him," said the sputtering voice.

"Catch who?" Klausen asked.

"Saw…saw a stranger with a weapon."

"Where?"

Hank Jones went on to detail his failed chase while Klausen walkie-talkied the command post. State Reserve jeeps soon arrived, received an update and sped off in pursuit. Others established a temporary roadblock across the six lanes. Two minutes later a posse of Grays joined the fracas.

On a hunch Klausen hurried to the backside of the tower where Jones had said he first saw the man in black. Nothing out of the ordinary showed itself at first. He started to return when he spotted a steel door ajar. The sergeant ventured over and pulled open the portal. A moan ricocheted off the cylindrical chamber. The beam of his flashlight followed an algae stained path past a colony of bats hanging within their wings. On the first landing of the spiral staircase, thirty feet lower, a clothed mass stretched across the platform.

The sergeant bounced down the steps. He flicked a shaft of light across the lifeless form. Tony Ponti's pupils stared back stone-like from frozen chambers.

Klausen's plea for help fell in a low murmur not far away. He freed a wad of saliva before shouting an unmistakable alert. Bats scurried away with a squeal, cantering and quartering upward. Men rushed to the tower's entrance and fled down the staircase single file. They looked past the sergeant to a pool of crimson.

Elmer Klausen's vision slid from his buddy's carcass to his fellow militiamen and back. For some unknown reason, a curious finding, insignificant and barely detectable, latched onto his meandering gaze. He fingered the torn breast pocket of Tony's shirt where his unit's brass insignia once resided. Upon further examination another fact struck him. There was little evidence of any resistance. The private's sidearm was holstered. He would've put up a fight, thought Klausen. Small for his size, yet as feisty as a swarm of bees, Ponti was not one to surrender easily. Must have been taken by surprise, he guessed. The sergeant draped his coat over his friend and cradled the body up the steps to the sidewalk.

"Horrific," Fredericks said. "Quite unfathomable to comprehend that one of our own would be the first." While half a dozen soldiers had been killed in training accidents near and around the Bay Area, none had as yet fallen by the enemy's hand. "Lieutenant Jones, did you happen to witness the offender?"

No response.

Fredericks shook him, drew him around. "Jones."

"Huh?"

"The attacker, did you see him?"

"Puny sort, all in bl-black." Jones held the flat of his hand against a wound that ran from the corner of his brow along the bridge of his nose

A jeep returned. A Reservist sitting behind the wheel reported in a non-pulse manner that he found a bloodied knife at the north end of the bridge. Grays drew in closer to inspect the weapon, which rested inside a sealed bag. It was approximately nine inches long, curved with exotic foreign characters written on its handle.

Fredericks studied the blade and said, "This could very well belong to the Black Dragons."

A recent article in the *Chronicle* emerged before Klausen's mindscape. The secret society was a Japanese paramilitary group, formed at the turn of the century for covert operations inside

China. He wasn't a student of history, didn't claim to be, but was aware that by the mid-thirties the clandestine organization had exported its talents to the West Coast.

"If it wasn't for Private Ponti here," confirmed the major as he motioned toward his fallen comrade, "that scoundrel might have perpetrated serious harm."

While the compliment sounded insincere to Klausen, Fredericks was right in paying homage to their slain brother. A grenade down a vent of the *Hornet* might have disabled the ship and its cargo of B-25s.

Klausen couldn't concentrate any further. His thoughts were all over the place. The fog reclaimed his attention, but he didn't put on his wrap. He couldn't, not with his friend splattered all over it. With the arrival of the coroner, he and the other Grays backed off. The sight of a body bag being loaded for transport sucked the air from them. With venom etched to their expressions, the militiamen fell in behind the slow rolling ambulance.

Klausen lingered behind with the investigative unit, not so much to assist as to figure out what to do next. He started off when something demanded his inspection. A familiar metal pin, the size of a half-dollar, lay on the ground. With the likeness of a Republican Gray etched on its front, there was no mistaking its identity. Must belong to Tony, he thought, and stuffed the brass medal into his pant's pocket and went, with no discernable haste, to nowhere in particular.

Chapter Eight

Rumors filtered through the corridors. In recent days Commander Minoru seemed edgy. Amidst the guarded veil of whispers, some expressed uncertainty in the man. Suspicions matured into concerns.

Everyone remained ignorant regarding their next assignment. Besides the skipper himself, one man alone had access to the I-25's fate—Navigator First Classman Nishino Kozo. The crew persuaded Airman Nobuo to tempt Kozo with fish delicacies. The pilot agreed and invited his fellow sailor to his cabin to help him with a taste test.

Men gathered outside, ears pressed to the conversation. Whether it was raw tuna in soba noodles or marinated puffer or Fugu blowfish that found Kozo's palette, the result was always the same—no deal. Then Nobuo remembered a gift from his daughter and retrieved a box of yōkan. Made of agar and sugar, it satisfied one's need for sweetness beyond measure. Before long, the navigator confessed all.

*   *   *

Air pressured saltwater from the ballast tanks. Stubby wings at stern and bow were set at the proper angle. The nose of the I-25 pierced upward with expediency, flopping on the sea with a thud.

Nobuo scurried up the ladder onto the bridge where the captain stationed himself under the starry night. A lighthouse on the northern fringe of Fort Stevens, Oregon, marked the mouth of the Columbia River but little else showed from the coastline. With blackout procedures in effect, Nobuo pondered what could possibly be the point of the exercise.

"Tell Mister Nazaro to check the gun access hatch," Captain Minoru ordered.

"Mister Nazaro has the word," reported the second-in-command.

"Gunner's mate to the bridge."

"Gunner's mate is on his way."

"Battle stations. Ready deck gun only."

The barrel of the five-inch cannon was loaded. A target, with a bearing of one two zero and a range of 6.2 kilometers, was confirmed. With the brilliance of a lightening strike, four rounds exploded from the high-angle weapon. The commander, fixed to his binoculars, testified to the wreckage of some sort of structure and shouted a victory for the Emperor. With the emergence of repeated flashes from shore, however, doubts crept into the crew's collective mind.

Minoru scanned his men with expectation. Instead of favor drawn on faces, hesitation had climbed aboard. In an attempt to stir emotions, he started to render an oration of some length when a steady drone from above approached. A flock of P-51's soared overhead.

"Rig for dive," ordered Minoru.

"All compartments rigged for dive," reported the control room.

"Secure deck gun. Clear the bridge."

"Dive, dive, dive."

An alarm sounded to confirm the command, but a valve at the bottom of the rear tank malfunctioned. The sea could not enter.

The stern sat light. Extra water was pushed into the forward ballast. No luck.

The Mustangs made another pass. The outline of the pilots' heads came into view. With the same suddenness with which they had appeared, the American squadron flew off.

The rear tank began to fill and the submarine descended as a B-24 Liberator arrived. The plane came in low and slow. The hydrostatic fuse was set at a depth of ninety feet, and a 325 lb. bomb was on its way. The experimental Mark 17 did not penetrate the water as designed and instead exploded upon impact with the flat blue.

Shock waves traveled down to the I-25, which continued toward the ocean's floor. Damage reports made their way to the control room: a broken pipe in the galley; electrical damage in the engine room; sparks and smoke filled the main gangway.

The Liberator came around for a second run. The fuse was reset, the device released. The round nose of the little-tested shell boomeranged off the Pacific and headed skyward, erupting not more than a hundred feet from the aircraft's starboard wing. Shrapnel pierced the fuselage. Flames shot from the right engine. The raid was called off and the bomber limped away.

*   *   *

Defenses from Alaska to Panama were put on full alert after the attack on Fort Stevens. Many feared that a full-scale invasion was imminent. Intelligence, however, was skimpy as long as the enemy's code remained unbreakable. Very few men in uniform were acquainted with the Japanese language. Wright knew the logical solution, but he was reluctant to ask for help from the very community that he so despised. In the meantime precautions were set into place.

Battleships *Colorado* and *Maryland* anchored just outside the Gate. Cannons were borrowed from the battle cruiser U.S.S. *Saratoga* and placed in various "burster courses", two-foot thick concrete shields sandwiched between layers of earth. Batteries at forts Funston, Miley and Scott on the San Francisco side as well as gun emplacements at Baker, Cronkhite and Barry on the Marin side staged mock warfare.

Dummy projectiles traveled more than twenty-six miles into the Pacific, just off Point Bonita where Wright and others of his staff felt that a strike by sea could inflict the most damage. In every quarter of the City, the echo of large guns redefined reality. Not since the American-Mexican War of 1848 had a foreign power dared to invade western United States. Over the next ninety-three years, its citizens had become soft, feeling impervious to outside threats.

Elsewhere, though, pandemonium and destruction were the norm. Socialists had turned Spain upside down. Hitler had annexed Austria. Japan was bulldozing its way through China, leaving a path of death in its wake—twelve million dead and counting. Perhaps the Japanese Empire was capable of such savagery here. The unknown had infiltrated the very core of society as it bent and twisted the minds of citizens. Fear had ratcheted its way into the American fiber.

*   *   *

A secretary in her WAC uniform showed a pair of militiamen into an office where they seated themselves in front of a massive oak desk.

"Can you believe this?" Lieutenant General Wright said as a greeting before slapping the front page of the *Chronicle* into Fredericks's arms.

The Gray's leader straightened it and began reading an article to himself:

A Jap is a Jap

"Congressman Welters of New Jersey states
that the Japanese American's loyalty to this country
is undeniable. He went on to say that accusations to

the contrary stem as much from racial prejudice than from evidence of any actual malfeasance.

"Lieutenant General John L. Wright, commander of the Western Theater of Operations, disagrees. 'Horse pucky. Prejudice has nothing to do with it. I simply don't trust any of them (persons of Japanese ancestry). A viper is nonetheless a viper wherever the egg is hatched—so a Jap American, born of Jap parents—grows up to be a Jap, not an American. They (Japanese) must be wiped off the map.'"

The commandant of the Fourth Army paced across the room. "Those yahoos in D.C. are stalling, trying to turn this into a debate. We don't need a damn national discussion on what constitutes a threat. What we need is action. Every Nip must be relocated from the West Coast immediately."

Fredericks placed the *Chronicle* down upon the desk as Wright came around to put a hand on each of them. "That's why I called you boys here today. Attorney General Warren and others in Sacramento are running into one delay after another in their efforts to get Washington to authorize internment camps for these outcasts. We may have to take another approach."

"Yes, sir," Fredericks said.

"Ye-yes, sir," parroted Lieutenant Jones.

Wright quick-studied the stuttering soldier. Curious fellow, he mused, as was his partner. Between the two of them there didn't seem to be enough distinction to fill a child's trophy cup.

The lieutenant general gathered himself and said, "The military has had a positive relationship with our civilian organizations in the past." A match found his pipe, and he puffed until a red blush showed in the bowl. "Now more than ever our country requires your assistance."

Jones became glum. Fredericks nudged him with an elbow to snap him out of it, but there was nothing there.

"All search and seizure operations have been denied," the commandant said. "Disheartening, gentlemen. Disheartening, I say," and he leaned into Fredericks, removed his pipe and said, "I want your Republican Grays to be...oh, how shall I say?" and he explored the ceiling for an answer before saying, "...to be my eyes and ears," not thinking that such men deserved any better verbiage. To instill a modicum of sincerity, he added, "The Native Sons and Daughters of the Golden West and the American Legion are already on board."

"What will you have us do, sir?" Fredericks asked.

"Perhaps you can befriend this Agent Harris fellow. Let him think that you support the FBI's conservative agenda, and..."

"...*and* report back to you," Fredericks volunteered while Jones stared out the window.

"Exactly. We're titling the effort 'Operation Dragon'." Wright started toward the exit, announcing that the meeting was over. "I'm glad we understand each other." Another thought came to him and he said, "By the way, Fredericks, I must apologize for that interruption at your organization's celebration a couple of weeks ago. The California State Reserve...they mean well, but they're a bit over ambitious."

"Well, there's no need to..."

"I'm reinstating your commission to colonial."

"Actually, it's major, sir."

"You don't say?" After digesting the statement, Wright said that the Grays might be asked to perform certain services that otherwise would prove awkward for the military. "As civilians your outfit will not be under the Fed's microscope. Do you understand my meaning?"

"Yes, sir, I believe I do."

The secretary met all within the frame of the door and handed over certain requested copies to the commander. He thanked her before passing on the pile to Fredericks.

"Here's a little homework for you." Wright apologized for the lack of clarity, blaming the poor quality on the new Dexigraph machine.

Before Fredericks could entertain a comment, the lieutenant general put the flat of his hand against the Gray's back to show him the other side of the entrance. "Good day," and returned to his office without so much as a salute or a handshake.

Fredericks huffed at the closed door before turning to Jones. "Can you comprehend the nerve of that man attempting to shortchange me of my proper rank? It sets the mind to pondering, I tell you. Yes, indeed."

No response from Jones except the fingering of his wound as if measuring its length. In an attempt to engage his partner, Fredericks held up one of the documents, a black-and-white photo taken from the December 22nd issue of *Life*. The picture showed a Japanese male with the caption "How to tell Japs from Chinese". White arrows pointed to different facial features with corresponding remarks such as "longer narrow skull", "higher bridge", "lack of rosy cheeks", and "parchment yellow complexion".

"Even with this aid," the major said, "it will prove difficult to distinguish one Oriental from another." He turned to see the doldrums attached to Jones and added, "What occupies you? Is it your boy?"

"Le-leave me alone."

Chapter Nine

Elmer leafed through the *Chronicle* until the obituary column quivered before him like some stirring menace. An old photo of his friend rose up large and consuming. An ancient smile was sculpted upon a skull, which rested aboard a pressed World War One uniform. Just a youngster, he thought. Hell, we were all young back then. Some of their boyhood romps came to mind: posing as priests inside the confessional at Saints Peter and Paul Church, listening to sinners tell all; standing atop Green Street, rolling bocce balls down upon unsuspecting tourists below.

And there was that summer of 1910 when they discovered the lone wooden street that existed in the known world, albeit a world calibrated within their limited ten-year-old experience. Nevertheless, it was a fine discovery. Below Julius' Castle, on the east side of Telegraph Hill, stood a dense collection of eucalyptus that hid alleys and an avenue built of timber.

Within the wooded grove, Tony and Elmer manufactured a tree fort. It was simple by design, consisting of a single open-air platform with an accordion rope ladder. From this perch they would prepare themselves for battles to come. Mud-pie grenades found various shacks below, which enlisted the ire of nearby residents. On one occasion a lady approached them in all her magnificence. Such beauty they had never witnessed before. Gaped mouths signaled their clumsiness when she invited them into her private domain for a peace offering.

She explained, while dipping her plunging neckline with a Coca-Cola in hand, that these *shacks* Tony and Elmer had poured their wrath upon, were in fact living monuments to the gold rush days when they were halfway stations for shanghaied sailors. Most of every hour of that August was spent in her resplendence, acquiring a better appreciation of San Francisco's historical charms.

At the time these adventures didn't seem like much, just the stuff of silly pubescence. Yet now, burdened with the stress of a conflict that promised to worsen, Elmer missed such innocence.

"How long did you know Mr. Ponti?" Anne asked.

He aborted the effort that conversations often demanded and read aloud the scripted bio:

> "'Antonio Giovanni Ponti passed away on January 9, 1942 at the young age of forty-three due to sudden cardiac arrest.

What? Cardiac arrest? That ain't right, he thought, and lowered the paper from his vision before continuing:

> "'Born December 24, 1898 in Palermo, Sicily, to Dino and Sophia Ponti. Graduated from Galileo High School in San Francisco with a life-long appreciation of San Francisco's past and the human form. He joined the Republican Grays in 1915, served in WWI and was honorably discharged on October, 28,1923. He is survived by his loving wife, Nicola, and five daughters—Dianora, Adriana, Mesolina, Fiorella, and Vedette—and one grandson, Aldo. Antonio enjoyed a good wager and Italian cuisine. His wit, verve and candor will be missed; his memory cherished. Services will be

held at Mission Dolores Cemetery on Sunday, January 14th, at 2:00 P.M.'"

Elmer skimmed through the newspaper—no mention of an assassin or the Black Dragons. Must be for security reasons, he guessed, and retired to his favorite chair, a rocker by the fireplace in the living room. A splotch of sun and a bottle of lager worked in concert to dull his troubled mind. After a second drink, he slumped to one side. The chair ceased swaying. With a gentle hand, Anne placed a blanket over his frame.

*   *   *

Inside the church's entryway, a stench assaulted Anne and she peered sideways. "Has someone had a couple of beers for breakfast?" She guided her nose to her father's uniform. "Whew," and fanned away the offense with a hymnbook, saying, "*The Lord shall castigate the drunken one.*"

"He can do that? *Castrate?*"

"What?"

"'Cause that sounds mighty extreme to me, not Christian at all."

"Not *castrate—castigate.* It means to punish."

"Why didn't ya say so?" Elmer said. "Usually don't give two hoots what threats the Lord puts out, but today's different," and he nodded toward a banner that stood limp nearby. Imprinted in flaxen thread upon the standard was an inscription—GOD BLESS ANTHONY PONTI / MAY HE REST IN PEACE.

"Was a good man and a devoted father."

"Too bad he didn't share his secrets," Anne said.

Elmer shot his daughter a sneer as he nudged her from the antechamber. "Let's park that highbrow attitude of yours near the front where God and everyone can get a good take on it."

Anne moved away from his guidance with a gimp.

"For a dancer ya move about as swift as a fully loaded bedpan," the father said.

The pair fell into a stiff rhythm, walking side-by-side, ignoring each other as they strolled past ancient columns, which flanked the center aisle. They came to the second row and sat behind Mrs. Ponti and her daughters.

While Mission Dolores withstood the crushing blow of the '06 quake, not so could be said for the opulence of the Financial District or the wickedness of the Tenderloin. Good had triumphed over evil, Anne believed, and then she puzzled why such men as the Grays were set free to reconstruct the mayhem all over again.

A band of light pushed through a stained glass window to put a spot on Father Harrigan. Dressed in white and purple vestments, the Diocesan greeted his congregation with the sign of the cross. *"In nomine Patris et fillii et Spiritus Sancti."*

"Amen," responded all with the exception of one.

Anne poked her father. "If you're going to be here, you should at least abide by the rules."

"Rules were meant to be broken. Reckon that's why you folks got confession, right?"

She glared back at him, ready for anything he might throw her way.

A gold leaf crucifix showed from the hold of the priest. *"Pater Noster, qui es in caelis, sanctificetur nomen tuum…"*

Father and daughter slid from pew onto padded kneelers. Anne repeated the prayer in English: "Our Father who art in heaven, hallowed be Thy…"

"Still intendin' to leave for L.A. after graduation?" Elmer said out of the corner of his mouth.

"Thy kingdom come, Thy will be done," Anne said, ignoring him, "on earth as it is in…"

"To continue ballet?"

"And give us this day our daily bread and forgive us our tres-pass-es." She drew out the last word to underline its meaning.

"Need your fanny here."

"As we forgive those who…," and she stopped herself and gawked his way. "The place is already overflowing with cheap booze and women." With the disappearance of her dance instructor, the scholarship was a dead issue, but she felt certain that she would move somewhere, anywhere, and soon.

Father Harrigan glimpsed at the prattle and tossed out a theatrical cough. Caught by surprise, Elmer's expression darted from priest to daughter and back. He shrugged and pointed at his child with a stealthy finger as if she was the sole source of the disturbance.

At God's insistence, an uncomfortable truce enveloped the pair as Latin phrases floated past. The Diocesan placed three spoons of incense into a biretta and closed it.

"*Benedicite Pater Reverende.*"

Nicola and her five girls hung their heads as the crucible swayed over them. The sweet scent of burning spices clothed each in a blessing.

At the conclusion of mass, "Ave Maria" flowed from a standing pipe organ, which was situated as close to heaven as possible—in the balcony. Anne witnessed Harry Mitchum gliding a bow over his violin while ceremonial gongs resonated in accompaniment from the bell tower.

Father Harrigan and two altar boys marched toward the exit followed by the congregation. Jesus peered down from nearby Stations of the Cross. Anne thought that He must be disappointed the way things have turned out. A spitting sky greeted all upon reaching the outdoors as if to validate her misgivings.

Elmer's comb-over provided little protection from the elements and he raised a bible to his head, saying to Anne, "Better skip the burial and go straight home."

"I see you found a use for the Old Testament."

"Shouldn't mock the Holy Book in such ways. Your mother wouldn't approve." His discourse mingled with the sour smell of booze.

"I'm not mocking the bible, daddy dearest," she said as she inched closer. "Just the fools that it tries to preach to."

"Can't talk to me like that."

She climbed on her tiptoes, spewing out venom and other matter. "I'm not the one who's tipsy, mister."

Elmer wiped a spray of spittle from his face. "Do you mind?"

Nearby, a clump of Grays lifted their judgment to the acrimony. Anne scanned the bunch and said, "What're you looking at?" and bounced past the buzzing to the side of the church.

*   *   *

The U.S. government had denied Nicola Ponti's request to secure a plot for her husband at the veterans' cemetery in South San Francisco. So they gathered in the diminutive graveyard behind Mission Dolores Church for a simple funeral where other Republican Grays were remembered, where their past was not questioned.

Boulders of darkness rolled overhead as Fredericks stepped forward in his double-breasted West Point overcoat and dress cap and stood at attention next to a bronze statute. After a salute to "The Missing Gray", he made a snappy about-face to the mourners.

"We are assembled here today in this humble place where so many of our brethren rest alongside other warriors…"

Anne thought it ironic that these vigilantes should mingle within the same soil as Ohlones, local Native Americans that succumbed to the tortures of civilization, to the tortures of men not unlike these Grays.

The major pardoned himself as he removed his cavalry cap and peered inside to its cardboard band. While the strap's original purpose was to maintain the hat's shape and integrity, Fredericks had invented a second purpose—to serve as a handy notepad upon which to scribe jokes and phrases. Upside down, the West Point headgear slipped back and forth before his vision until a poem appeared.

"For God and soldier we do adore, in time of danger, but not before..." and he paused, sliding the hat a quarter-turn, *"...but not before the danger passed and all things righted, God is forgotten and the soldier slighted."*

Fredericks, pleased with his effort, said thank you before parading over to Jones. To his lieutenant's blank stare, the Gray's principal confessed that he knew little of what Kipling was trying to say but hoped that the verse might have served a purpose.

The commander waited for confirmation, but when none came, he said, "Did I evoke a scholarly presence in your opinion?"

Jones squinted through one eye to better study his self-absorbed leader, saying, "Can-can't steal someone else's brains."

Anne, who stood nearby, pursed her lips and questioned why no one else saw through the act. She gasped out loud before sauntering off with her father toward a clutch of females near the rear of the graveyard.

"Mornin', Nicola." Elmer said hello to her daughters as well, who ranged in age from ten to twenty-three.

"I pleased that you came," the widow said with a heavy accent. "My Tony spoke of you with best emotions. Whenever I see a Klausen"— and she included Anne with her glance—"I think good thoughts mostly, except for foolishness with Grays. He was on adventure. Well, adventure caught up with him, *sí?*"

"Found this near Tony," and he placed a fraternity pin into the palm of her hand.

She thanked him before stuffing the medal into her handbag.

"Heard they clo-closed down the Green Valley Restaurant and Hotel Boheme," Jones interrupted as he drew near. "Some say all of Nor-north Beach will be boarded up soon." He sounded unyielding and acrid.

At this close range, Anne saw the bloodied line along his nose but regarded it with little significance and instead said, "I'm sure Mrs. Ponti doesn't need to know..."

The father stopped her before turning back to the widow. "Sorry, my daughter can forget her place sometimes."

"Naw, it fine," Mrs. Ponti said. "I hear same rumors."

Vedette, the oldest daughter broke in, no accent, adding, "The *Giornale L'Italia* printed that Joe DiMaggio's parents received a call from the FBI." She shared details of how a trio of sedans made a big show of it, pulling up in front of the ballplayer's house with efficiency, forming a neat line at the curb, of how a gang of men in suits marched along in an official way as if to leave no guesswork as to their visit. She relayed the newspaper's tales of greater misfortunes taking place in New York's Little Italy where three thousand citizens had been transported to military camps.

"Can they do that here? Can they take us away? Can they?" Vedette rattled her concerns atop one another until syllables ran into each other. Nicola pressed her daughter close to ring out the tension.

"What right they got to do such thing?" the mother asked. "And the Clipper, quitting Yankees like that to join fight," and shook her head. "What more they want?"

The DiMaggios grew up in the City along Taylor Street, just a block away from the Ponti's place. Everyone knew them. At one time Joltin' Joe and his brothers, Vince and Dom, started in the outfield for the San Francisco Seals, a minor league club of the Red Sox.

"I mean no disrespect whatsoever to the DiMaggios," Fredericks said to the widow, "but trust is not something one can easily manufacture."

The boxy matriarch stepped closer. The major could see her nostril hairs, her shadowy mustache.

"Never mind Joe DiMaggio." Her fingers jabbed at the space between them. "You know who do this to my Tony?"

"The dastardly deed seems to be the work of a Black Dragon."

"Do old lady a favor," Nicola said, her hand shielding the request from her children. "If you find *bastardo muto*, you deal with him straight away, *capisce?*" She grabbed his arm, squeezed it. "Don't let jerk-wad Feds get him first," and her look locked onto his.

"On my oath as the sworn head of the Republican Grays, your husband's death shall be avenged."

From the side entrance, a freckled figure in his Block Warden uniform appeared. What's he doing here? Anne thought.

"Hi, everyone," Curly said. He flashed a playboy smile at Anne before turning to the bereaved, his lips still bent upward. "Sorry for your loss, ma'am."

"Might help if take off that smirk," she retorted. "Show proper respect."

And he waved his hand like a magician over his mouth. His cavalier presentation served only to underline the foolishness before all.

While watching the sideshow, Anne felt the makings of evil inside her head. A maniacal scheme came forth in bursts. While still in its infancy, the thought harbored great potential. Not knowing what would be the outcome of such doings, however, a fear climbed from her bowels. Mucus soured the visceral tangling within, but she couldn't let go and slid her vision to Curly and blew him a counterfeit kiss. The boy returned a wink while she surrendered a mousy wave goodbye before he joined Fredericks and Jones to leave.

"Glad you're makin' acquaintances with the opposite sex," Elmer said to his daughter. "Didn't know if ya even liked boys anymore."

"Curly?" Anne rebutted with a cackle, and then she remembered her plan. "Yes, well, he, ah, has many hidden qualities."

With no response to his daughter's sudden interest in the dim-witted boy, the father asked if she was going home, and she responded by saying that she would be along later. He left with Mrs. Ponti on his arm and ushered the family down a cinder path to a waiting limousine. Along the way a troubling reminder occurred to him—no Gilbert Schmidt. In recent years he had been Tony's closest companion. His absence was peculiar, but Elmer recalled that Schmidt had indeed seemed withdrawn over the last week or so. When the man spoke, which was rare these days, he chose his remarks with care.

Elmer bade farewell to the Ponti ladies and shuffled down Dolores Street toward home. Not a half-block away, a black cutout, topped with a Fedora's shape, sat in an unmarked car parked on the other side of a row of palm trees. From the crease of the open window, cigarette smoke escaped in a lazy manner as if the stranger had nothing better to do with his day.

*   *   *

If done properly, deceit might provide a handy alibi for her new place of employment. She needed time to sort things out, though. For now Anne desired nothing more than to lose herself amongst the beauty of the cemetery's garden. Peach-colored trumpets spewed out a honeysuckle scent while a stand of roses swelled in deep red. Tucked in the western corner to capture the sun's full stature, ten-foot high cacti showed off their epic white blooms. Nature had gone mad, inviting hummingbirds, monarchs and bees. A breeze caressed its way through her loose fitting blouse. Her scheming mind began to unwind until the stark scene of men shoveling dirt into a pit stirred up the last remnants of a sharp tang within her throat, and she started toward the exit.

Before she reached the arched gate, a violin's purr rose above the clamor from the streets, above the quarreling of a couple from the looming tenement next door. The bewitching tune beckoned her to the old woodshop. A raspy voice asked who was there. She answered with her full name, pardoned her intrusion and inquired about the melody.

"It's from *Phantom of the Opera*," Harry Mitchum said as he lowered his instrument from his chin to his lap. "I'm glad you could drop by." He stuck out his cane, saying, "Please, clear a spot for yourself."

"The song is…," and she paused, wanting to make sure the next word was right, and said, "…haunting." Satisfied, she upturned an empty five-gallon drum and sat.

"Next to *Les Misérables*, the *Phantom* is the longest running musical in modern history." Harry took hold of a fresh stogie and bit off its end. The sexagenarian sat there, clothed in a wrinkled three-piece black suit, and gnawed on his unlit cigar.

"I always wanted to dance to that piece," she said. "Perhaps someday."

His milky eyes lifted and settled upon a spot where cobwebs took residence, off to Anne's left. "Have you ever seen the movie version?"

"I have to confess that I have not."

"Lon Chaney starred in the flick, which was made, I believe, around twenty-five. The feel of the music beneath my feet gets me going." An idea came to him and he said, "Would you like to go next Saturday? It's playing at the Castro."

"Can't, I have rehearsal down at the Music Box."

"Too bad."

Harry's easy style and the quiet timbre of his voice gentled the air around Anne. So much so that she put away her conspiracy with Curly and relaxed enough to utter whatever notion came next.

"Why were you on the bus at such an early hour the other day?"

"Insomnia." His cheeks ballooned with juice. A muddy stream dribbled down his chin. He mopped his stubbly face with the back of his hand but not before a stain had settled within the crook of his vest. Harry patted nearby objects until he found a suitable spittoon. "Sleep doesn't seem to agree with me much these days. So I ride the muni with my friend, Benny, the bus driver."

"Do you ride all night?"

"Sometimes. Better than sitting up until the break of morning listening to the mice play."

She wanted to ask if there had been a Mrs. Mitchum at one time but guessed that would be too forward and instead asked where he lived.

"Live over at Indian Basin near Hunters Point Shipyard."

"That's a long ways to commute."

"Place suits me fine, nice and peaceful. Just an old tavern and some warehouses nearby."

Her vision strayed backwards through the doorway to the statue in the garden. "What's the significance of The Missing Gray?"

"You sure are full of questions."

"Sorry, I didn't mean to bother you," and she began to rise, the barrel scrabbling against the floor.

"Haven't been troubled in a while. I miss it. Now please," and motioned for her to retake her seat, "remind me, what part of *bother* were we discussing?"

"The bronze bust outside."

"Ah, yes," and he began to tell of the thirties when a trio of dock strikers fell at the hands of hired thugs. "Thousands of mourners paraded down Market Street to honor the slain. Teamsters blamed your daddy's fraternity for the killings. But the Grays had a different take on things, claiming that the City owed them some appreciation for keeping open the fisheries along the Embarcadero. The statue represents not so much the idea of Grays missing in action as missing from history books."

Anne sat silent. She did understand, at least partially, why her father never mentioned the past. At the inclusion of Hank Jones in the story, however, Harry grew solemn.

"Are you all right?" Anne asked.

"Have you heard the rumors about Jones's son?"

"Not the particulars."

"A terrible tragedy. It would be hard to recreate a worse demise," and he let loose with a wad of spit. "The boy was killed in action at a place called the Bataan Peninsula, somewhere in the Philippines. Almost 75,000 American and Filipino troops were captured by the Japanese and force-marched sixty miles through the jungle to a prison camp. Evidently several atrocities happened along the way including the beheading of Jones's son and others by sword-wielding horsemen."

An image of the slain soldier's father came to her along with her insensitivity at the funeral. How could she berate a man who carried such a burden? She lowered her head with the worst kind of guilt, Catholic guilt.

Chapter Ten

The color guard marched on stage, pivoted toward the assemblage and halted. Servicemen on either end dipped their respective Marine Corps and U.S. Army standards as the Stars and Stripes and Bear flags remained erect. The throng recited the Pledge of Allegiance and retook their seats. Electronic shrieks from the public address system called for everyone's attention.

"I want to thank Mr. Warfield for offering his theater," Lieutenant General Wright said, "so that we may bring these various civilian groups together today. I sincerely hope that Mr. Hearst does not spend a lot of ink, however, venting his frustration on the postponement of his biographical debut in *Citizen Kane*." He paused for effect but the stillness told him to continue. "I also want to express my appreciation to the Wartime Civil Control Administration and the Office of Civilian Defense for hosting this affair."

The Western Command leader went on to praise everyone for the selflessness displayed during these troubling weeks. Not one for hyperbole, he came straight to the point.

"Yesterday at zero three hundred hours, Fort Stevens, Oregon, came under attack by an unknown number of enemy ships."

An edgy hum circulated through the auditorium. What did not accompany his speech was the extent of the damage, for such information was classified. Due to their adversary's ineptness or the antiquity of their weaponry, the only damage recorded was the destruction of a baseball field's backstop. This was surely not an example of the same savagery visiting China. The incident's wrath, however, would not be measured in terms of loss of life or property but rather in miles. The enemy was near.

Lieutenant General Wright raised his voice above the din. "We are no longer insulated by the vastness of our ocean. The Japanese Imperial Navy is here and we must be prepared. I have ordered the extinguishment of all lighthouses along the West Coast until further notice. What outcome this may have regarding the safety of our maritime shipping is yet to be determined. Nevertheless, as F.D.R. has said, 'desperate times require desperate measures'." While the commandant frowned on the President's leniency toward aliens, he would use Roosevelt's popularity when needed.

Without divulging specifics the lieutenant general mentioned the bravery of Republican Gray Antonio Ponti and asked that his widow join him on stage. Upon her arrival he offered an American flag folded in the shape of a tri-cornered hat, emblematic of those worn by colonial soldiers during the War for Independence.

"You have my eternal gratitude for your husband's ultimate sacrifice."

Nicola accepted the flag with a half-hearted smile, thinking that Tony's sacrifice wasn't *ultimate* enough to warrant a proper military burial. Flanked by her five daughters, she retreated down the aisle when a memory came to her and she stopped beside her late husband's comrade to hand him an envelope.

Elmer's stare followed the family through the rear exit. He returned his attention to the casing, picked out a note, and read it in silence:

"Dear Elmer / Good of you to attend Tony's funeral. Sorry I was bit cranky that day. Pay no mind to madwoman. Tony wouldn't want his death revenged. Enough misery occupies our home. Please find enclosed his medal. God knows Gray's insignia brought nothing but heartaches to girls and me. Perhaps you can find some good in it. Best regards / Nicola."

Elmer felt the offering to make sure the brass insignia was there as if all attachments to his friend would be lost without it. With his heavy thoughts he gawked at a training film.

A British documentary, *UXB*, filled up the screen. The government-sponsored cinema outlined the correct protocol when encountering unexploded bombs (duds and delayed action fuses). The various public agencies, after *UXB*'s conclusion, filed toward different corners of the theater to discuss the flick as well as to outline their organization's duties for the invasion.

Elmer saw his daughter sitting with a clump of Block Wardens and motioned his approval. Anne smiled back at him as he turned to join his fellow Grays. Pleased with herself, she sat there feeling smug, when a hand landed on her knee. In prompt fashion she took a swat at the offense to send a message.

"Don't get any warped ideas," Anne said. "It's just dinner."

Curly threw her a sinister grin as if his role in her duplicitous plot might warrant more in the future.

"A date in exchange for a civil servant's outfit is all you'll ever see, got it?" She would keep the *why* of it to herself.

"Fits you well," Curly said as he glanced up and down at her uniform.

Anne returned a smirk, feeling confident that she could handle such a dolt when a burly woman stopped beside them.

"Curly, quit your babbling and help the little lady with her mask," and banged a riding crop against her side before moving on.

"Thinks she's George Patton," the red-haired said as he fitted the protective headgear over Anne's auburn crown.

She scanned the area and signaled to her father again. He just laughed. She remembered the gas mask and stripped it off only to see him step to another. He and Hank Jones appeared to be in deep conversation. Her father seemed to try and comfort him, but from this distance she couldn't be certain. So sad, she thought. The man had lost a brother and now a son to violence. Did he have any other living relatives or was he the end of his family's line? Her vision strayed, thinking of her relationship with her own father. However fragile such coexistence was, it was *their* fragile relationship, all they had. Perhaps she could guard it more carefully, even try harder. With such conciliatory notions, Anne found Jones again, still talking with her dad, and she desired to offer her condolences. To her surprise the lieutenant brushed away her father's gesture and hurried on. As Jones passed by, a chill feathered up her spine and she pulled out a stick of licorice from her duffle bag.

Curly squirmed in his seat like a giddy kid. "My favorite food group. Spare a piece?"

She handed over the black rope in a deadpan manner.

"Must be fate," he said as he bit into the sweet. "Never knew we had so much in common. Drawn together by the confection of the gods. Ain't that somethin'?"

"That's something, all right," Anne said with a forged smile. Seeking a distraction, she went back into her pack and pulled out a walkie-talkie.

"Hello, anyone there?"

Billy sounded pleased by the call and admitted that a friendly voice helped. He vowed, after a brief conversation around school and girls and other light-hearted matters, to keep in touch and clicked off.

At the front podium Police Chief Delaney carried an exasperated expression. The Republican Grays should have been put to rest during the thirties, he thought, disbanded for its part in the dock strikes. The fact that once more he would ask for their assistance riled him. Not just because he didn't trust the Grays, but since he would be the one to take the fall if things went awry. He was angry for allowing himself to be caught in this position, a position bargained for by the manipulations of Lieutenant General Wright. While the police chief had no future designs on politics, he wasn't so sure regarding the commander of the Presidio.

Delaney described the strict parameters under which the Grays would operate and proceeded to put forth a long list of "don'ts". He stopped himself and took a gander at Fredericks who interjected that his unit could use the exercise to search for those murdering Black Dragons.

"No one's going to do anything of the sort," Delaney shot back. He reset both hands upon the rostrum, saying, "If you feel the need to take someone into custody, hold them until the MPs get there."

"We just…"

"There are to be none of your vigilante-like shenanigans."

Jones examined the frustration aboard Fredericks and laughed a silent laugh. He took delight in knowing that his superior's ego, if left alone, would do more harm than any indignities someone else could muster.

"Now, onto other business." The chief tried to update them on the happenings down in Little Tokyo, but Fredericks kept interrupting with questions and side conversations. Order began to leave the area. Jones laughed again.

The unseemly display drew heads from around the hall. Lieutenant General Wright heard the raising of voices and asked his assistant to summon Fredericks to the side exit.

"What in tarnation do you think you're doing?" Wright said upon the Gray's arrival. His voice rose and fell as passersby came and went.

"I had been given the distinct impression that the chief had acquiesced to our agenda," Fredericks responded.

"He has, but he knows better than to make an announcement concerning it."

"Well, sir, if you don't mind me saying so, he seems rather perturbed."

The lieutenant general withdrew his pipe to give the matter his full attention. "We've gone over this before, remember?"

"Yes, but my men are itching to bring Private Ponti's executioner to justice, if you know what I mean, sir."

"The only thing you'll be *itching* if you don't obey orders is a cellmate's pleasure. Do you understand *my* meaning, colonel?"

"It's *major*, sir."

"You best leave."

"Well, there doesn't have to be any…"

"Now."

*   *   *

The thrum of facilitators continued to roll over each other from different sections of the theater. A uniformed lady from the American Women's Voluntary Services (AWVS) told her female counterparts that they would assist the canteen corps and clerical divisions. In another corner a representative of the Red Cross stated that its equestrian division would be charged with the delivery of updates and orders and such from Western Command headquarters in the event that motorized couriers were immobilized. In the orchestra pit a lieutenant from the Fourth Army took charge of the Ground Observation Corps (GOC), instructing the citizens to log and report type, direction and altitude of all planes that might infiltrate coastal airspace.

It was fitting that the Civil Air Patrol took up residence in the balcony. Noncombatant aviators would offer the Army Air Force with twin intelligence from the skies. An officer reminded the group that under no circumstances were they to engage the enemy in battle. This received a large round of boos from the amateur pilots who were too old to enlist but with plenty of fight left in them.

One such man, wearing bib overalls and a baseball cap pressed down tight over his shaggy hair, stood up and said, "If any yellow Japs were to take a shot at my plane, well, I'd have Ol' Faithful at the ready," and extracted a .22 shotgun from a nylon bag under his seat.

"Sir, sit down," said the officer, "and put that thing away."

Another person, wearing a glass eye, objected with the shaggy haired man, not with the general principle involved but with the method. "We ain't goin' after no damn flamingos. We're gonna shoot ourselves a full-size Zero. If you wanna do some real damage, there's better ways'n with a scattergun. Maybe a Savage or Remington, both thirty-ought-sixes," and he passed over a bottle.

"Gentlemen!"

Shaggy Hair ignored the demand, taking notice of a Ruger Speed-Six .357 tucked inside the belt of the glass-eyed man.

"This ain't nothin'," Glass Eye said. "Got a pearl handle thirty-eight snub as well. Keep it under the mattress."

"Where's such a mattress call home?"

"Brookings. Up in..."

"Up in Oregon," Shaggy Hair said as he finished the other's sentence. "Know well where it's at. Fly outta there ever so often."

"Maybe we kin hunt Japs together."

The prospect of free booze invited others seated nearby. Over continued objections from up front, the conversation moved to other topics, to the condition of relatives and friends sharing time in Humboldt County Correctional Facility, a minimum-security prison for dinks, drunks and short-timers.

"Hard duty," said Shaggy Hair, working himself up, "is when you're holdin' a reservation up at Pelican Bay. Those boys'll chew your heart out for a nickel."

"Ah," Glass Eye said, waving him off, "all fudge-packers."

"You callin' me a homo?" Shaggy Hair started to rise.

"Lemme tell you somethin'," said Glass Eye as he went nose to nose, "if the skirt fits…"

An MP rushed over and escorted the fools out the nearest exit, saying, "Don't call us…Well, you know the rest."

The pair strolled through the parking lot jabbering, switching from Rebel Yell to a couple of longnecks.

*　　*　　*

Father and daughter met outside where businessmen and soldiers hurried about with purpose. Autos and military vehicles of different shapes and sizes zipped through the downtown area. Within the whirlwind of activity, Elmer expressed how proud he was of his little girl for coming around.

"Was there ever a doubt?" and she pushed out the lapels of her khaki jacket, the initials CD stitched within a white triangle on the breast pocket.

"Nice." A triviality entered the father's head and he said, "Seen my walkie-talkie anywhere?"

She shrugged to which he said to never mind, that it was a spare. That was fine with her and she let the dialogue amble on until they went their separate ways. Elmer lingered to make sure his daughter reached the other side of Market Street when he observed that she was heading up O'Farrell. Not knowing what possible business could be waiting for her in the blue-collar Tenderloin, he yelled his concern.

A passing streetcar's grinding wheels, the honking of impatient drivers and the general disharmony of the financial district swallowed up his question, and she shook her head to indicate as much. Worried, he caught up with her.

"I have to fill out some paperwork down at City Hall," she offered in quick fashion.

"It's the other way," and he pointed further down Market Street.

"Oh, yeah, right." In an effort to further hide her deceit, she asked if he would like to tag along.

"Love to."

Now what?

Soon they came upon the Civic Center Plaza. A circle of temporary barracks was splayed out across the square like spokes from a wheel's hub. Everywhere, soldiers had taken up residence. Beyond the encampment sat the fifth largest dome in the world.

"I shouldn't be more than an hour or two if you want to wait," she said.

"No thanks, meetin' up with Schmidt and a few of the guys at Original Joe's. Was Ponti's favorite restaurant."

And she took off before he could reconsider.

"Can bring home a plate of their spinach-hamburger omelet if ya like," he called out to her backside.

Without turning around, she nodded an okay before hurrying up granite steps to a wall of sandbags. At the top level, she pushed through wrought-iron glass doors, which stood under a sign that read: CITY HALL & AIR RAID SHELTER.

Anne threaded her way through the rotunda. A jangled noise whirled its way upward. An ill-sorted line cruised past the grand staircase. She used it as a sexton and followed the bunch as if some saving truth waited just ahead. A rear egress showed itself soon enough and she dashed onto McAllister Street where she zigzagged back over to Polk before continuing north toward the Tenderloin.

Chapter Eleven

Piano keys struck up a melody for a bawdy ballad. A tight-fitting evening gown accentuated Rose's curves as she shimmied to center-stage while singing in a story-telling voice: "I used to bare my derriere / down to my bikini / But now I wear a feather there / created by Cassini / I used to down a quart of gin / and zip would go my zipper."

A sea of white caps flew from young heads. Orders had arrived to expedite the repairs on the *Lexington*. The carrier would sail out to sea soon enough, but for now the boys were ready for a little razzle-dazzle.

"You know people say I'm gifted / since I take it off with class / But to me I feel the same / since I still show the same old...," and she swung her backside to all, bending over, throwing up her dress.

Trumpets and drums escorted Rose as she roared with a baritone's gusto. Servicemen tried to outdo each other with their approval. Howls and whistles shot onto the stage. The club's icon sashayed sideways while bellowing out the last bars. Upon arriving near the right wing, she wrapped the curtain around her torso and blew a kiss to the throng.

The number was the owner's last of the evening. She would mingle with the crowd while orchestrating the comings and goings of employees.

Backstage, others prepared for the night. In one cubicle a pair of teenagers gathered. From their very first encounter, Anne knew she would like Mishi. Perhaps it was because they were both outsiders with their fellow peers: the dancer for her obsessive-compulsive behavior, the Oriental for her physical features.

Mishi glanced at a pair of matching khaki pants and jacket hanging from the makeshift closet and said, "You're not going to get away with it."

"Get away with what?"

"Your little masquerade, pretending to be a Block Warden while dancing at the Music Box."

Anne continued to apply makeup.

"Fathers know these things," Mishi persisted. "Besides, your dad and Rose's relationship seems to be on again. Sooner or later he's going to make an unscheduled visit and catch his not-so-innocent daughter prancing around in something a lot less dignified than a Civil Defense uniform."

"Not to worry. Miss McNally has agreed to schedule my performances on nights when he's pulled duty at the Golden Gate." Anne puffed up a sly grin.

"Think you're pretty smart, don't you?"

"I think Rose is a lot smarter than some old soldier-boy. Besides, I'm practically a legal adult. Who says I owe him any explanation at all?"

"*Legal* has nothing to do with it."

Anne dabbed a tar-black compound onto her face and neck and brushed all to an even dull surface. Mishi assisted with a hooded skin-tight top, which matched the hue of her facial powder, and pulled it up and over Anne while tucking in any loose strands of hair.

"I heard the Japanese were seen up in Alaska," Anne said as she slithered into the outfit. "Oregon, too."

"Think they'll be moving south?"

"That seems to be the consensus. All over the news."

Mishi's hands trembled as she tried to help with the stitching of a fresh heel into a slipper's pocket. Clumps of oxygen accompanied the effort.

"What is it?"

No response.

Anne spun around to see moist eyes. "Talk to me."

"Things at home aren't good," Mishi said as she accepted a Kleenex. "Grays have been snooping around Little Tokyo, asking a lot of questions. Two of them, big ugly brutes, were stopping residents, demanding I.D.s and addresses." She brought the tissue to a fresh tear.

"Bastards," Anne said and slapped the dressing table. She realized as an afterthought that her anger had gotten the best of her, and she apologized. "Sorry, shouldn't use words like *bastards*."

"*Bastards?*" Miss McNally repeated as she entered the cubicle. "Someone botherin' you girls? Just let ol' Rose know and…"

"These men," Mishi said, "they…"

"*Men?* Well, of course it would be men. They're all bastards. Don't ya fret over any of them, honey. Ain't worth it," and she left as quickly as she appeared.

Anne pushed into her ballet shoes and stepped to a rosin box for a thorough dusting. A thousand needles of pain shot up. She winced as she stiffened her posture.

"You wear too many slippers," Mishi said with a shake of her head.

"What?"

"There is an ancient saying from our native island of Hokkaidō—*mono sen zori wo hakitsubusu hodo no jikan ga tatta*—the bygone wears out a…"

"You're up," interrupted Rose as she peered back in. "Let's go," and latched onto the performer's inky costume.

Anne glanced over her shoulder and mouthed an apology. In response Mishi held up two fingers entwined in luck.

*   *   *

Notes from Puccini's *Madame Butterfly* floated from the orchestra pit to fill the darkened theater. The ballerina glided across the stage as infrared spotlights picked up the fluorescence of wings, a feathery headband and shoes. The glittering pieces took flight as if the product of some cinema trickery. The solemnity of the number caught the patrons off guard and they suspended their talk. The performer fluttered and soared, acting out the story of a fifteen-year-old Japanese girl who forfeited her ancestral traditions to marry an American naval officer. The room pulsated with the gentle quality of oboes and violins. The tempo heated up to announce a shift in the mood. A bass drum released a crescendo's roll. Cheated of her love, the girl flapped her wings in remorse and rushed up a cliff to a raised perch where her feathery appendages engulfed her with finality. Her neck stretched out to the audience with a farewell before leaping sideways to her death.

Anne fell with a thump onto a cushion behind the raised platform. The ensuing quiet choked her. She sat there with her disappointment. A few claps could be heard. She looked sideways to see Rose applauding. Then another pair of hands joined together and another until the entire theater shook with approval.

Anne returned and bowed and skipped offstage to the adulation of the entire company. She held onto Mishi, twirling around, until Rose came by and scooted grip men and others along with rapid-fire claps.

"All right, that's enough. Let's get back to work."

The pack began to dissolve from Rose and Anne, one person at a time. "Classy," said the boss. "Particularly enjoyed the piece where..." and she heard the clang of crashing kitchenware. "What in the name of Jesus," and left, cussing down the full length of the hallway.

A lumpy figure in a crumpled three-piece suit, a Labrador and a Negro appeared in the wake of the exodus.

"Gaspar!" Anne knelt on one knee and held out a hand to beckon the critter. The Lab came, lolled out its tongue and moved into position for strokes. While digging into the shiny coat, she looked up at Harry. "What're you doing here?"

"Well, we were..."

"Did you see my number?" Excitement hung in her voice.

"As a matter of fact, we..."

"What did you think? Did you like it?" Her fingers twitched in crazy-eight patterns across Gaspar's rump. The dog's hindquarter shuddered upward to confirm the spot.

"Enjoyed it very..."

"Thank you." Unable to contain the sensation, she went to embrace him. Shouldn't be anything new. After all, just three months previous she had made a guest appearance as a cast member of *Coppélia* at the Opera House. This was different, though. Was it the reckless attitude of the patrons or the adrenalin that came with performing at an altogether different venue? Didn't matter. More than ever she was convinced that she had made the right decision to dance at the burlesque club.

"You remember Benny?" Harry asked as he pointed in the general direction of the bus driver.

She extended her hand. "We kinda met on the muni one day. I'm Anne."

"Oh, I know who you are, all right. Harry's told me all about you," and took her greeting into his, saying that it was nice to meet her as well.

"Benny is on his lunch break," Harry said. "Thought we'd stop by and see how our girl is doing." Except for the fact that it was ten P.M., lunch seemed appropriate given Benny's nocturnal schedule.

"Are you on one of your all-night bus rides?" she asked.

"You got it," Harry responded. "We're taking in the sights, studying the devil at work."

"He sure can get busy," Benny said in agreement. "Yes, indeed."

A slice of a banana-pickle-peanut-butter-sandwich was offered to Anne who refused and joked regarding the weird food concoction, asking if Benny was pregnant.

"No, but the wife is. Again. If this keeps up, we're gonna have to start usin' the dresser drawers as bunk beds." He stared down at his lunch as if she might have a point and said, "Must be sympathy pains, no other explanation."

The boys started on their second course, sardines marinated in soy, when a slender Oriental in a white apron stopped to inquire as to the foul odor. Benny repeated his menu to the sound of sporadic clacking.

"Sardine beautiful fish. No need to spoil with sauce," the Oriental interjected.

"This is Number One," Anne said with a smile, proud that she had remembered his alias.

"That's some moniker you've got attached to yourself," Harry said.

"It serve me well."

"Is Mishi still around?" Anne asked.

"You mean Number Three? She leave with Number Two. Why you ask?"

"Mishi, I mean Number Three, wanted to share this thought when Rose came in to...," and she saw the boredom on everyone and said, "I'll catch-up with her soon."

"How you *catch-up* a person?" Number One asked.

The overhead lights flickered. Everyone, military men and employees alike, flinched, ogled one another. Sirens sounded an alarm.

"Just another air raid," Rose called out. "No need to...," and she suspended her reassurance as the electricity failed altogether.

Within the blackness, gasps grew into sharp screams. Chairs scuffed across the parquet floor as troubled voices made their way to the exits.

Afraid that her request to turn on the generator might have fallen into the chaos, the owner weaved her way backstage and flipped a switch. The sirens ceased their fright in some strange confluence with the reincarnation of the houselights. Sailors returned, jumpy. Nervous laughter circled the room.

*   *   *

Anne noticed the hour and left early to hitch a ride with the guys. While the #20 rumbled south along Van Ness Avenue, the bellow of horns started up again. Glimpses fell upon the lady in the Block Warden uniform.

"Duck and cover?" Anne suggested.

Grown adults checked the small space beneath their seats and responded with addled declarations and snorts. Anne pinched up her shoulders as if to say that was all she had to offer.

Benny proceeded one block to a white six-pointed star upon the blacktop and turned off the engine. A violin played Vivaldi in an attempt to quiet the tension, but the effort proved of little value. Not even the rendition of great composers can wash away the ugly side of man. A few moments later the "all clear" sounded, and the bus rumbled back to life.

At the corner of Folsom and Twenty-fourth, Anne said her goodbyes and disembarked with her duffle bag. She kept to herself as much as possible and proceeded under the safety of what little illumination presented itself. While much of the Mission District remained strangled by the night, patches of brilliance escaped from diners and pubs as customers came and went.

A pair of hardhats banged out of nearby O'Keefe's Tavern, tittering within a thrown box of light. "Where're you off to, lassie?" one of the men called out in a slurred voice.

Anne crossed over to the other side and picked up her pace. The night grew darker as she passed under a row of five-story apartment buildings. Muffled sounds of life pushed past blackout shades from above. A mother shouted at her disobeying children while a man in a sleeveless T-shirt leaned out a window to curse at the racket. The voices offered Anne some comfort until she heard a different kind of noise from behind.

94

"Do you be needin' some company now?"

The grumbling followed her, but she dared not turn around. If she could make it to Mission Street, she'd be safe. There'd be plenty of people milling about, businesses open.

Glass broke upon the sidewalk in the background, followed by sounds of disappointment. Coated in a new edginess, their language turned harsh.

"Hey, we be talkin' to you."

Anne sprinted off the curb. Her vision fixed downward, she was unawares of an advancing frame and crashed into him. A pothole caught her wayward step and sent a catch of muddy water upward. She scanned her soiled uniform while a young man let out a groan.

"Watch where you're goin'." Then the pedestrian recognized the owner of his aggravation and said, "Sweetcakes, is that you?"

At the relief of a familiar face, Anne ignored her haggard presence and said, "Curly, so good to see you!"

"It is?" he said before seeing her mess and began to hand-wipe her outfit.

"Stop that." She realized the sternness in her voice and said instead, "Please, allow a clumsy girl to tend to herself."

From back over her shoulder, she could see that the two hooligans had hesitated. Rough-hewn stares withdrew back into a huddle.

"Don't you look just divine," Curly said as he spied the fire-red lipstick, the mass of blue eyeliner and the blush on her cheeks. His fantasies began to stir.

Forgot to wash off the makeup, she thought. Damn. The heel of her hand whipped across her lips before an idea came to her. "Would you mind escorting a girl home?"

"Been out partying, haven't you? Now don't lie, wouldn't be right," and he stepped back for yet another view. This saucy side of Anne intrigued him, even awakened his loins, feeling movement.

Wanting to put some distance between her and the Irish wankers, Anne picked up her duffle bag with one hand while the other curled around Curly's arm to lobby her intent. "Please, can we go?"

"Could have that date right now if you've a mind to," he suggested. Something was definitely beginning to awaken inside, and he reminded her of an earlier promise, a promise sealed with a handshake at the OCD Conference.

"We can negotiate," she said.

They restarted. He driveled on, eager to know more of her adventures that night.

They came upon Mission Street, weaved between passersby, past liquor stores and pawnshops and a police station. A few blocks further, they hurried across the four-lane boulevard and continued up Twentieth. At short intervals Anne checked behind her. When she was convinced that the hardhats had most likely opted for another tavern, she untangled her arm from his and thanked him.

"I can take it from here," she said.

"What about the negotiations?"

"It's a work in progress," and she hurried away.

He studied the fading female. A hard species to figure out, he thought, and started walking back toward his original purpose, toward a smoke shop and the latest issue of *Razzle*, when his lust selected a closer option. He regarded its usefulness and made a U-turn.

Anne pushed along the edge of Dolores Park. Fronds of palm trees swayed at the introduction of a breeze while a gauzy swarm of stars swung east in the company of a fingernail moon. A pall of light reflected off a white picket fence, which framed a Victory Garden nearby. On the far side of the sloping meadow, the jagged roofline of her Mission High School poked up from a strip of fog that spilled over Twin Peaks.

At reaching Liberty Street, she put the balls of her feet to the pavement and trudged up the terrain to her driveway. She padded over the crabgrass to the side of the bungalow. An overgrown hydrangea hid a faucet and a coiled garden hose. Mired in muck, she turned on the water and dragged the rubber tubing through snapping branches and rustling leaves.

The hose cuffed her around the ankles. She fumbled into the bushes and slid sideways and crashed into a wheelbarrow. The freed line shot funnels of water everywhere. With difficulty she managed to get to the nozzle and shut it off. Her saturated uniform clung to her while mascara and rouge ran unchallenged.

She peeled off her Block Warden jacket and blouse and rummaged through her pack for replacements when a cry ascended from the direction of the doorway. Heavy footfalls thudded down the porch and along the gravelly path toward her.

She flung her coat back over her bare breasts like a shawl, uprooted her CD cap from the ground.

"Show yourself," a man said alongside the sound of a cocking gun.

"Just me, dad." She thought a little levity might help her cause and added, "Don't shoot."

"What're ya doin' out here?"

She stayed within the darkness, afraid of revealing her tawdry condition. "Wanted to check that leaky faucet." She gnawed on her lip.

"Leaky faucet?" Too tired to investigate, he lowered his rifle and demanded that she get inside. He started to retrace his steps when he called out, "Don't forget to close up the house...I'm goin' to bed."

Relieved, she waited for him to settle back into the bungalow. Satisfied that enough time had intervened, she let her wrap fall from her when another disturbance could be heard from across the street. Frantic, she fished for a dry shirt and hurried into it, cajoling buttons into whatever eyelets presented themselves first.

Chapter Twelve

The Ishigawas walked fifteen blocks from the Music Box to Japantown and approached the Geary Boulevard inspection point. Hajime handed over his driver's license and provided papers as well for his wife and daughter. The MP checked off the names from a paper instrument and noted the time—1:35 A.M.

The family shuffled north along Webster Street to the corner of Bush where the late hour activity caught their attention. Mother and father flanked their daughter as they hurried between the comings-and-goings. The trio hastened sideways into a store's entranceway to avoid the rush of a couple of ruffians dressed in gray. At the disappearance of the men, they moved on with care.

After another block, they came to their house and climbed the front steps. The door stood ajar. Hajime motioned for all to remain behind and entered with a cautious gait. Voices crisscrossed each other from upstairs. The father retreated to the foyer when military uniforms started his way.

Two cardboard boxes, which weighed down the arms of the lead soldier, hid his face from view. The other carried nothing except his cavalry hat, his concentration stuck on its cardboard band.

"My wife is an earth sign. I'm a water sign. Together we make mud."

"You ne-need new material."

The pair whisked past the Oriental as if he wasn't there and walked into the living room and sunk into a futon couch. Not sure if an accounting was in the offing, the owner of the house approached and said, "Who you?"

Surprised, one of the Grays bolted up and drew his revolver. "Stan-stand back."

"No understand." Hajime raised both hands to show that he posed no threat and in a soft voice asked for calm, saying, "Woman and child are present," and motioned toward the entrance, past an antique tansu cabinet to where Sato and Mishi stood.

The Grays holstered their weapons. Jones started to state their purpose, but Fredericks cut him off.

"In the name of the Republican Grays and all that is just, we are confiscating your camera, two phones and certain files as well as various letters written in someone's personal hand."

Mishi broke loose from her mother and sprinted into the living room. "Those are my things," but Fredericks snatched up the communiqué and handed all to Jones who placed them into one of the boxes, securing it with wires and a small lock. A name was written on the carton's top and side. It was not their family name, but something similar—ISHIGAWAN.

Hajime protested in an effort to correct the matter. Bureaucratic ineptitude had taken him and Sato hostage before when they immigrated in 1910, resulting in an additional month of detention on Angel Island. He feared worst for his belongings. Agitated, he spoke in a hurried manner. Mishi cried and pawed at the box. The mother yelled around the room.

Fredericks surveyed the situation before him and said, "Jones, we best be going."

"No shi-shit. Figured that on your own, did you?"

Down the front steps they scampered as complaints chased after them all the way to a panel truck, which showed within the glow of another transport's headlights. Mishi recognized a shadowy figure framed by the rear dual doors. To confirm her suspicions, she drifted from the protection of her mother's grasp, went to the curb and peeked into the pit of the vehicle. Her next-door neighbor sat on a wooden bench, his head slumped. Horrified at the spectacle of chains linking his hands and ankles, Mishi turned and banged into Fredericks.

"If you don't desire a seat with your friend, I suggest that you remove yourself," and he pushed another cuffed male past the teenager and up the bumper-step.

Mishi sprinted away in clumsy fashion back to her parents. She tried to speak, but her words jumbled together under her fright even as her mother hand-combed her hair.

Japantown was wide-awake now. Strangers came and went with little explanation. Six-inch colored numbers were tacked on each place of residence.

More red, Hajime thought, and then he inspected his own entranceway, his own number—**416.** Flashbacks of similar actions loomed up before him, of his country's goon squads patrolling the streets of Tokyo during the suffocating rule of the Meiji family.

Sergeant Klausen glanced upwards and spotted an older woman on the portico. Rose's helper, he guessed. And the younger one? Seen her down at the Music Box as well. Fredericks marched past and ordered him to get a move on.

"Yeah," echoed Jones, "get a move on."

Fredericks slapped Jones across the head with his cavalry hat as if annoyed by the constant imitating. A tightened expression fired back.

The turmoil on the street began to unnerve the Ishigawa women. Hajime could see the panic in their eyes and escorted his family back into the house, into the living room where they sat on the couch still warm from their uninvited guests. Everyone conversed in their native language for fear that someone might interpret their talk as treasonous.

"Why don't they need a warrant?" Sato asked. "Others have rights. Why don't we have these rights as well?"

"Absolutely correct, mama," Mishi said. "Random search-and-seizures belong to thugs and dictators. This is America, land of the.."

Before the teenager could finish the slogan, the father interrupted, saying, "It will be okay," and slid along the sofa to her side.

"No, it is not okay. We leave tomorrow," Sato said and got up in a huff. "We will accept the government's offer to live elsewhere," referring to D.C.'s one-time proposal allowing any Japanese-American to relocate inland.

"But this is our home," Hajime countered.

"We get ready now." Sato started upstairs to pack for the trip.

"Where shall we go?" Hajime asked.

The question stopped her in mid-stride. She gazed upward toward the second floor landing, past an accordion shoji screen to her bedroom where her things were stored. With no answer in hand, she pulled back and wallowed to the kitchen to prepare dinner.

*   *   *

At the main checkpoint rested an unmarked sedan. A slender man in a black fedora disembarked and walked to the white gate. He flashed his FBI badge to the MP and waited near the guardhouse.

A couple of trucks and four autos approached from the bowels of Japantown. The G-man put a hand up.

The motorcade came to a stop as the driver of the first truck rolled down his window. "What is it that you require of us, Agent Harris?"

"If it isn't Major Fredericks," the Fed said. "Or is it *General* Fredericks? I hear promotions are a rather informal affair these days within the ranks of the Republican Grays."

"I would advise that you stand aside."

"Mind if I have a look-see?" and Harris pointed with his chin to the rear of the panel truck.

"I don't suppose you possess a warrant."

"Get one easy enough."

"You do that," and Fredericks waved along the others.

Agent Harris stood there and studied the caravan until it disappeared down Geary toward Van Ness, toward Polk Gulch.

*   *   *

Coupons landed a dish of black beans, sliced pears, scrambled eggs (of the seagull and tern variety from the Farallon Islands) and the flesh of some animal. There was no coffee or sugar or cheese in the pantry as the Office of Price Administration (OPA) apportioned those with care.

Elmer, letting his meal cool, examined his ration book: fifty black and forty-seven green stamps, enough to get by for another week. Anne put a fork in her father's hand and sat opposite him with intentions of a normal conversation, free of the stress that the conflict had brought to their door.

She asked what he thought of "White Christmas", which last week had climbed to number one on the music charts. The long day wore on him, and he fell quiet to eat, but he had as much difficulty digesting the mystery meat as the babble from across the table.

"Bing Crosby wrote the tune while staying at the Bohemian Grove in Monte Rio. You remember Monte Rio, don't you, daddy? Along the Russian River?"

His look hovered over his food.

"They're filming Bing's movie, *Holiday Inn*, at the local lodge. We had a fabulous dinner there last summer, or was it the summer before last?"

He gulped down a can of Schlitz to wash away the disagreeable taste. "Whaddya call this?" and pointed with his fork.

"The Hormel people call it Spam, but that's not important. As I was saying, the eating establishment has changed its name to…"

"What's in it?"

"What's in what?"

102

"This jello-like stuff you're servin'."

"I don't know. Probably pork and ham and...," she exhaled her frustration, adding, "See the label."

And he did, noting the addition of potato starch before asking what "aspic" was. Anne snatched the can from his grasp, saying, "Never mind about that."

"Guess you're right. No time to wish for better," and he nudged his food around his plate.

She guided his chin upward. "Look at me."

There was a pause before the father said, "Well, I'm lookin'."

"They've changed the name of the eating establishment in honor of the film. Pretty cool, huh?"

"Who's *they*? What establishment?"

She rolled her head backwards. "Forget it."

"Works for me," and he gestured for a bowl of fruit.

It was not until after supper while cleaning up—he washing the dishes, she drying—that the father offered some parley and inquired as to the name of her schoolmate who worked at the Music Box.

"Excuse me?" Anne couldn't recall mentioning her friend's name to him.

"Mishi Something-or-other."

It was Anne's turn to fall quiet, uncomfortable where this might be going.

"Whaddya say her family name was?"

"Mishi's?"

"Who've we been talkin' about? "

Elmer Klausen was not the typical adult. He was far more clever, devious even. If Mr. Piner or Miss Threadgood had been on the other end of this dialogue, Anne would've let them run amuck until they tripped over their own tongue to reveal their true intentions. With her dad, however, she had to tread with care.

"Mighta seen her over in Little Tokyo today," he said.

To avert any personal connection with the burlesque theater, Anne decided to throw out some truth. "I don't recall her last name, barely talk to her. Think she's a sophomore. Not sure. You know me and my memory," and a skittish tee-hee.

He viewed the clock. "Time for *The Lone Ranger*," and wiped his hands dry and left for the living room's radio.

Anne returned a tight nod, all she could summon, her mind a mush at the close call. She stared at the floral patterns on the wallpaper, her vision stuck within the grasp of painted daisies and daffodils. A towel hung suspended from her hands as the faucet ran for no reason.

Chapter Thirteen

A knock on the door echoed a dull clunk.

"Come in. By all means, come in," Nobuo said in Japanese. Maybe one of the crew, he thought, but his grin flattened at the presence of his captain, and he stood with a salute.

"At ease, airman," Commander Minoru said. He slumped into a chair, plopped his feet onto the alloyed desk and took a long pull on his cigarette. "The gods smile upon you."

"Sir?" Nobuo grew uneasy at his skipper's cool demeanor.

"INS has come up with an interesting strategy concerning the use of submarine-based seaplanes."

"I'm afraid I don't understand."

"Navy Intelligence is suggesting that your E14Y be available not only for reconnaissance but for combat as well. A very innovative approach, wouldn't you agree?"

"Well, sir, I..." Nobuo fanned his hand at a passing cloud of smoke. "...I don't really know if it's built for such purpose what with its weight-to-speed ratio. Its aerodynamics are designed for stability not..."

The captain interrupted the blather, asking, "Is it ready for battle?"

"Well, I suppose so. The pushrod is back in place. The lifter for the cam plate is working." An afterthought rattled up, and he said, "*Battle*? What battle, sir?"

"Why, America, of course," Minoru answered before leaving.

Nobuo waved at the soot that hung where his superior once sat. Disgusting habit, he thought, and hacked up phlegm. He pivoted toward his samurai sword and said, "Satisfied now?"

The weapon's legacy had traveled a great distance to reach him, some four hundred years. In abrupt strokes Nobuo spoke to the heirloom.

"Blood on your tip for all eternity. Sixty men you have put down. You are not worthy," and he shoved the killing machine to the bottom of its sheath and flung it across the table, knocking over the framed likeness of a bygone owner. Nobuo gazed upon the disarray before him, paused to reflect and returned the picture and the sword to their rightful place. Order was the cornerstone of all wisdom. If anarchy ruled supreme within the confines of his tiny cabin, what sort of mayhem awaited outside in the big world?

*   *   *

Shrimp nets hunted for pink gold through "free" water. The sun rose full after another hour and the *Mystic Isle* lowered its anchor. Seamen brought up their catch and busied themselves with the separation of trash fish from crustaceans. Turtles, a dolphin and other by-catch were swept overboard to form an avenue of blood. A pair of boats arrived within the chum and set out their bait for tarpon and shark.

Nobuo soon realized that his target was not a ship of war but rather one of commerce. The craft's innocence struck him. With the netting splayed out port and starboard, the trawler took on the appearance of a giant butterfly.

I didn't come to murder insects and fishermen, he thought. Didn't come to murder anyone.

The E14Y approached from downwind not more than twenty meters above the blue water and came up sudden on the boat's stern. With a jerk, Nobuo pulled back on the wheel and thundered over the *Mystic Isle*. I can't do this, he told himself, and released his hold from the trigger.

The crew, startled by the explosive buzz, left their stations and hollered at someone in the pilothouse. With commands given, everyone darted to free tube-shaped objects from a storage locker.

Nobuo steadied himself and circled around. He returned a quivering finger to the toggle switch. Two hundred meters, hundred and fifty, seventy-five, fifty and...Blasts from several shotguns filled the sky. Pellets caromed off the fuselage and the floaters. In his panic the pilot engaged his weapon. The 80 kg incendiary bomb splashed ten meters aft of his quarry.

Another round of pings entered the fray alongside a different kind of explosive, widening his fright. Red bursts appeared on either side of him. Dark clouds followed with the smell of phosphorous. Flare guns? Throwing everything at him except their teacups. Men hoisted up their weapons in victory.

"The gods smile upon you." He gagged at his commander's prediction. The airman abandoned his composure altogether and added, "The gods can kiss the tip of my sword with their *fundoshi*."

Two minutes later the plane parted the sea and coasted alongside the I-25. Loud pops shot balls of exhaust from the mufflers. With a final wheeze, the plane fell silent. The pilot removed his goggles and hat to clumps of noise. Whistles cascaded over the side of the submarine to him. At first he thought that they were the stuff of jeers. He sunk in embarrassment. The battle was close enough to capture with the naked eye. Can't escape your fate, and he braced for the worst. He realized, however, by the mounds of smiles peering down upon him, that the jeers had morphed into cheers. Chants of *"shouri, shouri, shouri"* met him in celebration as he and the E14Y rode the crane to the deck.

Nobuo didn't understand. He brought to his mind the attack run and remembered the unexpected report of firearms and the release of his bomb and the subsequent fire and smoke. Wait, he thought. Of course, that must be it. From this distance, his mates could have misinterpreted the red phosphorous clouds of flare guns as a hit. There was no reason to lower the crew's expectations with unnecessary details. Besides, the ship's morale could use a boost.

He straightened his flight jacket, wetted his pencil mustache and stood up in his cockpit. His hands clasped together in a high nod to the right and to the left as might a prizefighter after his triumph. The deception felt good. Well, not really deception, he thought. He did what every pilot was trained to do—confront the enemy. His ancestors would have been proud.

Later, a few sailors gathered below to party. They offered up salmon, caught on hand-lines in true sashimi tradition. Nobuo pierced the fish's brain with a sharp spike and divided it into thin slices. A wasabi paste added a little zing while a daikon garnish dressed up the affair. A knot of hungry men cluttered the galley. Further down the narrow passageway, Commander Minoru leaned against the hull, studying the scene.

Chapter Fourteen

Two Grays walked under a vapor bulb. A bluish tint blurred the edges that divided Polk Gulch from the Tenderloin. A row of trendy coffee houses, restaurants and antique shops stood in mark contrast to the pool halls, strip joints and gin mills that gritted the next block. One could not discern which district was winning the tug-of-war. If history were any delineation of such a forecast, sin would reign victorious over virtue. For certain men, however, the distinction remained mute as long as they were sitting on top of the pile. The substance of such pile didn't matter much either.

Little life roamed the avenue at four A.M. What human forms were present—addicts, bums, unemployed, meager wage earners (prostitutes, musicians, poets and such)—meandered toward O'Farrell Street and the Tenderloin with different purposes except one, to survive another day.

"We must do something regarding that hellacious marker," Fredericks said as he gestured toward the "Polk Strasse" signpost.

"Neigh-neighborhood doesn't belong to them anymore," Jones said.

The lane had been the main commercial fairway for German immigrants since the late 19th century. Square buildings stood simplistic in form with foreboding edifices.

"The gumption of these outlanders," Fredericks said, "erecting these concrete fabrications as if they were of the mind to stay."

They paused at a butcher shop's window, which was set tall and deep within semi-circular arches. An array of sausages sat below a note that boasted fifteen hundred varieties.

"Where would one acquire such a plenitude of pork during these conflicting days?" Fredericks said.

"No-nobody's got any right to that much food."

Two doors down, a bookstore's display rack showed a sampling of the Grimms' fairy tales. *Cinderella, Snow White, Hansel and Gretel,* and *Rapunzel* sat there with an air of royalty.

"Those pantywaisters dare not compare to Paul Bunyan or Casey Jones or John Henry," Fredericks said.

The lieutenant let his superior rattle on.

"And what kind of designation is Grimm, I ask you? Is that a fit label for a teller of cheer and fantasy?"

A painted message over a diner's entrance read: BREAKFAST LIKE AN EMPEROR / LUNCH LIKE A KING / DINE LIKE A BEGGAR. In a few hours the place would be open for business. There was no time, however, for breads or cold cuts or cheeses or boiled eggs. Not this morning.

Fredericks gazed beyond the neighborhood as if digesting the fate before him and said, "Today will be witness to a grand and noble accounting of my immortal legacy."

The self-adulation continued as they passed a music store, a beer hall and a pastry shop featuring *Schwarzwalder Kirschtörte* (Black Forest cake). Jones slumped under his superior's reminder of how he and he alone was responsible for persuading the San Francisco Labor Council to evict Nazi Bund members from the German House, which they now climbed the steps of.

Three knocks sounded off the honeycombed door. An eye peered through the peephole as Fredericks motioned his presence. Latches and bolts slid from their strongholds. A guard in his West Point uniform stood in the entrance with a stiff hand at his forehead in address.

Jones and Fredericks strolled through the lobby. The major meandered past photos of former Republican Gray leaders, hoping that someday his headshot would grace these walls as well. The pair entered the main hall where forty or so militiamen mingled. Liquored up, their anxious chatter rang hopeful. The lieutenant preceded his commander who waited in the back of the auditorium. Jones mounted the stage, ran through a series of gestures and asked everyone to remain erect for the Stars 'n' Stripes. All joined in, but the oath ended in different cadences as the men tried in vain to follow the stuttering. They seated themselves only to hear the command to rise once more.

Fredericks mouthed hellos to men on either side as he walked down the center aisle. He took his rightful spot behind the podium, banged a gavel and said, "This meeting shall come to order."

Backsides and haunches began to lower themselves at uneven intervals, unsure if another call to stand was forthcoming. Major Fredericks plucked his "lemon squeezer" from his head. Bronze acorns dangled from the wide brim as he flipped it upside down.

"'A bomb fell on Italy...and slid off.'" He shook his head with laughter as if he owned the one-liner and then lifted the hat's cardboard band back up. "'Why does the *new* Italian Navy have glass bottom boats?'" He looked up for effect and then said, "'To see the *old* Italian Navy,'" and a singular chortle sifted through the first couple of rows.

Sergeant Klausen withdrew, surprised by the indelicacy before him. His friend's corpse lay warm while ethnic jabs ascended freely and without hesitation. What the hell?

Lieutenant Hank Jones sat nearby with his bowed head, showing his disbelief not at the inclusion of racial insensitivity but at the introduction of another stale joke. He looked in the direction of the podium and let loose with a chain of talking-coughs: "E-N-O-U-G-H. E-N-O-U-G-H."

Fredericks swiveled around to see a hurry-up-wave from his second-in-command, shot him a glare and whispered, "Do you mind?"

"I do," Jones said.

"Be still, you're making a buffoon of yourself."

"I thi-think you got that ass-backwards," and Jones pointed toward the audience.

The major turned around to witness a restlessness circulating the hall. Earlier, his ego had allowed him to interpret such as nothing other than approval. Upon closer examination, he could see the meaning behind the clatter and decided to move onto other matters.

"As you are well aware, the issue of our headquarters' namesake is long overdue for a formal vote," Fredericks said. "This building was constructed a half-century ago when different nationalities saw a need to preserve their heritage. This no longer rings popular within most sections of the City. The German Concordia Sport Club, the Deutscher Musikverei Music Society, and the Freundschaft Liederkranz Men's Choir have been ordered to disband. The German Hospital is now Franklin Hospital. Furthermore, their language is no longer taught in our schools. In tune with such sentiment, this distinguished assemblage should be permitted to gather without any foreign stigma attached."

Fredericks measured the group's interest and said, "Therefore, I do hereby propose that the official name of this structure be forever altered from the 'German House' to the 'California Hall'. The floor is now open for discussion."

Not seeing a single hand to debate the issue, Fredericks asked for a second to his motion, which Lieutenant Hank Jones offered. The major raised the small mallet and said, "All those in favor, say 'aye'." Deep-throated calls shot forth to confirm their wishes. "All those oppose." He scanned the hall for any traitorous declaration and to his surprise he found one. He squinted to double-check his finding.

Klausen and others followed Fredericks's frown to the bold person in the back where one of their own raised his arm and registered a loud "nay". Jones started toward the man but thought better of it and stopped short.

Proud of his German heritage, Gilbert Schmidt felt that his kind should remain steadfast when it came to their contribution to the American fiber. In addition, whenever the subject of Hitler came up, he was quick to join ranks in denouncing the dictator as a crazed fanatic. He and his brother, Felix, had fought on opposite sides during WWI. Upon Felix's demise last month, his two German Iron Crosses were mailed across the Atlantic to his sole remaining kin. Private Schmidt sent them to the Salvage for Victory Committee and often quipped that perhaps his brother's medals would find their way back to Hitler on the backside of a bomb. The gesture held sway with most of his fellow fraternity members but not all.

Klausen admired Schmidt's tenacity but thought that such outspoken stubbornness would invite trouble. What would Tony have thought? he wondered.

With the banging of the little wooden hammer, the vote was final and the vulgarity of the word "German" wiped from the site forever.

"Yes, well, I must say that I am a bit disappointed that the vote was not unanimous," Fredericks added, his look still fixed on Private Schmidt. "Nevertheless, it is time to move on," and his vision slid wide to include the entire assembly. "I wish to applaud everyone on Operation Dragon. Your seizure of illegal contraband and suspected foreign agents has proved invaluable. Needless to say, Lieutenant General Wright was more than pleased to be given the opportunity to interrogate these aliens. As a result he has given his full endorsement to our next mission."

Fredericks waved a document before his men. "I have in my hand a manifesto from the Joint Immigration Committee of the California Legislature which will be tomorrow's headlines." He read aloud the declaration, which argued that Japanese Americans were "totally inassimilable", that they remained loyal subjects of the Emperor. Furthermore, the document declared that ethnic after-school programs were "bastions of racism", advancing doctrines of foreign superiority.

"This will come to its just end today," he called out, straightening his arm in exclamation as he marched off stage. The others fell in behind him, hooting as if it was a parade.

Out back Sergeant Klausen ordered two of his men, Jarvis and Hondo, to help with the loading of supplies onto the ten-wheelers. They were brutes of men, siblings actually, wearing tattooed arms and punchy smirks that told all others to take a wide berth.

"Think we're gonna kick some butt tonight?" Jarvis asked, his breath rank with the smell of booze.

"How should I know?" Hondo responded.

$$* \qquad * \qquad *$$

Three camouflaged trucks rolled to a quiet stop. Beams were extinguished, motors left running. Canvas flaps flung open as Grays dismounted. Some carried boards while others carted tools. All armed.

Bolt cutters snapped a gate's lock. A cluster of men rushed toward a two-story building while Lieutenant Jones's unit sealed the perimeter.

Hondo pressed plywood sheets against a window as Jarvis worked a screwdriver. The brothers felt anxious, ready for some action. Their eyes darted to and fro like drunken fireflies, but the night remained still. Disappointment grew proportionate with the passage of time. Without warning, a faraway drum tipped over and rolled out along the asphalt playground. The pair jerked up at the prospect of battle when Jarvis spotted a trio of foraging critters.

"Nothin' but raccoons."

"Are you daft or just plain stupid?" Hondo argued. "Can't tell a coon from a dog? I swear to God."

"Whatever it is, it's a sight prettier than that mug you got on."

"Looks is something we share. Bred from the same mother if you remember."

"Even mothers make mistakes."

Fredericks ordered the brothers to cease. He exhaled his disdain and put a wooden match to his cigar before promenading up the main steps. With the heel of his revolver, the major hammered a "Permanently Closed" announcement onto the entrance of the Shinjuku-ku Language School. Men began to retreat when a loud bang pierced the air.

Jones yelled from a short distance away. All rushed forward to see Gilbert Schmidt's skull resting on the lap of their lieutenant. Unable to speak his meaning, Jones signaled down a darkened alley with the barrel of his smoking pistol.

Five minutes later Hondo returned. "Found this behind a trashcan," and surrendered a crimson-covered knife.

"Wasn't no trashcan," Jarvis corrected. "Was a holding bin."

"Held trash, didn't it?"

Fredericks called for the bloodstained blade. "This would be a shun knife, a centuries-old Samurai weapon. Same species that killed Private Ponti."

He raised the weapon to let the gruesome scene imbed itself upon the memories of his men. They passed around the death-tool, each wiping a portion of their fellow Gray's sanguine fluid onto their palms.

Fredericks approached his lieutenant for an explanation. Jones said that he saw Schmidt struggle with a much smaller man, a man who wore black from head to toe.

"I fi-fired a round, scared him off, but it was too late." Swallowed by the turmoil, he could offer little more.

"There is no need to go into every particular at this juncture," Fredericks said in an attempt to show a common front.

While Sergeant Klausen did not share boyhood romps with Schmidt as he had with Ponti, the pair had struck up an acquaintance as of late with their common fondness for Original Joe's rich fare. While saying a silent farewell, the sergeant glanced at the coat lapel of the deceased. Threads poked out from a darkened patch once reserved for the Republican Grays insignia. Same as Tony's, he thought. Wanting to express this observation, he returned to the faces of the others, but hatred had taken up residence there. He retreated from the vehemence, fearing where such emotions might take these men.

Porch lights flickered on, one by one. Dogs barked. Herds of men in pajamas and sandals came pouring out from dwellings toward the early hour ruckus. They spotted the boarded windows and doors of the school. Indignation replaced questions. Fists shot up. Shrieks charged through the block. Now awake as if the day had moved to noon, scores of others arrived as well, armed with bottles and bricks and pipes.

A handful of Grays formed a ring around their fallen brother. Pinned against the building and outnumbered four to one, alarm sculpted their motions. Then a curiosity unfolded. Several of the younger Japanese began to argue with their elders.

The sergeant ordered the men to relax their rifles. One, however, cocked his weapon and drew a bead on a frail man in his sixties. The Oriental stumbled forward with a baseball bat. Sergeant Klausen kicked away the Gray's barrel. A discharge pinged off a signboard, sending an old woman to the safety of indoors.

The Orientals ceased their debate, seeking meaning behind the report. Stares were fixed onto those in uniform.

In the background, trucks growled their presence. Smoke billowed from vertical exhausts like the snort from awakened beasts, and the mob parted from their advance. Two wide-eyed vigilantes leaned their tattooed arms out the windows of one, yelling, brandishing rifles like mad warriors.

Klausen lifted Schmidt onto his shoulders and all scrambled aboard the slow rolling vehicles. Sighs of relief sounded as the distance separating them from the mob grew. Elmer surveyed the turbulence that filled the street behind him. Figures scudded everywhere with wild gestures, but it was difficult to tell if their anger was meant for the Grays or for each other.

*　　　*　　　*

The muted shuffling of slippers made its way down the hall to the kitchen. Unsettled thoughts from the previous day's events burdened him, and he shambled to the counter for a cup of joe.

Different sections of March 15th's *Chronicle* lay strewn across the table nearby. Elmer flopped into a chair with his coffee and skated through the headlines until he caught one that sounded familiar: "Immigration Committee Reports on Japanese Schools". The article reiterated what Fredericks had mentioned at the California Hall—that the Oriental educational system was a "bastion of racism" and a "hotbed of ethnic superiority".

Upon a more thorough perusal, there was not a syllable concerning the closing of the school or the violence, just the long drawn out sermon of judgmental bureaucrats.

His confusion drifted past the printed page as he tried to get an idea straight in his head. In the middle of his deliberation, Anne walked in and said good morning. She saw him reach for a refill and told him to stay put. With kettle in hand, she reached around the raised tabloid and filled his cup to the rim. But she did not withdraw. The black gunk ran over the side of the saucer, onto the table to the edge of the Formica and beyond.

"Hey!" The father bounced up, wiping his robe.

"That was you and your mercenaries down in Little Tokyo yesterday, wasn't it?" she said and slapped the pot down.

He threw a towel to the linoleum and dropped to his knees. His head remained lowered upon the brown streak, hand-mopping. Not much of a place to hide, but it would have to do. He didn't know what to say. Should he tell her that he was conflicted as well? In the end he decided that the whole affair was none of her business and rose.

"I called Mishi last night," Anne said as she threw a glare at her father who had moved to the sink to ring out the towel. "She told of these soldiers who boarded up the neighborhood school. Shots were fired. A riot almost broke out."

"Thought you two barely talked," he said.

"Were you there?" she persisted, not caring where this bold effrontery might lead her.

"Best if ya don't see the Ishigawas anymore. You're only gonna get hurt."

"What do you know?" Anne said with intentional vagueness, pondering which way he would go with it.

"For chrissakes, they're under investigation."

"What do you mean *under investigation*?"

"Father had a ham radio in his possession. Strictly forbidden according to the new alien laws."

"They're not *aliens*. They're residents just like you and me." She rattled on in a sharpened tone paraphrasing Mr. Piner's civic lesson regarding the American Civil Liberties Union's stance that such treatment approximated totalitarianism. "Get it?"

"What I *get* is that a Gray was killed—Gilbert Schmidt." He paused before adding, "Still wanna take sides with your Oriental friends?"

"I'm sorry for the Schmidts, sorry for the Ishigawas."

"Can't see how someone could support such different families."

"And what about the *Klause* family? Or is it pronounced *Klausen*? Remind me, because I'm often confused."

"*Confused* is the product of minors of which you're still one. How's that for a reminder?"

"Not for much longer, daddy dearest," she said before leaving.

Elmer opened his mouth to rebut but told himself that he had never before won an argument from the backside of a woman and saw no reason to try such folly now. Instead, he stood there and studied the emptiness that occupied the room.

Chapter Fifteen

Anne had hoped that a sense of refinement would win over crassness. Yet the *Chronicle's* performing arts critic stated: "…tutus have no business prancing through the Tenderloin".

Showbiz was a fickle mistress. An audience's allegiance shifted with the latest hot act. "Must stay ahead of the pack," Rose often reminded everyone. In sync with such thinking, the theater's conservative *Madame Butterfly* was dropped in favor of something more "modern".

Anne wavered, but she needed the coin. Just last week she discovered a stack of unpaid bills stuffed in the back of a desk drawer. Whenever the subject of finances came up, her father would avoid the topic, too proud to admit that he had gotten laid-off from Acme Brewery Company. His male ego, however, would not keep a roof over their heads.

The dancer fluffed out layers of silk upon her frame. The dress was cut high along the thigh. She peered into the mirror. A cobra headpiece sat atop a black wig while strings of gold bands decorated her wrists. Caked creams and aromatic powders accentuated the rift of her cleavage. She maneuvered her breasts upward and leaned back to inspect. Feel like the star in a lecher's fantasy, she thought. Then a rational ploughed through and she recalled how *A Midsummer's Night Dream* and *Copula's* bawdiness carried the day. No matter how she phrased it, though, she felt her father's condemnation. He knew something. Just how much she couldn't venture a guess. A trumpet's note sped to her and she fumbled with the hook of her jeweled bra.

*   *   *

At the VIP table, the usual dignitaries held court.

"You can't just turn a blind eye to those questionable search and seizures," Police Chief Delaney said to Lieutenant General Wright.

"Sure you can, so long as the other one stays open."

"I don't know," countered Mayor Rossi. "Those Grays tend to go their own way."

"Listen, boys," Wright said, "certain liberties are allowed during wartime."

"Washington doesn't see it that way," Delaney debated. Sooty rings materialized with his speech as if the smoke from his cigar forewarned the stirring of some new thought. "Hoover is hanging a mountain of morals over Congress's head."

"D.C.'s righteousness continues to interfere with my efforts to corral these Japs, I'll grant you that," Wright said before adding, "My sources tell me that the Black Dragons have gone on the offensive. Might need all the help we can get."

"The times don't call for the use of civilians in these types of operations," Mayor Rossi persisted. "One got himself killed during the closing of a language school. Not good PR," and rolled a cigar between his lips. "Don't need to give the Feds another excuse to snoop around."

The lieutenant general hated kowtowing to the local authorities and said, "Gotta keep 'em on a short leash is all."

"Everything good here?" Rose asked as she came over and squatted on the police chief's knee.

He pinched a matchbook's cover from the linen and held it up to the owner. "Thought you didn't care."

On its front was scribed: LET'S GO!! / SAN FRANCISCO PORT OF EMBARKATION; its flipside read: HANG ONE ON NIPPON with a picture of a yank socking it to a Japanese infantryman.

"Hey, don't get me wrong. I'm all for the red, white and blue. Just don't advertise it," and she noted the name of the bar below the picture—Gold Coast. "The help brings in the souvenirs from the Silver Rail, Tadich Grill, Buena Vista, Far East Café, all over. Say it's good for business. Who'm I to argue?"

"Darlin', stay awhile," the mayor said at seeing the owner rise.

"Can't, got a business to run," and she went over to the silver-haired politician and fondled his few strands of hair, saying, "Anything else before I leave?"

"Now that you asked. My glasses are dirty."

The standard joke was reserved for special guests. Rose wrapped her hands around his head and brought his bifocals and hawk-nose and all to her bosom and gave everything a good dusting.

Delaney, wanting in on the fun, said, "My mustache is soiled."

She slapped him across the chest and wagged a finger at the trio. "Behave yourselves." She threw the VIPs a kiss and jiggled her hips as she pranced away, feeling the heat from their stares.

"Nice workbench," Wright said to the murmur of agreeing voices.

The boss walked backstage calling out the minutes to the next act. She peeped inside a cubicle and noticed Mishi brushing the hair of Anne.

"Enough with the pretty, already," and clapped her hands to hurry them along.

"Give us a minute," Anne blurted.

"Everyone's a prima donna," and she left.

Anne thought of telling Mishi how sorry she was to hear of the closing of the language institute, of the Grays' involvement. But where would she start? With not enough time, she said, "You must stay strong." The sentiment sounded hollow, yet nothing else came to mind until she spotted various costume pieces hanging from a nylon line.

"Here, try this on," Anne said as she jostled a feathered headdress atop Mishi's scalp.

The teens squinted into the vanity mirror and traded playful grins as if the world was right once more.

*   *   *

Anne stretched her neck, nervous. I have to do this, she thought. While paying the bills was paramount, there was another reason for staying at the Music Box. If she ever hoped to reunite with ballet, it was imperative that she continued practicing, learning new steps—even if those steps revolved inside skimpy outfits, skipping to the shrill of catcalls and taunts.

In the middle of her performance, however, her confidence waned with the demands for more skin. Anne missed a beat and fumbled over a cardboard fern. She rolled into a *cabriole* and a *jeté* in an attempt to conceal her mishap. Gliding closer to the front of the stage, she slid the strap of her brassiere down her shoulder. With the onslaught of howls from the audience, her muscles began to tighten. Stiff and out of rhythm, she started to hyperventilate. Get a grip, girl, and reached for the clasp of her bra. She couldn't bring herself any further and came to a standstill, gazing into the blinding glare of the houselights before rushing off stage to a chorus of boos.

*   *   *

He sipped his beer before hailing the cigarette girl. She looked spiffy in her white and black corset with ruffle top, matching apron with back-bow and pillbox hat. She lowered her tease to him and said, "Hi, Elmer. Would you like some Camels?"

"Naw, gave up smokin'. Just wanted to see that pretty smile of yours."

"My smile isn't down there."

"Was workin' my way up," he said as he placed a Washington on her tray. His grin deflated as a painted talon flicked his earlobe from his blindside.

"What's that for?" Elmer complained as he turned halfway around.

"Happy with yourself?" Rose said.

"What?"

"Don't play games with me, Mr. Klausen." The owner stood over him like a perturbed mother.

He pulled over an empty chair with the toe of his boot and patted its oval cushion. "Sit down before ya alert the authorities," and gestured toward the VIP table below. "Place is full of riff-raff tonight."

She lowered herself to the seat, crossed her legs and straightened her dress, taking her sweet time. "How long have ya known?"

"'Bout a week."

"Enough is enough."

"Meant to have a talk with her last night, but…" His voice faded to nothing.

"Anne's happy. The place keeps her spirits up. Lord knows there's enough doom and gloom goin' around. Besides, she can make a decent contact or two here, maybe restart her career when this silly fight is finished."

Bored, he drummed his fingers along the linen.

"There're two things I've learned in this life," Rose continued. "First, don't pet a burning dog. Second, don't play with a relation's trust." Her voice grew with determination. "Get over yourself and have a proper sit-down, understand?"

"Thought I'd have a little fun first. Not everyday a father has the upper hand."

"No talkie, no nookie." Her hands took up residence upon her hips.

"Usin' sex to blackmail. Oughta be ashamed of yourself. 'Sides, you can't bribe someone with somethin' that doesn't exist."

The pair had not consummated their relationship, the courtship one giant tease-fest.

"Be careful what you wish for, mister," and she sauntered off.

Elmer brought his vision back around to his empty bottle and searched for a server when he recognized a figure rushing down the side aisle toward the exit. He hurried into his overcoat and followed.

Outside, the darkness and the incoming fog masked much of the Tenderloin. The door from a flophouse across the street swung open and placed a slant of light upon Anne. The father started to cross O'Farrell when he realized that she was not alone. A young man appeared from the shadows to offer his arm, but she wouldn't have any of it.

"How did you know to find me here?" Anne said to Curly, full of vinegar.

"You ain't the only one with connections, sweetcakes."

He stepped back to inspect her frame. High heels brought her statuesque length to a fine finish while saucy colors lit up her face. A civil servant's uniform had been replaced by a trench coat, the slit of which exposed a pair of black stockings.

"Mind if I steal a look?" and his fingers hooked onto her wrap.

She bent his pinky to the breaking point. "Might want to rethink what you do next with that hand of yours. Less, of course, you don't mind having one less tool to wipe your Irish rump with."

Elmer strained to hear, catching only snippets of their quarrel. The couple, after a moment or two, appeared to have hashed things out as they slipped underneath the mist.

The guy doesn't have a chance, Elmer thought. Poor sucker. The father hadn't pulled all the pieces together but knew there was a connection between Curly and his daughter's sojourns down to the Music Box. Different recipes for his future enjoyment came and went. He headed toward his Chevy while treating himself to a good laugh along the way.

Chapter Sixteen

The crew assembled the E14Y in sixty-seven minutes. Even by Nobuo's meager standards such a performance would not suffice. These thoughts occupied him until a sailor rushed forward. In the cradle of his arms lay the aviator's family heirloom. With no alternative, the airman bowed, accepted the cursed sword and climbed into the cockpit.

*   *   *

The floatplane veered away from Cape Blanco Lighthouse, the westernmost point of Oregon, and headed south. The pilot scouted the rugged coastline. Volcanic boulders, transported here ions ago, dotted beaches, which gave way inland to low lying wetlands, hidden ponds and lakes. Wind-sculpted sand dunes towered a hundred feet or better. Bay spits and ragged cliffs protected remote fishing villages. He pondered if their citizens were much different from his compatriots back home, if they wanted nothing more than to provide for their families. Earth would be a better place if mankind stuck to his own plot, he thought. Mired in such distractions, a key landmark suddenly appeared.

A jetty in the shape of a giant elephant seal showed off his left wing. The E14Y banked over the flinty black rock and came to a populated bench of land. Must be Brookings, he thought, and checked his map when he glanced up to see a swarm of quadrilateral shaped objects assaulting him. He jerked on the yoke, but not before realizing that his attackers were simply a parade of kites. He laughed at his madness, released the tension from his grip and brought the photo of his Aiko to him. Her smile usually wrung out his paranoia but not this time.

He traced the Chetco River for 4.8 kilometers and headed northeast where the temperate rainforest separated to receive golden pastures. The farmlands did not prevail for long as the terrain soon returned to its wild state. Streams carved out gorges, which ran free and unmastered. Now here lays a land under a wise ruler, he thought, a place where one can move about without offending his neighbor.

His finger slid across a wrinkled map's demarcation line of forty-three degrees north latitude to the Kalmiopsis Wilderness. No opposition showed, but his heart sprinted like a racehorse. Was it his nerves or the six cups of coffee he downed that morning? He squirmed, pressing his thighs together. Pressure built in his pants. He snatched onto an empty water jug and began to relieve himself. By the time he finished with his business, he was approaching Wheeler Ridge. Too low, he thought, and started to climb. Urine spilled across his lap.

"*Bonkura!*"

A tower, manned by black silhouettes, emerged on his right. There was no way they could've missed him. Bad luck. Gathering what remnants of concentration he could find, he pushed aside another urge and banked left over his target.

Not more than three hundred feet above the thick mat of pines, two 80 kg incendiary bombs dropped from their supports. He circled back around. A black plume of smoke appeared as a forest fire began to build. While he could not comprehend how such a meager conflagration could help win the war, he was comforted by the fact that his assignment did not encompass a civilian area. With the absence of another explosion, he realized that the second device must have been a dud.

He cut west toward the coast and followed the Rogue River to avert Brookings. Another five minutes clocked by without any sign of the enemy. Just one more ridge and the Pacific would show itself.

His baleful look landed on his sword. "You've buried every owner that has honored you, but not this one, not today."

And that is when he heard the first strike. On his tail was a pair of crop dusters, Waco Upf-7's, he surmised. He pushed on the wheel and dove. The biplanes stayed with him as he did a half-roll before flattening out with the tree line. Panic began to climb his frame. Air pushed through his nostrils heavy and hard. His mettle began to unravel. He searched for his *gaman*, his levelness, but it remained hidden.

He went vertical and headed for the sun. Another ping. "I curse my ancestors. I curse this blade of death."

Not built for dogfights, the seaplane strained to obey his commands. The enemy was below, coming up fast. In his panic, Nobuo lifted his weapon as one might a spear, but a sudden shift in the attack-plane's behavior caused him to suspend his desperate intentions.

"Got my sights on a genuine Zero, no damn flamingo," one of the Americans said over his radio. Both hands remained steadfast on trigger and barrel to deal with the Remington's kick while his knees steered in erratic fashion. "Little booger's mine. He's right above me. Got a clear shot." But his twitching knee put the biplane on a convulsing course and another volley went awry.

"Get outta there and gimme a turn," responded his sidekick over the transmitter.

"I'm threw makin' losers happy," and the pilot of the lead plane returned his hands to the wheel and pushed his Waco into a snap roll and looped out on the Zero's tail.

"Tryin' to say I'm a screwup?" and fired at his buddy.

"Sum-a-bitch!"

*   *   *

Commander Minoru pulled out his stopwatch from his coat pocket and timed the retrieval and dismantling. The crew pushed the four sections of the E14Y along the track and into the hangar and secured the latch. Click. Sixty-five minutes.

All hurried below deck and moved through the wheelhouse and past their skipper's scowl. To everyone's consternation, more practice drills were promised.

Inside his cabin Nobuo made the two-step journey to his desk and hoisted the portrait of a bygone relative to his vision. He asked forgiveness for his earlier tirade, thankful to be alive, and promised to be faithful to the code of his ancestors. He laid the samurai sword in its place of honor, next to two praying candles.

A knock summoned Nobuo. Excited by his narrow escape, Japanese spilled from his mouth to his commander. "You should have been there. Air whizzed by on the tail of bullets as I executed a perfect barrel roll and..."

"The Empire," Minoru interrupted, "launched nine thousand incendiary balloons over the Pacific. A meager three hundred have landed in North America."

"Yes, sir, that's all very interesting but..."

"Hirohito had hoped for greater success. The I-25 will have to assume a bigger role in our country's strategy."

"Aha, aha," Nobuo said in a flat tone.

"I've received an official communiqué from Admiral Yamamoto. He will organize an attack on the Alaskan archipelago to build airstrips in order to give the impression that our main force is massing there. To further the illusion, we shall speed up our activities along the West Coast to divert our adversary's attention from Midway."

I just risked life and limb for my country, Nobuo thought, and this egomaniac wants to regale me with strategy and numbers and faraway places.

Minoru rose to leave but hesitated and turned around to reprimand the pilot and his team for their sloth-like dismantling of the seaplane. "Such behavior puts ship and crew at great risk."

Nobuo did not respond to this rebuke. Instead, he restarted his tale, but the captain was quick to remind him of his place, a place where personal boastings did not belong, and then he departed.

Rigid codes of conduct placed great emphasis on appearance and "face". One never showed, at least in public, his emotions. This was the second circumstance that day when the airman had failed to find his *gaman*.

*   *   *

Once into safer waters, the I-25 emerged from the depths. Still seething, Commander Minoru vented his frustration upon his men. Complacency would be the anchor that dragged all to the ocean's bottom. For the next five hours, the pilot and his unit assembled the floatplane, catapulted it from the deck and tore it down upon its return—a submarine aircraft carrier's version of "touch-and-goes".

Within this weary scene, a sailor rushed to the bridge to deliver an urgent dispatch. Minoru cut the flap with a fingernail, blew the envelope open and lifted out a decoded message. He organized his thoughts before plucking a bullhorn from its cranny.

"The Emperor extends his most gracious blessings upon the crew of the I-25 for their successful attack." He read on, omitting his pilot's name. "You honor your homeland. The enemy shall crumble before this great collaborative effort."

In appreciation of the flattering news, the captain called off the balance of that day's exercises and invited everyone below for saké and bean curd dumplings. In the mess hall, the throng raised their glasses in the direction of their leader. Minoru retained a humble posture and stated that Buddha deserved all the credit. While enjoying their treats, the navigator dialed up radio station KKSF out of San Francisco. The American disc jockey had named the invasion "The Lookout Air Raids" and stated in disbelieving tones that the attack was the first aerial bombardment of the U.S. during its long and illustrious existence. The announcer went on to say that little damage occurred as a forecasted shower had quickly extinguished the flames.

A sally of boos ran through the steel carriage. All American lies. To prove the point, the ship's operator passed along several deciphered reports coming out of Tokyo. "America in Flames", "U.S. Burns in Hell" and other exclamations made the rounds. More cheers. Nobuo, thinking he had heard something of import trying to break through from the American channel, requested everyone's silence.

> "...The lone casualty appears to have been a five-year-old girl on a camping trip. Apparently, she became separated from her parents and started to play with an unexploded bomb when tragedy struck. In other news Lieutenant General John L. Wright of the Western Command continues to apply pressure on FDR and Congress for greater powers in dealing with the removal of..."

The remainder of the broadcast slipped away as the image of the slain child imprinted itself upon Nobuo's psyche. He excused himself and made his way to the privacy of his quarters.

Chapter Seventeen

On the other end of the phone, concern echoed from General Mark Clark's voice. He regarded the growth of underground espionage groups to be a serious threat. Lieutenant General Wright agreed and shared an article written by Walter Lippmann that the West Coast "...is in imminent danger of a combined attack from within and without". The commander suggested accelerating Operation Dragon and hung up.

*   *   *

The kansho (a handheld imitation of the much larger bansho bell) tolled once. The worshippers, sitting cross-legged on their meditation cushions, bowed their heads and recited in unison: "Dharma is deep and lovely / We see it / We hear it / We practice it / We vow to learn its true meaning."

Dressed in gold and red robes, a Yamabuse monk by the name of Manjusri responded, "May we create a spirit of awakening and understanding to live a life of peace and harmony."

The kansho tolled twice. All lifted their heads toward a statue of Buddha, which sat on the altar's top level.

Anne let her vision roam over the tabernacle. Beneath Buddha stood representations of the Four Elements: candle (fire), incense (air), bowl of rice (earth), and a thimble of tears (water). At least that's what she was told.

The venerable Manjusri tolled the kansho thrice before walking to a raised dais where he peered out over his fold. "A simple life, without the clutter of material things, shall introduce you to your inner love. Harmony shall plant the seed," and he raised his hands in a gesture of invitation and said, "but you must tend to the garden."

Anne whispered into Mishi's ear, "Back at the Music Box, you started to share a proverb from your native land."

Mr. Ishigawa glowered at the show of disrespect. Anne mouthed an apology before steepling her hands in prayer.

Outside, a gang of Grays marched through an iron gate along a walled perimeter. Near a lotus fountain, a mythological king met them with a warning carved into its face. Hank Jones returned a snarl of his own before slowing at a second statue, similar to the first. Bits of wetted paper stuck to its surface, reminding him of spitballs, which once decorated the ceiling of his childhood classroom. He brushed several to the ground and pointed out the oddity to Fredericks, but the major threw out a look and hurried him along.

A three-foot chime hung exposed from a trestle pole under a decorative roof, BONSHA engraved on its brass shell. Jones could not resist and pulled on a rope, attached to a heavy wooden beam, and the bell struck a deep and solemn chord. Fredericks thumped his subordinate's skull.

"Cease your foolishness."

"Do...do that one more time," Jones dared, kneading his head.

*　　　*　　　*

"May all beings be free from enmity / May all beings be free from ill treatment / May all beings be free from troubles / May all beings be free from suffering / May all beings be..." and without warning an unsettling bong sounded. All peered toward the impropriety, in the direction of the sacred bell that rested in the courtyard.

The bansho rang on one hundred different occasions in the old year, just eight times in the new—one hundred and eight the total number of worldly desires to be driven away. Other than that, silence should reign. Not a trivial matter, Manjusri beckoned another to investigate.

A fellow monk walked to the square where he encountered a knot of strangers. He asked if he could be of assistance when Fredericks pushed him into the arms of a Gray. Within this hold the priest beheld a sacrilegious sight. Prayers, in the form of swabs of paper, lay scattered at the foot of one of the mythological kings, and he struggled to free himself.

*   *   *

Voices caterwauled their way from the rear of the temple over shrouded heads to the front. The offering of rice was halted as all looked backwards.

Fredericks pointed his rifle at the assemblage. "You are to clasp your hands behind your heads." He stomped to a man who was slow to obey. "Surely you don't desire to tarnish these proceedings, do you?" and he pressed the barrel of his Springfield against the alien's chest.

Hajime did as requested while throwing a sneer at the Gray. Sato observed her husband's malfeasance and scolded him with a shaking gesture.

Hank Jones strolled toward the altar. With nonchalance, he cuffed a monk by the collar. Anne bowed her head to hide but not before witnessing the cut along the soldier's nose, which had healed to a scar.

"May I ask the meaning of this encroachment?" Manjusri asked.

The butt of Jones's rifle hit him across the jaw. "Is that mean-meaning enough?"

The religious man lay on his side, his limbs sagged without purpose or design. He pushed off from the marble floor with one hand while bandaging his wound with the other. His dazed head tilted as if to spill the infliction from his countenance. With calculated movements he ascended and repeated a prayer to his followers: "Protect your happiness."

Fredericks moved forward to retake control and announced, "Your Mr. Manjusri here is a member of the Military Virtue Society, a cell of the outlawed Black Dragon Society." He surveyed the assembly and added, "He doesn't possess the eponymy of virtue now, does he?"

No further explanation was forthcoming as was customary with those of military background. The major instructed his sergeant to take a couple of men to search the back room. The remaining vigilantes stood guard, blocked all exists.

Hondo and Jarvis combed a rear storage area while Klausen stood there with his jumbled thoughts. Fleshy furrows ran over his sunspots. Filled with ambivalence, his mouth took on a hard line. The brothers maneuvered around the old man, ignoring him as if he had long played out his usefulness. Within ten minutes maps of West Coast cities as well as a short-wave radio were discovered and taken away.

The evidence soon rested before the militia's chief. He sifted through the matter with a condemning eye before turning to the congregation. "If any of you is found complicit in the organizing of these Fifth Column brigades, you will know our wrath. My name is Major Mikael Fredericks," lifting his gun with a warning, "and we are the Republican Grays."

With the tip of his weapon, Lieutenant Jones nudged the priest forward. He inhaled long and purposeful, drawing up small steps to insure his steadiness as he began the journey toward the exit.

Sergeant Klausen scanned the space for any suspicious movement when the auburn head of a young Caucasian woman showed itself. Her alabaster face appeared for a brief glimmer before turning away. No, it can't be, he thought, and joined other Grays as they marched past posted guards to the street.

"Mr. Manjusri," Fredericks said near a dead streetlight, "you are being charged with possession of illegal materials with the expressed purpose of perpetrating acts of espionage upon these United States. How do you plead?"

No response.

Pints of Jim Beam circulated the militia. Cries of revenge charged through murky heads. Infectious anger swelled up and soon evolved into such unruliness as to force Fredericks to suspend the proceedings in a call for order.

"Now, where was I?"

An uneven voice sounded from behind. *"How...how does the Jap plead,"* Lieutenant Jones said.

"Ah, yes," Fredericks said, rendering a condescending thank you.

Jones returned a smirk.

"Mr. Manjusri," Fredericks said, somewhat distracted, "do you comprehend that the penalty for the dissemination of classified information to the enemy is punishable by death?"

Silence.

"Hang him," shouted someone.

"Skin him flat," added another.

"Since this man presents no defense of any suitable nature, it leaves this court but with one conclusion. We find the defendant guilty as forthwith declared," and directed the priest forward.

He did not move.

Fredericks gestured to Lieutenant Jones who guided, with little resistance, the monk to his fate. Another strung a rope over the lamppost and tied a hangman's noose.

Sergeant Klausen had seen this before—back in the thirties, during the dock strikes. Same liquored threats, same faces for the most part. Not good, and he started to push his way toward Fredericks when a disturbance interrupted his purpose. The faithful had forced their way past the lotus fountain to the outer gate.

Manjusri surveyed his parishioners and said in a loud and meaningful voice, "Tend to your garden. Be at peace."

The worshippers kneeled at a bell's toll and bowed in rhythm to their chants: "May all beings be free from troubles / May all beings be free from suffering."

Lieutenant Jones approached to kick a crate out from under the accused when a single person revealed herself from above the canopy of raven-haired heads and shouted, "Stop, you have no right." The woman slipped under the reach of armed men and sprinted to the Gray's leader.

"You should be ashamed of yourself," the protestor said.

"Miss Anne Klausen, what an inconvenient surprise."

"This man's case should be heard before a military tribunal, not before a bunch of hoodlums trying to recapture the past."

"We...we don't have time for this," Jones warned.

"And you," she said to the stuttering, "hasn't your son's death taught you anything?"

"You no...no good German slut," and raised his hand to strike.

Sergeant Klausen latched onto the arm with a death-grip. "Sure ya wanna do that?"

From nearby a man in a black suit and tie arrived. "Good morning, everyone."

His self-assuredness quieted the bold verbosity that drifted about. Voices began to rise and fall in the form of disgruntled inquiries.

Agent Harris took in the scene around him. "Appears we got ourselves an ecumenical event." He steered his contemplation to Fredericks. "Uniting churches of the world, are we, major?"

"The Republican Grays are on official business, sir."

"Now whose *business* would that be?"

"Why, the business of the United States of America, of course."

"That outfit," the Fed said while gesturing to the imitation West Point uniform, "as natty as it may be, doesn't give you the proper authority that's required in this circumstance."

Heads began to swivel with questions for which answers remained hidden, and they fell back into their jumpy talk.

"Unless, of course, you possess papers from Lieutenant General Wright," Harris offered. "Now that would be an altogether different situation," and he waited for a nibble.

The lieutenant general has indeed approved of the mission, Fredericks would like to tell him. *How else would we have come by the information regarding the monk-spy?* But he remembered that Wright had made it clear that any implication, which might compromise the Fourth Army, would be denied. Fredericks didn't take the bait and retreated.

Within the Gray's hesitation, Anne ran to the lamppost and loosened the rope. Manjusri, unable to secure his balance with his tied hands, fell from the crate to the sidewalk. Anne guided the priest to his feet and brushed the earth from his robe.

The monk nodded a thank you to the auburn haired girl before Harris hooked onto the man's bound hands. The agent turned back to Fredericks and said, "Major, you and your men might want to consider joining the twentieth century. Just a thought," and he left with his prisoner.

"You're pathetic," Jones said to his superior.

"Now is not the time, lieutenant."

*   *   *

Anne was building a SLT (Spam-lettuce-tomato) atop the Formica when she said to her father, "A holy man, how could you?"

He wanted to tell her that Fredericks should be answered to, that he was abusing his authority. What about the monk? After all, he was on a "wanted" list. And those files detailing the layout of several West Coast cities? No reason to have those in his possession. Called for some type of action, he thought.

"You're no better than those who attacked Hawaii," she said. "Worse. At least they didn't rampage a holy place like bloodthirsty savages."

"Plenty of good boys sacrificed their lives at Pearl, on a day of worship no less."

"I'll agree with you there. They held a higher standard than those gangsters you pal around with, that's for sure."

"Maybe, maybe not, but that's not for you to decide," the father said.

"Who has the right to make such decisions if not the citizens of this land?"

"Those who have decided not to sit amongst foreigners, who don't pray to false gods, that's who."

She didn't know how far to press the issue. She left the table and tossed her uneaten meal into the trash.

The father brought his plate and silverware to the sink before plodding to his rocking chair in the living room. To help calm his mind, Elmer flipped through a mound of literature, which rested on the ottoman. He read the feature article in *Readers Digest,* entitled "The Battle for the Philippines". The news, however, dragged him down further, and he reached for the lamp's chain when mail and other papers loomed up before him. At first nothing of importance seemed to be present, just the usual collection of unpaid bills and requests for donations. A handwritten note slipped onto the oval carpet. He recovered the correspondence, held it to his bifocals and looked at it one more time. The last bit of the widow's sentiments wouldn't let go: *I hope Tony's medal brings you closure. God knows it brought nothing but heartaches to girls and me.*

He retrieved the brass insignia from an old cigar box and explored its dimensions as if the object harbored magical secrets. In concert the images of Ponti and Schmidt appeared before him and he started to reconstruct their tragedies. There were many similarities between the two—the torn lapels where a fraternity pin once resided, the discarded samurai knives, the ensuing secrecy in the media. Something, however, escaped him, something that tied it altogether. Riddles, brainteasers and a puzzle's missing piece besieged him.

Chapter Eighteen

Quarantine of Japanese

"Effective Sunday, March 29th, no persons of Japanese ancestry are permitted to leave Zone 22. Furthermore, curfew requires residents within said zone to stay indoors between the hours of 8:00 P.M. and 6:00 A.M."

San Francisco *Chronicle*
March 24, 1942

For all intents and purposes, March was over but where was spring? Old Man Winter never cottoned to such arbitrary schedules, figuring that he was here first, that humans were the ones who had to adjust. The Ishigawas bundled up against the fog's sting as they walked down Buchanan Street.

Hajime wrapped his arm around his sullen wife and said, "I buy you cream puff."

"We lose house and you wanna buy sweet?" and Sato shook off his warmth.

"No lose house," the husband retorted. "Government take care of everything."

"Yeah, and I am Tooth Fairy."

As they crossed Sutter, Mishi took in the brokenness before her. It was not the hang-your-minister kind of disarray but the cancerous kind that spreads from the inside out, choking the breath from a community one lifework at a time. Plywood covered up the windows at Sakagura's Restaurant as well as Ushwahamua's Fish Market and the local Laundromat. Next came the Shinjuku-ku Language School where a "Permanently Closed" sign hung from its chained entrance.

How often had Mishi passed under their collective shadow? How long had she judged their simple existence to be insignificant, even trivial? The thought saddened her, not just the idea that pieces of her heritage had fallen in such undignified grace but that she had taken such pieces for granted for so long.

Mother, father and child moped past a caravan of forty or more motorcars rowed along Post. A skirt of spare tires ringed their chassis for the arduous journey to the hinterland of America. Chairs, ironing boards, tools and luggage of different sizes hung from various handle-holds. A young child pleaded with his mother for the inclusion of his Radio Flyer. The tattered scene reminded Mishi of her last reading assignment as a Mission High School student—John Steinbeck's *The Grapes of Wrath*—where farmers had fled the dust bowl of a decade earlier to venture west. Now her people were retreating back along the same path, back along a road of discrimination and hardship to compete with Mexican braceros for handouts and scraps, all outsiders occupying a lifeless land.

Further along the street, well-dressed residents from other districts haggled with brown-skinned women over the price of furniture, clothing, kitchen appliances and other articles. Two doors down, abandoned chattel lay exposed for the taking. Things and possessions and personal articles disappeared in clumps. Mishi reached up and fingered her feathered headdress to assure its presence.

The Ishigawas walked into their favorite ramen shop and ordered the house special—tonkotsu—a pork bone broth with wheat noodles flavored with miso, green onions, dried seaweed and corn. Different ramen were imported from different regions of Japan. This particular brand hailed from their former island of Hokkaidō. Within this harmonious reflection, the father could not help but contemplate if he had done right by his family.

The shop's owner poured green tea. He was a weathered looking man in his seventies; his wizened face dabbled with worry. "Your family leave soon?" he asked in Japanese.

"Like you, we have stayed, hoping that reason would fill the day." Hajime had rejected his wife's plea to accept the government's offer to move out of the area, to homestead property in Nevada or Kansas or Oklahoma. "Too old for such an enterprise," he added. "Now, our fates rest with the authorities."

The owner shared accounts of how his enterprise had gone the way of other businesses. "Foot traffic and tourists now take their money to other neighborhoods. Without the frugalness and industriousness of Little Tokyo, nearby competitors flourish."

He cited other examples of things to come, of relatives from Los Angeles who had bolted their doors behind them, walked to a collection center and were never seen again. "Many tell of the separation of household members, of brother and sister, of husband and wife, sent to different camps."

"The military and the Grays are to blame," Sato said.

Hajime countered with a wicked glare. "Emperor Herohito's lust for foreign oil has as much to do with the conditions." In conclusion he said, "The JACL (Japanese American Citizens League) has urged all to comply with the internment order."

As if to cast his support to this attitude, the shop owner said, "*Shigatoa jan-ai* (It cannot be helped)." It was a phrase that issued often from the lips of fellow Issei during these past weeks. Sacrifice must be made for the greater good.

"Old people with old ideas cannot make fresh pot of coffee," Sato persisted. Fed up with the Issei way, she was more in agreement with the younger Nisei thinking and shot her daughter a malevolent stare.

"What?" Mishi said in English.

"You bring your schoolmate who bring her father who bring Grays to our temple."

"Annie's only fault was that she befriended me, befriended us. She should not be condemned for the actions of her father."

"Grays almost hang our spiritual leader."

Hajime took cognizance of his daughter's bowed head and sought to lift her melancholia. He promised that they would one day return to their normal life, to their jobs and home.

Mishi shot up. "Stop, all of you. Just....," but she could not complete her consideration and stormed out. In her hurry the headdress flew from the crown of her head.

Father and mother retrieved the memento and caught up with their daughter. In silence the family shuffled along Webster Street single file.

Chapter Nineteen

Instructions to all Persons of Japanese Ancestry

"By order of the Wartime Civil Control Administration, each head of household will be allowed to leave Zone 22 tomorrow, April 2nd, between the hours of 8:00 A.M. and 5:00 P.M. to insure delivery of proper credentials to the Civil Control Station."

San Francisco *Chronicle*
April 1, 1942

A queue ran north along Van Ness Avenue past O'Farrell Street. Men in blue patrolled the busy thoroughfare. Hajime, after three hours had passed, worked his way up to the front where a pair of armed infantrymen stood at attention.

The representative of the Ishigawa family took small steps down the side aisle of Commerce High School's auditorium, his eyes adjusting to the dim. Males of similar colored skin stood lifeless, their glassy stares fixed on the back of the person in front. With the exception of a singular bark from near the stage, dead quiet choked the hall.

Hajime came to a uniformed lady with a mouth that was much larger than her paperclip frame. She handed him a packet, rifled off some instructions and roared, "Next". Intimidated by her brass and patches, Hajime withdrew certain questions and climbed a group of stairs to a stage where tables stretched its length. Unsure what to do next, he ventured toward the letters **F-M** pinned to salmon colored drapes.

"My name Hajime Ishi…"

"I.D.," a State Reservist interrupted.

No response.

"I.D. I-den-ti-fi-ca-tion." The officer drew out the word, motioning with his hand for compliance.

"I most honored to." Hajime sifted through an old canvas vegetable bag he used for carrying just about everything.

"C'mon, old man, before Hitler surrenders."

"I almost there," and uprooted his California Drivers License (though he never owned a car) and presented it with a grin.

"Other relatives' papers?"

Hajime dove back into his bag.

Another long exhale. The soldier's countenance crunched up in disbelief.

The Oriental pushed objects aside before lifting a pomegranate, saying, "You like?"

"No like. Papers…now."

Hajime kept digging. Pens, a PGE bill, an old receipt, and a forgotten sock rose up before discovering his wife's picture I.D. as well as his daughter's birth certificate.

The tightlipped trooper stamped the legal instruments in red and directed the Oriental to the far corner of the stage, to yet another line. More waiting, more nothingness came and went before Hajime sat in front of a mountain of a woman dressed in a business suit two sizes too small. Flesh spilled over her waistband as she bent to the worker beside her. They were in the middle of a conversation, yapping away regarding the constant air raids, the shortage of canned goods, gasoline and cigarettes, and the world's predicament in general.

The She-mountain swiveled from her co-worker to the pencil of a man standing in front of her. "Papers?"

"I give papers to...," and Hajime started to point back down the line but the lady did not follow his motion.

"No, the other papers...bank statements, creditors."

"You Federal Reserve Bank?"

"Honey," she said, smacking on a fresh stick of gum, "if I was the Federal Reserve, I'd be in Caracas, drinking a Mai Tai, licking the sweat off some cabana boy. Just work for 'em, sweetie."

He dug up the pomegranate once more and made the same offering as before.

"No thanks, sweetie. Gotta watch my figure," and pinched her tummy to prove the point.

A document with the embossed seal of the assessor's office caught her eye and she gathered it in, surveying its contents. "So you're one of the 'lucky' ones, huh?"

He knew what she meant but didn't respond. Nothing lucky in it, he thought. Worked double-shifts for decades to be in debt. The Alien Land Law of 1913 prohibited Asian immigrants from owning land or property. He and Sato arrived in San Francisco a few years prior, able to scramble together the down payment of $150 on their Western Addition fixer.

"Sweetie, where's the itemized list of your household belongings—furniture, jewelry and such?"

At the glimpse of his shrug, the She-mountain handed over more forms and pointed down to the first row. He muddled away to others with like expressions—confused, lost.

Hajime started listing his possessions. Halfway through, he tried to see how such insignificance might affect the path before him. The future remained clouded, and he mumbled to himself, "*Shiranu ga hotoke* (not knowing is Buddha)." He repeated the saying in his head before diving back into his task.

The wait before the Federal Reserve employee had grown to the back of the auditorium. Undaunted, he collected his things and took his place at the rear once more. Every five minutes or so, he scrabbled a few feet forward. The one thing Americans and Japanese had in common were lines, lots of lines—lines at bus stops, train stations, checkout stands, schools, even lines at public restrooms. This was something he could do.

After another three-quarters of an hour, he arrived at the She-mountain who, without acknowledging his return, signed-off on each document. The government would be keeping the original deed to his property until the appropriate time.

"What mean *appropriate*?" Hajime asked.

"When you and your kind are no longer a threat to these United States. That's what that means, sweetie," and she popped her gum.

His discernment tracked the document as it left her meaty hook and disappeared amongst hundreds of other files. Much too much filled his head.

Not knowing how to express his worry, he retreated toward the exit. Hajime retraced his steps north along Van Ness before turning west on O'Farrell to Webster Street, a sleepy lane that housed a three-story brick textile factory, a café and other nondescript buildings. A tattered box spring and bedding blocked his path, and he stepped into the gutter to get around.

A pair of Republican Grays was arguing with each other as they left a gun shop when one of the brutes spotted the Oriental. "Hey you, halt."

Hajime kept his vision straight ahead, quickened his pace.

"Understand English? I said halt." Tattoos showed from his thick arms.

Hajime darted down a blind alley, not sure of where he was, and arrived at a twenty-foot-high cyclone fence. Disoriented, he rushed back to the nearest entrance, tried the knob. Locked. He banged on it, gave up the effort and dashed next door to a barred window. Nobody. He guided his vision back toward the alley's mouth. Boxy silhouettes glided past, and he relaxed a bit. A Gray, however, soon returned to peep down the passage.

"Hondo, over here," the militiaman yelled to his buddy.

Hajime flitted about for an escape. None found, his panic turned back toward his pursuers who had slowed to a steady march, cocky.

"Jarvis," the other said, "looks like we've found ourselves a Jap."

"For once, I think you might be right."

A window creaked open from above but did not attract much attention until a female's voice called out to the uniformed brutes. "What you do?"

"Go back inside, old woman. This is none of your business."

"Who you call *old?*"

A fiery exchange ensued with each side·voicing their opinion on the subject of age. Hajime used the distraction to scan the area once again. Something appeared that had escaped his earlier inspection, and he scurried toward a small tear in the fence. He splayed out the metal screen and shoved his bag through the opening.

A pot of dishwater cascaded down upon the Grays. The portal slapped shut and the militiamen, after hand-drying themselves as best they could, returned their attention to the Oriental who appeared to be tangled within the galvanized barrier.

At the realization of the muscular men restarting toward him, Hajime kicked harder to free his trousers from the wire. A grin slid across the faces of his would-be attackers as they heard a bulldog's growl from a clapboard residence on the far side.

"Hondo, which part should we save for the mutt?"

"Ain't much to go 'round," responded the other.

In his panic Hajime unbelted his snagged pants and jettisoned them and slid through the small hole. He hustled to a standing position wearing nothing but a pair of boxers, cotton socks, a baggy shirt and a red knit cap.

The bulldog bared its teeth and bounded toward the trespasser. Hajime hurried through his bag and retrieved a round vermilion colored object. With a mighty windup, he threw the pomegranate back toward the whitewashed structure. The pet swirled around and gave chase as if the ball of fruit provided better entertainment.

Unable to slide through the slender opening, the beefy Grays shook the fence as they promised hell's damnation. "This ain't over."

"So sorry for inconvenience," Hajime said as he bowed before them, doffing his cap, and whistled a tune to a nearby gate.

*   *   *

Neighbors crowded Webster Street. "Good afternoon, Mr. Ishigawa," a portly lady said.

"And a good day to you, Mrs. Kinshika," Hajime said with a slight inflection so as not to be discourteous.

"How is Sato? Is she…," and the woman saw his bony legs sticking out from under a pair of white skivvies. Embarrassed, she glanced away and scampered down the sidewalk.

Upon arriving at his address, a small boy, perhaps three, sat in a shopping cart crying up a storm. The child goggled at the half-clothed man and ceased his torment.

Pleased beyond measure, the mother said, "Thank you, sir, thank you very much."

"You are quite welcome," and Hajime grinned as if nothing out of the ordinary had occurred before sauntering up the limestone steps to his front door.

"Isn't it a glorious day?" the father said to his daughter who was sitting on the futon.

Mishi said hello before a realization hit her. "Did you forget something?"

In an attempt to cover his entrance with flair, he said, "Nope, need little for such a simple journey," and continued to his bedroom.

Sato, who had stolen a glimpse of her fleshy-legged husband from the kitchen, went on chopping celery, rolling her eyes. "Only matter of time."

Chapter Twenty

Pilot Akita knocked twice. The skipper called for him to enter and the pair began a heated discussion, speaking in Japanese.

"I can no longer kill innocent civilians." The death of the Brookings girl continued to haunt Nobuo. Could not survive the loss of my child, he thought. Unfathomable how someone else could either and he said, "I fly reconnaissance only."

"You'll fly whatever missions your Imperial Navy sees fit," retorted Commander Minoru as he tossed his fountain pen to the daily log.

"These citizens that we bomb are much like our parents, wanting nothing more than a decent fare upon their plate, a dry floor under their bed."

"Again, I remind you that we exist to serve our Emperor. Your destiny is forged on your body, an eternal reminder of your commitment."

With a sweep of his fingers, the aviator felt the back of his neck where a Rising Sun with wings resided. "Nevertheless, such an outlook requires…"

Minoru hammered the desk with his fist. "Do not question your superior."

"Yes, sir."

Minoru ordered his pilot to sit. The air began to settle. "Your family is from Bihoro in the prefecture of Abashiri in Hokkaidō, correct?"

A nod.

"In the beginning your village struggled to build a successful industry on the rugged landscape. With the irrigation system and other particulars, there had to be cooperation. Your people had to work together."

Nobuo could see where this was going. He felt trapped.

"Space has always been a premium in our motherland. People have learned to share. Selfishness, as anywhere, exists, but our countrymen have come to appreciate social harmony over the American value of independence. One must subjugate personal desires."

The pilot sat still.

"Do you want to disgrace your legacy?"

Nobuo did not have to think long on the matter. A dishonorable discharge would blackball him from any sort of meaningful employment upon his return to civilian life as well as shame his family forever.

"Now, is there anything else?"

"No, sir."

"Then let's get on with the war, shall we?"

*   *   *

Nobuo brought the floatplane around on a heading of five degrees south by southeast. "All your fault," he said to the sword beside him. Just give me my sweet native grasses, my precious Aiko and a cookbook, he thought. Not too much to ask for, and then he said aloud, "Apparently it is...*Imperial Navy* this, *Emperor Hirohito* that. If I don't want to be a professional baby-killer, that should be my decision, right?"

He was rambling again. Emotions flew scattershot. He leaped from one thought to the next, disjointed, one run-on sentence after another.

"Blah, blah, blah," he scolded himself, "nobody's listening, nobody cares." And a pop. Tendrils of smoke arrived a ways off his left wing. Another boom and then another. Perhaps someone *is* listening, he thought. Due to the distance, however, concussions from the reports did little more than cause the seaplane to quiver.

He realized the main focus of the anti-aircraft guns. Three weather balloons in the form of dirigibles drifted unteathered on the air current. They must think they're the enemy, he surmised, and chuckled. But the trail of bursts approached closer and closer. His laughter collapsed at the realization that the enemy had now included his plane in the felonious attack. He jerked back on the yoke. A heavy concentration of anti-aircraft fire traced his ascent, dotting the sky black.

Below, the bunkers of Santa Monica came alive. Sixteen-inch cannons pointed their barrels out to sea, waiting for intelligence to direct their wrath upon the nearest enemy vessel. With machine guns linked together on half-track beds, a parade of Quad Fifties sped to support the oceanfront defenses. 20mm artillery alternated with their much larger 90mm counterparts, shooting just ahead of the invading forces at different altitudes, adjustments made manually.

Nobuo's jaw tightened. Thoughts raged toward whatever images occupied him. That is when the engine sputtered.

*   *   *

"Horrific!   Powder flashes fill the sky with their thunder…Nobody…where…came from…"

Lieutenant General Wright adjusted the knob until clarity displaced static. He pressed his ear closer.

"Santa Monica is overrun with military personnel. Their guns lash back at the assault as thousands of rounds blanket the heavens. Zeros dart in and out of the smoky horizon. Ladies and gentlemen, the Battle of Southern California surges toward an ending I cannot predict."

Wright silenced the radio, turned around to his legion sitting at the conference table and said, "Recall all military personnel to the base immediately; make contact with the radar stations atop San Bruno Mountain and Marin Headlands; mobilize all Quads to Ocean, Baker and China beaches; alert Moffett Airfield."

Due to the overwhelming activity at Oakland and Hunters Point shipyards, the Navy found it necessary to moor much of their fleet in the middle of the bay off the Embarcadero in tidy rows. Pearl Harbor, however, had instilled a valuable lesson upon military strategists, and the Commander of Western Operations gave the order for all ships to disperse out to sea with haste.

*   *   *

Jeeps roamed San Francisco as bullhorns directed citizens off the streets. Overhead, Civil Defense sirens roared in agreement. The thump from Anne's chest reached her ears where blood throbbed in peculiar sensation. The no-nonsense blares contrasted with the uncertainty in her teacher's voice. Cries rang up from the courtyard below as if the enemy was steps away.

The unknown scalloped the face of a nearby pupil in fear. Whimpers wallowed upward until she crawled under a desk to Anne's side. With the sounding of the all-clear signal, Anne convinced her classmate that it was just another false alarm.

Mr. Piner instructed everyone to retake their seats. The teenagers leaned into one another with their chatter when a familiar tone came over the P.A. system. Anne could almost see the phony Cheshire-cat-smile through the speaker. It brought a remembrance of that day when Miss Threadgood and the local police escorted the Japanese students away. Anne had not seen Mishi for quite a while, their last conversation cut short. Distracted, she did not hear the vice principal's announcement that there would be an early dismissal.

Fellow seniors rushed past Anne who sat there with her absorption. Mr. Piner waited within the doorway in his houndstooth hat, his leather satchel hanging from his hand.

"Well, Miss Klausen," he said as he turned back to the empty classroom minus one, "are you coming?"

Anne shot up and fumbled for her text and binder and pens and things. She exited with her messy thoughts and hurried down the stairs to the outside where she crossed 18th Street to Dolores Park. It was not before arriving at the Victory Garden that she snapped out of her daze. Anne paused to orient herself, but disparaging notions continued to define her concentration. They were not those of self-preservation, but rather concerns for another that consumed her. Recent rumors told of Japanese students restricted to "home-schooling" and of curfews not unlike those that inhabited Jewish ghettoes across Europe. She lumbered up Liberty Street, her vision sliding along the perforated lines underfoot.

*   *   *

Nobuo departed from the cockpit to another round of cheers and whistles. Though he sought none of the fawning, the appreciation felt good and he began to question an existence without such. He manufactured a smile while winding his way through the crew until coming to his commander who stood on the bridge. They traded salutes. Doubt appeared aboard the skipper's face.

"How many bombs did you return with?" Minoru asked.

"None, sir." Nobuo said.

"Hmm," the commander said. He squinted as if seeking any representation of betrayal. No such folly surfaced, and he retreated to his cabin.

The revelry resumed with more congratulations and sallies of "victory belongs to Nobuo". No one foresaw that this timid man could own such a conquest, let alone return alive, given the numerous radio accounts of unimaginable resistance.

Delighted to share his laurels, the aviator regaled the crew with his adventure, an adventure fraught with a faulty engine as well as a solid parapet of anti-aircraft fire to rival any battle in history. To align himself somewhat with the facts, he confessed about the weather balloons. At this juncture of the story, an apparition of the Brookings' girl advanced before him. Contradictions swirled around inside his mind. He decided to sequester further fabrication and withdrew from the din of lascivious song and card games.

Chapter Twenty-one

The whereabouts of the U.S.S. *Hornet* and its cargo of B-25s remained conspicuous by its omission in every periodical. No longer did the *Chronicle* have the aircraft carrier arriving in Honolulu or linking up with other forces near Midway or New Guinea. The daily had decided not to give way to constant speculation. As a substitute, it kept the public updated on the overdue repairs to the *Lexington,* which sat in a restless state at Hunters Point Shipyard. The delays were bad for the war but good for business. Music Box tickets continued to compete for every serviceman's dollar. "The sauciest show along the strip," announced columnist Randolph Brice.

*　　*　　*

THE 1933 CHICAGO WORLD'S FAIR appeared in candy-apple letters above a backdrop of painted skyscrapers. In the foreground a mini replica of the Sky Ride walk-bridge dangled from one end of the stage to the other. Nearby stood a cardboard image of the Old Morocco Saloon. In the recessed archway, a king sat in a velvet high-back chair, wearing a white flowing robe. A scarab beetle plate adorned his neck. Concubines flanked him, fanning him with giant ostrich feathers.

A spotlight switched to the Sky Ride overhead and Miss Egypt who hid behind a purple veil. Flutes, harps, double clarinets, lyres and lutes presented their melodic notes to the traditional folk beat of Sufi Dhikr.

Up on her slippered toes, the maiden skipped across the footbridge. Finger-symbols clanged as the performer reached the far side and danced down a spiral staircase and passed a pair of palm trees to twin mistresses. With choreographed swats of jealousy, the beauty felled the women to the floor. The king's objections dissolved bit by bit as articles of Miss Egypt's clothing landed on different parts of his frame. She swayed with the music while caressing the king's sappy face with her lacquered nails. Her carriage shimmied with gelatinous seduction, her upbeat tempo running with the small band of musicians.

At this moment the performer saw a gesturing Rose who was standing just off-stage pointing to the audience. Confused, Anne returned to her act, tossing a waist-scarf and a translucent skirt from her fluid frame onto the throne of the king. Servicemen joined ranks in their uncontained lust for more. Chants met her, carrying the familiar demand to bare all. A scant brassiere and hip-hugging panties were all that remained.

Frantic now, Rose's lips formed a hurried warning while a finger bent toward the first row. Determined to correct all the wrong that accompanied her last performance, the ballerina blocked out the distraction. Moving to the sound of percussions, her hips jutted out to one side and then the other. She came forward in a suggestive angle and dropped a grape into the potentate's fleshy aperture.

Rose waved her hands, stamped her feet. No longer able to ignore the disruption, the dancer swiveled around in a pirouette-like move. Anne's glare widened as she followed the owner's body language to a table in front. Her father wore a devilish snicker. The daughter hurried to cover up her cleavage, inventing steps along the way. She pulled his eminence from his seat, used him as a screen and guided him sideways past plywood columns and paper fronds. Her finger-symbols knelled scattered and disjointed.

Upon reaching Rose, the performer grunted, "I thought you were going to handle him," and vanished to her dressing room.

"What happening?" Number One asked.

Without the energy to sort out another squabble, the owner said, "Better get back to the kitchen, orders are stackin' up. Number Four is havin' a cow."

"No human can do such a thing, let alone a scrawny Chinaman," and he marched off.

"Who let the fight in?" Rose said to no one.

*   *   *

"That was some nasty business down in Little Tokyo," Chief Delaney said. "Your worst public relations disaster. Even if the Buddhist was a spy, no one likes to see a priest almost hung. Too many martyrs spoil the soup." His eyes swept across the VIP table to determine the others' accord.

Lieutenant General Wright hummed a soft ditty, pleased that Congress had finally heard his voice. Executive Order 9066 authorized the evacuation and relocation of "any and all aliens" from "exclusion zones".

"Now that your office possesses authority to expel the Japanese from the West Coast," Delaney said, "there is no longer any need for the rough-handed tactics of your Mr. Fredericks and his Grays."

With a slow turn of his smoke, Wright wasn't so sure that he didn't agree with the police chief.

*   *   *

Outside the theater the area grew quiet. Anne brought her arms close to chase away the chill while guilt put an exclamation upon her gloom. Her father had tripped across her little secret, just as Mishi had predicted. But the night still promised further embarrassment and she saw no way around it. If absolution were to find her transgressions, she had to fulfill her pledge to Curly. Such was the way of the church upon one's sense of right and wrong. Damn.

"Hey, sweetcakes," Curly said, arriving on foot.

"Where have you been?"

"Was inside."

"Inside the theater?"

"Got a gander at your act. You're a bad little girl, aren't you?"

No response.

"Had no idea you were a stripper. Naughty," and he threw out a tsk-tsk. "Thought you just cleaned tables."

"Let's get this over with."

Small talk labored forth as they shuffled toward the nearest muni stop. A sly grin formed on him, but she refused to acknowledge its presence as he expounded on how he was there for her, how any secret of even the most scandalous nature was safe with him.

Anne searched in the distance past bleeding neon signs, wishing that the yellow face of a public bus would show itself. No luck as he rambled on about his procurement of a couple of hard-to-get reservations for the Tonga Room. She craned her neck away from the gloating when a dark blue Chevy sidled up next to the Plexiglas walls. A lumpy, balding man with kind eyes reached over and cranked down the passenger window.

"Need a lift?"

Anne dropped her head behind her raised palm, not so much to conceal her identity as to acquiesce to her destiny.

"Hi, Mr. Klausen," answered the freckled face. "That would be swell," and guided his date into the front seat.

The sedan rolled along O'Farrell Street. Anne crouched away from her father, but there was nowhere to hide.

"Curly, seen Anne's Egyptian act?" Elmer asked in a casual way as if his daughter wasn't present. "Traded in her fufu for a trollop's outfit."

"It's pronounced *tutu*," Anne corrected with a yawing of her head.

"Right. Sorry, dear."

"Saw the act for the first time tonight," Curly answered. "Somethin' else. Wished she would've...," and he paused before saying, "You know...finished the act," raising a sinister look to indicate his meaning.

"Hopin' for the same thing. Nothin' like a daughter naked in public to make a father proud."

A knowing grin formed on Curly, thinking that the men in the car were on the same page, bonding. The trio motored through the Hyde Street intersection and managed a left onto Taylor. Elmer downshifted. Tires latched onto the blacktop as they headed skyward. The scenery metamorphosed from seedy to resplendence within the space of four blocks. Yet that was the way of the City. Such confined quarters tended to define themselves in a hurry.

Architectural wonders crawled past without Anne's notice as she let her sour mood run amuck. In fact, at the vehicle's every hesitation, she choreographed her escape: reach over her babbling date to the handle and do a rolling plié into the night. As the scene rewound in her head, however, she saw nothing but further humiliation.

"To think," Elmer continued, his insincerity obvious to his child's ear alone, "that she still has time to help her country in need."

The sarcasm forced Anne to show the back of her auburn crown. Crammed between the two, she didn't know which was worse—her father's smug posture or her date's sunblock-cologne.

As the conversation deepened, Curly grew confused by Anne's sullen attitude. He knew that she had reserved the Block Warden uniform for some skullduggery but never imagined that her father might be an unwitting victim of such fraud. Then again he never spent much energy on the matter. It was her doing, her affair.   He just wanted an opportunity to peek beneath her mischief.

"Just the idea of you two patrollin' the streets until all hours of the night gives me enough comfort to get a good night's sleep," the father carried on.

Curly detected what Anne had witnessed earlier—a syrupy condescendence. Now he was guilty by association. He fanned the flat of his hand over his scalp. Had he known of his companion's previous plot, he would have gladly assisted in her escape. Ignorant of such facts, he slid further down along the vinyl and pressed up against the door panel.

They made a right onto California Street and followed a cable car's pealing bell. The former mansions of the privilege slipped past. "Snob Hill" took a lofted seat above the tawdry Tenderloin, as well it should. After all, the area was the former address of the Big Four of railroad fame. The Union Pacific Club rose up in all its brownstone magnificence. Curly gaped at the block-long edifice. Were the rumors true as regards to its scalloped fence? Patina had been allowed to settle upon the enclosure to conceal untold value. If brass truly lay underneath, he thought, one could make a small fortune with a hacksaw as an accomplice.

They rumbled past the Mark Hopkins Hotel, turned left onto Mason and entered a brick circular entrance. The Parthenon facade and Corinthian columns belonged to the Fairmont Hotel, a survivor of the 1906 earthquake and the place to see and be seen. Workmen in their orange jumpsuits bunched together sandbags to secure ground-level windows. The bunker-like appearance, however, did not deny the rakish charm that smothered the entranceway. A strawberry colored carpet ran along a path flanked by velvet rope railings. A valet stood at attention in his black tailcoat with squared cut front and top hat. His white-gloved hand stretched for the Chevy.

Anger fixed Anne's disposition as she disembarked. She spun around and leaned back inside to her father.

"Entertained yourself, did you?"

"Not really," but a shitty grin announced his true emotions and he confessed, "Yeah, a little."

"You knew and never said a thing. Just watched your daughter shame herself in the company of such a doofus," and pointed with her chin toward her date.

Curly's antenna stiffened at the reference before falling back into his previous concentration, deliberating where he might acquire a hacksaw at this hour.

Elmer disengaged the brake. "Have a grand time, kids."

Anne's scorn followed her father's retreat when she noticed a pair of lights flick on from a nearby burgundy panel truck.

Chapter Twenty-two

A brilliance shot from the uncovered windows, but no other signs of life appeared—no fuzzy outline of a lanky old man or a maniacal female, no Chevy in the driveway. Under the cover of a clouded moon, Curly sprinted across the street and over the crabgrass to the side of the house. He pushed through hydrangeas, cracking branches along the way, and leveraged open a stubborn window and slipped inside. A dish-cluttered sink, a pantry door and a white tabletop came under his inspection. Drawn by a collection of personal items scattered atop the Formica, he stepped closer.

Photo albums, notebooks and other personal items came and went without promise until a manila envelope with a foreign seal cropped up before him. He undid its clasp and plucked out a blanched photo. The faded pic offered a challenge but soon his conviction settled upon a young black-and-white figure standing next to a matriarchal-looking woman.

"Gotcha. Play me for a sucker, huh?" Keep your psycho daughter as well, he thought. Don't need the aggravation.

He put the photo back into its casing and prepared to leave when he heard metallic doors slam shut. Uncertain as to the ownership of such arrival, he listened for validation. Quarrelling voices traveled toward the house.

"You left me no choice. I had to get a job after you got your sorry-ass fired," a female's voice blurted.

"Didn't get fired. I quit. There's a..."

"Yes, I know—*there's a war going on.* Patriotism won't pay the bills, daddy dearest."

The argument carried them across the threshold when a different kind of disturbance from further inside the house unnerved Anne. She tried to hush her father, but he continued to babble on, changing the topic to her poor choice of suitors, to the shortage of brain cells Curly brought to their relationship.

"Is your .22 loaded?" she whispered, motioning to the Springfield resting beside the fireplace.

"What?"

"Where are the cartridges?"

"What the hell you want..."

And she snatched up the firearm and slinked to the kitchen. Disorder did not present itself until she noticed a photo album on the floor. The breeze pushed a peculiar scent around the room. Mingled with Spam and beer, the sour aroma baffled her. She glanced past the sink to the fluttering curtains and rushed to the window and stuck the barrel into the darkness. The hydrangea stood disfigured, not as she remembered. Alarmed, she rushed back through the living room, past her baffled father to the porch, and scanned the front yard. Empty.

"Have ya gone bonkers, woman?" Elmer said to his daughter upon her return.

"Someone's been rummaging around in the kitchen."

"Of course someone's been rummagin' around. That would be you and me."

"No, somebody else."

"Perhaps it was the whisk-thief or maybe the appliance-thief. Our Toastmaster might fetch a nifty price down at Mick's Pawn Shop."

"Go ahead, make fun, but I tell you someone broke into the house," and she pointed with the rifle to the opened window.

"Careful, girl," and he freed the .22 from her grasp. "With all you crazies roamin' around, wouldn't surprise me if we killed off our own kind before the enemy got here."

*   *   *

On the corner of Geary and Van Ness, a "Welcome" sign perched above a hofbrau's entrance. Though the midnight hour fast approached, a line ran outside.

"Le-let's go someplace else," Jones complained.

"Relaxation is an acquired skill, lieutenant," Fredericks responded.

"I'm hungry."

"A distraction might do you some good. Did I ever regale you with the parody regarding...,"

"Ye-yes," Jones interrupted as his stomach growled a dissent.

Fredericks removed his cavalry hat and began reading: "'A drunk went before a judge. The judge said, *You've been brought here for drinking.* The drunk said, *Well, let's get started.*'"

Fredericks poked his buddy. "Henny Youngman shall provide all the nourishment your soul requires."

"If you say so," and Jones pushed through the revolving door.

Hot food and cold drinks parried the atmosphere. No frills here, just good eats. Jones sidestepped down the buffet, sliding his tray along an aluminum railing, examining lamb shanks, roast beef and pastrami. He settled on a certain plate after spotting the head of a horned beast upon the wall wearing a note— "Where Buffalo Is King".

"Waddya getting?" No stutter.

"The brisket seems to be calling to me."

"What about your pledge?"

"Pledge?" Fredericks ladled up bean salad from atop ice chips before switching to mash potatoes.

"Nothing German, remember?" Jones asked.

"Brisket is of Jewish origin. It does not present a dilemma."

As they maneuvered between customers, Jones added, "You'd be happy to know they're building a prison for Krauts down in Crystal City, Texas."

"Do tell." Fredericks seated himself under an antique penny-farthing bicycle and picked a fork and knife from a tin can.

"Expect they'll fill up the joint in no time," Jones said. "Give those redneck cowboys something to chew on."

A young man wearing a civil defense uniform sauntered over. "Got something you might be interested in," and he flopped a manila envelop upon the red-checkered tablecloth.

Fredericks peered up at Curly. "You're interrupting my evening repast."

The kid nudged his discovery closer.

The Gray's leader licked his fingers clean and pinched out a Kodak and studied it. With the photo held up to his eyes, he said, "So?"

"See the sign on the building behind them."

HAMBURG TOY FACTORY showed from the glossy print. "Is that our sergeant in the knee-high socks?" Fredericks asked.

"Prob'ly. Bet that's his mother with the smock. Looks just like him, don't she?"

"That's it?" and Fredericks flipped the photo to the table. "A picture of a woman and her floppy eared kid? Hardly the stuff of incrimination."

"There's more," and the Block Warden pulled a water-stained certificate from the envelope.

Fredericks accepted it, thinking this was all a waste of time, his brisket getting cold. He had trouble with the small type and asked to borrow his lieutenant's reading glasses. The major moved the bifocals, as one might a magnifying lens, back and forth before his vision.

"Alice Anne Klause, born 1875 in Hamburg, Germany." Fredericks singled out the surname, said it aloud once more.

"*Klause*...Hmm. It would seem that our sergeant has forgotten how to spell his family's label." He dismissed Curly, told him to keep up the good work. "We might make a Gray out of you yet."

The boy said that he would be honored to be a bigger part of the war effort when his examination fell upon the mound of food. He hovered over all until a fleshy digit reminded him of where the exit was.

Chapter Twenty-three

Commander Minoru looked up from his desk and said in Japanese, "He who creates the illusion of reality is a magician. He who carves that illusion into stone is truly gifted."

"Well, early esoteric cosmology," Nobuo added, "was based on the Chinese philosophy of yin and yang, even earlier when…"

"Silence!"

"Yes, sir. Just thought you might…"

The captain held up his hand.

"Yes, sir. Very well, sir," and the pilot took a seat. A nervous tick squirmed up his left cheek.

The skipper paced back and forth between a framed academy picture of himself and a glass bookcase crammed with tomes of historic sea battles. "We shall strike while fear grapples with American sensibilities."

Preoccupied, Nobuo heard only the last word and wanted to critique Jane Austen's *Sense and Sensibility*, more comfortable leapfrogging to the nearest available topic rather than remaining inert. Speech was his salve, his ointment for a ruddy world. It didn't matter whether ideas or phrases were connected in any logical fashion. He resisted his natural instincts, however, and locked his twitching fingers under the weight of his legs.

"Using a two-prong attack might achieve our goals more fruitfully," the commander said.

Goals? What goals? No more goals, please.

"We will hit the Richfield Oil Facility west of Goleta near Santa Barbara. The American fleet in San Diego will be paralyzed. Our brave sailors in the Pacific shall proceed unimpeded."

The discipline that showed from his skipper's desk fascinated the pilot. Pens and ink bottles and binders and other items arranged themselves in perfect symmetry to one another. Then the drone from the other side of the cabin brought him back.

"We shall lay down a barrage from our deck gun while you attack from the sky."

From the case, a book's title rose up to announce Nobuo's worst fear. "Your plan, while clever in its simplicity, reminds me of the Carthaginian Navy caught in a crossfire between the Romans and..."

"Get your team ready. We launch at sunrise. Dismissed."

*   *   *

From the conning tower came the order for full speed ahead. The I-25 responded, doing twenty-five knots dead into the wind. Third Classman Akita constructed a brave face as he saluted his unit. Sailors returned the gesture before removing the blocks from under the E14Y. The shuttle blew white plumes of steam into the air and then slingshot the warrior on his way.

Timing was essential to the success of the operation. The I-25 would venture to within 6.4 kilometers of the fuel dumps for its five-inch deck cannon to be effective. To synchronize efforts, Nobuo estimated he had to stall for forty-five minutes.

No reason to circle over this endless ocean, bored to nothingness, he thought, and set a course for the source of his childhood fantasies. Might buzz Tinsel Town, he joked. Ever since the advent of "talkies", Nobuo idolized the movies. He and

Aiko never missed an American flick that came to their town of Obihiro on the island of Hokkaidō. *Gone With the Wind*, *Wizard of Oz* and *Stagecoach* were their favorites, all produced in thirty-nine. But the Emperor soon condemned Hollywood as "...a nesting ground for vile and immoral conduct". The denouncement came too late. Clark Cable, Judy Garland, John Wayne and others had already left their indelible mark.

A series of canals and boardwalks and pedestrians soon came into view. He waved hello with a tip of his wing. At 90 km per hour he figured the seaplane would be just a blur, its red zero unnoticeable—just another ace out for a joyride. Next, artsy towers of woody vines, shells and hubcaps reached upward, and he marveled at the whimsy of American culture. Five minutes later a one-of-a-kind landmark popped into view. He picked the photograph of his daughter from the control panel and pointed to the gigantic letters planted into the hillside: H-O-L-L-Y-W-O-O-D.

"See, my little one, we're in the land of the stars," he said to the black and white. "Remember our first movie together, *Popeye the Sailor*?" He ran down a list of their shared experiences at the cinema, or as many as his mind could recall.

The E14Y whirred past the famous signpost when its pilot looked at his wristwatch. Better head back, he thought, and swerved north by northwest. On the return an interesting edifice with a shell-shaped dome materialized. He switched on the mounted camera. Snap. Snap. A child-like grin appeared with the revelation of the Hollywood Bowl before him. His hand did figure eights to the rhythm of a symphony conductor's swagger.

With no great considerations cluttering his thoughts, he cruised up the coast while gazing at people lazed on the beach. Distracted, war took a backseat to the enchantment that played below.

*　　*　　*

The I-25's gun lobbed thirteen-pound shells onto Goleta, but the enemy was quick to return fire. The sound of concussions came from the sub's stern. Steel balls dropped from the heavens. A wall of water sent a man over the bridge onto the deck. The barrage lasted for another thirty seconds until the order was given to submerge. Sailors scampered down the open hatch as the Pacific rushed after them.

*   *   *

Nobuo scanned the scene along the Santa Barbara waterfront: nothing except the lapping of waves and caravans of military vehicles. The perceptible absence of the booming echo from American guns told him that he was fashionably late, and he headed back out to sea to unload his bombs.

The floatplane, after another twenty minutes, arrived at the rendezvous point. The endless blue, however, was all that he could see. Nobuo double-checked his compass. Where is everyone? He kneaded his forehead, rambling to the row of dials and instruments. With his calm drifting in the same direction as the fuel gauge, resignation began to shape his countenance. Melancholy steered his vision to his daughter's face. As if stirred by the eternal gleam in her smile, an election of a different sort presented itself. He sat up ramrod, shook the bleakness from his mind and entertained a renewed determination. At this early junction of the war, Nobuo felt secure in the assumption that his navy's code was safe. He acted on the risk and broke radio silence.

"This is baby chick calling blue heron. Over."

No response.

"Baby chick calling blue heron. Over."

No response.

He tried to reassure his comrade that this was truly he, not some U.S. trickster and said, "No more sushi for you, Charlie Chan." The radioman, Ensign Charlie Chan Kashimoto, enjoyed the American movie classics as well. His favorite was a series from the early thirties featuring the fictional Chinese-American detective. He would watch them over and over until one day his fellow shipmates tagged him with the film's hero.

Silence.

"Come in, Charlie Chan."

After another minute, a static-filled reply carried directions to a fallback position. Nobuo exhaled his relief.

On "empty" he sat his single engine down upon the rough seas. The crane began to do its job but gusts pitched the I-25 violently within the swells. Tick-tock. With a final lift, the aircraft banged onto the deck. Crewmen dashed forward, folding the wings back into their horizontal position. Tick-tock. The floaters made their way to the hangar, but the cowl and elevator resisted a mechanic's tool. Tick-tock. An alarm warned of approaching hostiles. With insufficient time remaining to complete the dismantling, Commander Minoru ordered the destruction of the E14Y. Nobuo streaked across the deck and rescued his sword from the cockpit before the fuselage slid overboard.

Chapter Twenty-four

Bare feet tiptoed down the inky staircase. Hajime continued toward the foyer and the antique desk where he slipped into his sandals. The latch receded with a click and the front door moaned open with a turn of its knob.

"Going out?" a voice said from the living room. Boom lights pushed their glare through the drapes to silver the edges of the futon couch where a propped up frame came alive.

"Mishi, that you?" Hajime said.

"No, it's the Shadow. Of course, it's me, but where are you..."

"Quiet, you wake up household." Reassured by the ensuing silence, he returned his attention to his daughter when a curiosity arose. Scribing instruments rested on Mishi's lap. "Why you write at this hour?"

She put aside her quill, rice paper and a strand of red ribbon and stood up from her resting place. "Tell me where you're going or I'll..." and her eyes moved in the direction where her mother bedded.

"Shhh." With the flat of his hand, he smoothed out his tension and whispered, "Need to talk to boss lady. Important."

"It's after curfew. MPs are everywhere."

"I back by sunup," and before Mishi could raise another objection, the door eased shut behind him.

*　　*　　*

The dance ensemble squeezed into the cubicle. Anne scanned the ladies and said, "Anyone seen Hajime?"

Quizzical looks were the only responses.

"Number One," she said to clarify.

"He's not coming," Fifi said.

"He's not coming tomorrow night either," Dirty Martini added and then went on to explain that the evacuation had started on April 7th, that soon Little Tokyo's 5,000 residents would be gone.

Anne nodded with recognition, embarrassed by her forgetfulness. Her head dipped at the realization that she didn't say a proper goodbye to Mishi.

Yet not all were saddened by the news. Lieutenant General Wright was delighted that he could finally present a proper defense of the West Coast by evicting every Japanese from the "exclusion zones". Rose McNally and others, however, had grown dependent upon the hard working immigrants. After all, they were reliable, not to mention cheap, their salaries well below the minimum wage of thirty cents per hour.

The troupe poured out from the dressing room not unlike clowns spilling from a circus car. A cacophony of broken sounds crowded the nearby corridor as they rehearsed for the next number. Everyone danced out of step, matching the discord that rang up from maracas, bongos and rainsticks. Edgy, Anne exhaled a yell and ordered everyone from the area. The backup quartet shared their confusion with each other and left to practice elsewhere.

Anne retired in a huff to apply the final touches of makeup. She never understood the need for war, and now that this horror sought to sweep up her friend, she was outraged. Feelings began to multiply, consuming all that was not right.

Before long, another disturbing image snuck into her perception. Her father had forgotten her birthday. But not just any birthday, her eighteenth. Scumbag. This is not how she imagined her entrance into emancipation. She should be holding court, celebrating with family and acquaintances, with Mishi. Damn.

A man, dressed in loose fitting pants and a red knit cap, entered the dressing room. "You look for me?"

"Hajime?" Anne said in surprise. She balked before stumbling out, "I just heard of the evacuation. I'm so sorry."

"There no place for *sorry* in world," he said without reminding her of his number.

A concern came to Anne and she said, "Shouldn't you be home?"

"Our block not leave for eight more hours."

"But…"

"*Butt* only important to jackass."

The last word reminded her of another. "Damn him."

"Damn me?" Hajime said, confused.

"Not you, him."

"Who him?"

"*Him* is a big, ugly Kraut with sunspots."

"Ah, your father."

"He was suppose to come down and wish me a happy birthday, maybe even give me a gift or something." She witnessed his befuddled face and added, "I bet his liquor cabinet extended a better invitation."

Before she could cut the air with another curse, Hajime pulled Anne up from her seat. "On birthday you must help someone else to be worthy. You come with me."

"I can't, I have to…," she started to say, but he tugged onto her robe and towed her out into the hallway, searching the area before seeing Rose heading for the kitchen.

*   *   *

175

"Wings need hoisin sauce. Reheat spare ribs," shouted Number Five as he returned a pair of fully loaded plates to the kitchen counter.

"Tell customers they can feed off scraps in alley if they like," Number Four answered before ripping off the next request from a rotating stainless steel band.

"You no can cook like One, that for sure. Don't care if he is Japanese."

Number Four lunged at his helper with a pair of snapping tongs. Startled, Five jerked backwards into a pot of pocky egg soup, sending "The Specialty of the Day" to the floor.

"See what you make me do." Five bulged with rage. "You big idiot," and snatched a ladle from the utensil rack.

The pair circled each other with their weapons, growling in Cantonese, promising each other eternal damnation.

"What in the good name of Jesus?" Rose said as she swung into the kitchen. "Could hear the racket all the way...," and her patent leather shoes flew out from under her. Her backside landed flush upon noodles and broth and chocolate-coated biscuit sticks.

Hajime walked in with Anne, studied the food-splattered scene and said to all, "You practice new skit?"

Five rushed over and embraced Hajime as if he was a long lost relative. "Four no know how to cook. You come back. We forgive your place of birth."

Hajime accepted the greeting with discomfort, not knowing what to do with such affection from his sworn enemy. He freed himself and put up his hands as if to say that was enough when Number Four reached across and snipped at the exposed arm of Five. Hajime clutched away the tongs and separated the pair. Four began to argue, but Hajime admonished such poor behavior as if he was still in charge. Behind the lecture, a voice sounded from the floor.

"Gotta do a better job of keepin' my feet under me," Rose said as she started to rise.

The help left their wrangling, expressed their apologies and hooked onto their boss, righting her. A flurry of bows and apologies followed.

"If you boys wanna see the light of 'morrow, better get your *feng shui* together." They were the few Chinese words she could pronounce. Didn't matter that she had forgotten their meaning, her tone delivered her purpose.

Hajime, realizing the hour, said, "Rose, I speak with you, okay?"

"Thought you were gone."

"No report to demarcation center until 8:00 A.M. Need to talk."

"Need a consideration is what you need. That's why ya brought along Little Miss Muffet here, correct?" and she gestured to Anne.

"Maybe, but I…"

"We'll talk later. First, help these two muttonheads get this place back up and runnin'," and without waiting for a reply, she departed.

*   *   *

The owner worked the bendable neck of a desk lamp as if a brighter beam might show the way to solvency. "No matter how ya look at it, the bottom line doesn't get any prettier," she said to the pair as they entered.

Anne prodded Hajime forward with a stiff arm. He removed his cap, held it in the fold of his hands and said, "Number Four be all right. Just need second cook."

"Good cooks are hard to find. Found debts is what I found." She lowered her head under the weight of these thoughts before saying, "Can't afford anymore dissatisfied customers."

"No, *mamasan*," he said with an apologetic bow.

"Quit callin' me *mamasan*. Makes me out to be somebody's sumo wrestlin' grandma."

"So sorry."

"All right, what's on your mind?"

"Need favor."

"Got that part," Rose said.

"Family leave tomorrow."

"Knew that."

"Go to Tulare."

"Just grew another wart. Get on with it, man," and she slammed shut the ledger as if one aggravation at a time was enough.

"Need someone to watch house." There, he said it.

"Get real and get gone."

Hajime stood in abeyance while Anne suggested, "Miss McNally, perhaps you could have one of those army boys keep an eye on his place, just until this conflict is finished." She approached in soft tones so as not to exacerbate things. "It might provide a bit of comfort."

"Listen, I'd love to help out. Truth of the matter is, I owe Hajime. Kitchen never ran smoother under his guidance. Orders were always delivered promptly. Food was presentable. Nevertheless, Lieutenant General Wright is pretty peeved 'bout the Music Box sellin' alcohol to his boys after curfew. No way to get around that."

In addition it was impossible to forecast the Ishigawas' fate regarding home and other property. Even God, Himself, was most likely in the dark, Rose guessed. If He had doubts, why should she pretend to know any better? She apologized and wished Hajime good luck before returning her gaze down to the column of figures.

Hajime exited and roamed the hallway where performers, stagehands, waiters and dishwashers said their farewells. Number Five leaned against the kitchen's doorjamb and waved goodbye with his ladle as if salvation just boarded the last train out of town.

In the foyer Anne said in clipped fashion, "Give my best to Mishi."

"I miss you most, Miss Anne Klausen." With a final nod he departed and became part of the City.

178

Chapter Twenty-five

Hajime hurried through the Polk Street intersection, mindful that the Grays' California Hall was just a half-block away. Van Ness Avenue came and went, and he continued west until he dead-ended into Gough. He zigzagged south onto Turk Street where boom lights poured over a roadblock. Razor wire extended across the street. A pair of MPs' skittish looks appeared from the guardhouse. Their edgy chatter filled the space as if the night promised the unexpected.

Hajime's sojourn at the Music Box lingered longer than he had hoped, and for what purpose? Nothing gained. Another thought came to him—his absence from home might soon be realized. Distracted, he stumbled into discarded furniture.

"Who goes there?" The guard's vision fanned the area. A feral cat emerged from the shadows to offer an answer. Satisfied no threat lingered nearby, the restless MP returned to the warmth of his shack.

Hajime snuck down an alley, skirting bands of uniforms. Members of the 184th Regimental Combat Team, the National Guard, the State Military Reserve and the Republican Grays took up posts along the perimeter of Japantown. Rumors had filtered through the Hearst newspapers that nearly 120,000 Japanese residents along the West Coast were ready to strike up against the sovereign United States. Lieutenant General Wright felt assured that the vulgarities of anything going amiss would vanish with the consuming presence of authority.

Hajime snaked back toward the rear of a closed enterprise as voices approached, which soon faded along with their stretched-out silhouettes. He peeked from behind a dumpster when another group marched down the passageway and past him.

Must reach home by daybreak, he thought, or risk being separated from Sato and Mishi. His place of refuge, however, had mutated into a cellblock. Trapped. Soldiers everywhere. Retreat not an option.

In frustration he rapped hard on a nearby entrance. An echo chimed as if from a crypt's hollowed insides. The pangs reverberated off the crisp night air until the rumble of trucks swallowed the disturbance whole. He breathed easier. Must be more careful, and then he felt the hurt from his bruised knuckles and scowled at the door.

Within his glare an idea appeared without forewarning, as bits of awareness often do, and he studied the metal slider, not with the blindness of his anger but with hope. This was the delivery entry to his friend's former ramen shop. He and the owner would slip away to the storage room for a game of Koi-koi, hiding from the bickering of wives, the sound of which he now pined for.

Hajime felt along its frame until a loosened block of clay confirmed his memory. He removed the brick from a cavity, retrieved a key and blew it clean. A sharp click set free the bolt, but rust resisted his initial efforts. Fingers hooked onto the slider's seam and he muscled it open. He found a switch but as expected there was no response. No reason there should be. His friend would have cancelled PG&E before their departure. Worth a try.

A gauzy stream of light from outside led him down a familiar path between wooden crates and a card table. Material possessions lay around like so many forgotten objects, things that over time had retained little meaning other than to give purpose to attics and basements and storerooms.

The glint from the alley ran out and darkness engulfed him. He shuffled forward, feeling his way, when he knocked over a dolly that clanged against standing cartons of empty bottles. The crash of glass caused him to crouch to his knees. He softened his breath, listened. After a moment, he continued to a door's knob, turned it and stepped into the diner. The sharp glare of floodlights poured through windows onto covered furniture and bare counters and shelves. He padded across the room to the front. Pressed against the wall, he leaned sideways and stole a glance outside to a wash of illumination. Where'd the night go?

A string of jangled noises sounded from behind, from the storage room. Rattled, Hajime flew out onto the sidewalk, looking back over his shoulder, when he rammed into a fleshy wall.

"Well, well, if it isn't the little Jap…in the red knit cap." The Gray became cognizant of his outburst of poetry and repeated the rhyme in boasting form.

"You very talented," Hajime said. "I go now. Bye, bye."

"Whoa, not so fast," and the brute snatched onto the Oriental and lifted him up to his inspection. "No where to go, no where to hide. Told you there'd be another day."

"American resident. No right to…" Then Hajime heard the steps of another. He twisted his head on his captor's grip to determine if help had arrived.

Instead, a second Gray exited from the ramen shop wearing a predator's smirk. "Hondo, whatcha got there?"

Hajime recalled the duo from his narrow escape a few weeks previous—same boxy frames, same tattooed arms. Not good, and he tried to slough to freedom with a kick to the shins of his holder but to no avail.

"Whaddya wanna do with the twerp?" Jarvis asked.

"Best we teach him some manners," Hondo answered.

"Sounds right."

Jarvis bound the Oriental with shoelaces, and the Grays dragged their trophy back to the privacy of the restaurant. The alien yammered out a series of complaints in a foreign tongue.

Irritated, Jarvis pushed him into an aluminum chair and told him to shut up, but the Oriental kept rattling on until a balled up fist cracked him across the jaw. His head fell limp to the side.

"That fixes that," Jarvis said.

Hondo went to the backroom. Not a moment passed when the sound of heated words hailed his brother. They explored the storage area together, lighting one match after another, when the discovery of a six-cell battery gave Jarvis an idea. "Could brand him so he don't get lost no more."

A knowing grin built upon the other's face. "It'll do." They had heard of Grays during the previous war swabbing the end of ice picks with acid and tattooing **G** on the foreheads of German-Americans.

Jarvis whistled the theme song from the movie *Stagecoach*, cowboying up. Hondo joined in as they made their way back to the dining area where they spotted the vacated chair. The pair fell silent in their surprise before scurrying about, searching.

"Could've tied up the sum-a-bitch to something," Hondo said as his eyes probed possible hiding places.

"Thought he was out cold," Jarvis said.

"Shouldn't have thought. That was your problem."

"If it's a *problem* you're wanting, how's this?" and Jarvis hoisted up a chair as a weapon.

Hondo raised an arm and bent his head in defense when a train of crimson tracked up before him. "Hold on," and he knelt to inspect. "What's this?"

They followed the blood trickles to the street and an unmarked black sedan that rested at the curb's edge. A face eased part way out from the driver's window.

"Hondo, Jarvis," the man said in greeting. "Fine evening, don't you think?"

The brothers were taken back by the sound of their names from this fellow, his identity hidden within the shadow of his fedora's brim. They decided to wait him out to see what information might be forthcoming. The stranger spoke with unnerving ease, complaining of the boom lights, how such contrivances wreaked of an overzealous man's doings, obliterating God's intentions for the night.

Impatient, Hondo squinted past him, saw the outline of someone in the backseat and blurted, "You got our boy in there?"

"Didn't know he belonged to anybody."

"Well, we saw him first. Guess that's good enough reason as any to claim him."

"If *first* had anything to do with it, guess we'd all be loyal subjects of wild Injuns," the man said.

"Don't care 'bout no history lesson."

"Well, you might care about this," and he lifted himself from the sedan and displayed his FBI credentials to their fallen expressions. A trio of police officers climbed out of a nearby squad car. Agent Harris switched out his Japanese prisoner to the black-and-white and then opened the back door of his auto for the Grays, not with the motions of an invitation but with the assertion of a greater authority.

*   *   *

The absence of snoring and wheezing woke up Sato. Her blind touch felt the cold sheets. She wiped the sleep from her eyes, crouched up onto an elbow and waited for her brain to come alive. Different sections of the bedroom began to appear.

"Hajime?"

She repeated his name and, when there was no rejoinder, pulled the covers off her frame and journeyed downstairs. A darkened profile sat in front of the picture window.

"Hajime?"

"No, mother, it's me."

Sato strolled to the futon where her daughter's long face showed the stress of the day. "Not to worry. Everything be all right. Your father make special arrangement for us. You see."

The attempts of her parents to placate her with running "all rights" had become a platitude, and Mishi turned away. Her quaking body, however, told the mother that something else was afoot, and Sato leaned an ear toward the heart of the house. No jostling of glasses, plates or a refrigerator's handle, and she said, "Where your father?"

No response.

Leery that not all was as it should be, Sato palmed her daughter's chin and repeated her query but in a more demanding voice. "Where he?"

*   *   *

With a pair of rifles slung over his shoulder, Agent Harris escorted the handcuffed Grays and Mr. Ishigawa up granite steps past fan-shaped arched windows. They entered a four-story stone building under a chiseled address—HALL OF JUSTICE / 750 KEARNY ST.—which sat opposite Portsmouth Square and Chinatown. They filed through security where weapons were tagged and stored. The quartet fused with the hurly-burly of the ground floor that also served as police headquarters.

Policemen came and went with purpose. A bunch carried the weary eyes of the graveyard shift while others cradled cups of coffee as they headed out into the new day. MPs, lawyers, men-in-blue, junkies, prostitutes and visitors weaved their way through the cavernous lobby.

"John Wayne's horse could carry a song better than you," Hondo said to Jarvis.

"Horse's name was Banner," the brother said, showing off.

"Wasn't. Was Cochise from *Riders Destiny,* first singing cowboy movie."

"Singin' got no place in westerns. Don't care what…"

Harris spun on his heels and hawked at the racket. "Don't say another word, either of you."

At the elevator the agent waved a knot of uniforms to the next stall. The ride to the third floor proved to be a challenge. The Grays whispered, whining to each other as regards to which horses belonged to which cinema stars: Dale Evans and Buttermilk, Gabby Hayes and Calico, Tom Mix and Old Blue. They couldn't come to terms on much except Hopalong Cassidy and Topper. Harris pulled his hat further down.

Hajime tried to steal a peep at the agent's wristwatch. Sato's probably up by now, the Oriental thought. Should've listened to Mishi and stayed home.

With a mechanical bell's single toll, the elevator came to a jarring halt. Shiny doors skated open. The tiled walkway and the buzz from the fluorescent lighting gloomed up before them like some subterranean passage. The otherworldly glow matched well with the manacled brothers' murmur, which kept a steady pace until they came to a pebbled glass entrance with gold lettering announcing Chief Delaney's quarters.

The clerk, who was expecting the group, swung open the hinged counter and admitted the party to the back office. Without waiting for each to settle into the leather chairs, the chief heard the FBI's account of that night and admonished the Grays for not taking heed of earlier warnings.

"By following the renegade practices of your Mr. Fredericks, you have placed yourselves outside the law. The Republican Grays no longer have carte blanche authority to roam the streets of the City with their own agenda." At this point Delaney had to silence the hazing that floated between Hondo and Jarvis, not sure what cowboys and ponies had to do with the issue of insubordination. "Despite a direct order from the governor himself, many of you Grays still refuse to wear the uniform of the California State Military Reserve."

"*Stagecoach* was the first movie shot in Monumental Valley."

"Wrong again. Filmed along the Arizona-Utah border."

"Same thing."

"Ain't."

"Is."

"Silence!" Delaney yelled and then paused to sling whiskey from a coffee mug into a potted palm before hailing his clerk over the intercom. Five minutes later MPs marched in and took custody of the brothers.

Agent Harris began to unwind under the stillness of the mundane. He browsed around the room, studying various headshots that lined the wall. Mayor Rossi, Lieutenant General Wright, Joe DiMaggio, the queens of Roller Derby and others hung pictured with the chief in different poses.

Hajime followed Harris's inspection when he spotted a familiar snapshot. "That *mamasan*," and he bolted over and sidled up next to a surprised Harris.

The agent hiked up his shoulders and skipped back a step, putting his hand up to ward him off. "Easy there."

Everybody moved through the day a stitch disarmed. The emptying of Japantown was sure to upset some. No telling what the Black Dragons had in mind or for that matter a simple family man like Mr. Ishigawa.

"Everything all right, Harris?" Delaney asked.

"Yeah, he just wanted a closer look at the photos. Keeps rattling on about a *mamasan*. Mean anything?"

"Japanese for 'boss lady'." That's when Delaney realized the subject of Mr. Ishigawa's interest and said to him, "You know Miss McNally?"

"*Mamasan* been very nice to family. All work there. Cook up tasty beef sukiyaki and teriyaki chicken."

"Love the teriyaki, a sauce to die for."

"Good, yes?"

Delaney gathered together pieces of the conversation before saying, "So, if I've got this right, you are," and then corrected himself, "you *were* a chef at the Music Box, correct?"

"Very correct," and a bow.

"Hmm." He returned to the file and thumbed through for a second study. "Says here that contraband was seized from your house, in possession of a ham radio."

"Not ham radio. Crystal set. Tune in different stations by moving contact up and…"

"And tonight," Delaney interrupted, "violating curfew." He closed the folder. "These are serious charges. Normally, you'd be shipped to Heart Mountain, Wyoming, a high security prison for spies and protestors and such."

"No spy. No protestor. No such. Must get back to family."

The police chief and Harris stepped to the far corner to confer in private. After another moment, Delaney reached for the phone and made a couple of calls. It was during this time that a woman's bark could be heard from the lobby. The disturbance grew until a pair of frilly dresses busted in.

"Hello, Charrr-lie." Rose dragged out the greeting, knowing the usage of the familiar irked him.

Frazzled by the sideshow, Delaney exhaled his bewilderment. "Miss McNally, what brings you and your associate here?" and he included Anne Klausen with his query.

"Nothin' brought us, Charrr-lie. We managed the trip all by ourselves."

Her vision shifted to the Oriental and in a theatrical voice said, "Number One, whatsoever are you doing here?" and placed her gloved hand over her mouth in feigned surprise.

Delaney pursed his lips into a thin line. "All right, enough with the dramatics."

No reason to ask how Rose found Mr. Ishigawa in such quick order. The Hall of Justice had more leaks than an incontinent old fart. Besides, many of the chief's men were loyal patrons of the Music Box. No doubt someone profited handsomely this night.

"As much as I've enjoyed your boy's cooking," and Delaney pointed to Hajime, "there are several complaints here," and held up a ream of paper for emphasis.

"Oh, Charrr-lie, is all this fuss really necessary?"

"Got protocol to follow."

The striptease artist felt along the frame of his wife's portrait. "You weren't so worried 'bout *protocol* when I cleaned your bifocals with my bosom or introduced you to our feature attraction, Miss Alexis. I'd hate to…"

"Stop already." He went to sip from his mug but it was empty. "I'm in communication with Wright's headquarters to work out a compromise," the chief said.

Hajime, hoping events had turned in his favor, called out, "Can go home now?" The third-story window showed the malignant dawn graying the financial district, and he worried that not much time remained.

"Not yet," Delaney answered.

"Why not?" Anne demanded, not able to remain quiet any longer.

Others joined the protest, causing an uprising. The clerk and a few officers poked their heads into the office, but the chief swooshed them away with a wave.

"Let's all calm down," Delaney said.

Rose glanced at the others and said with a meaningful expression, "The man's right. There's no need for hysterics. After all," and she turned back around to retouch the picture of his wife, "you did have more to say, isn't that so, Charrr-lie?"

Not a subtle point she was making, Delaney pushed the frenzy from his brain and regained his composure. He outlined Hajime's future, beginning with his Presidio assignment, the details to which were still being forged with Western Command. Though much information was not available, one thing was certain—Lieutenant General Wright requested Mr. Ishigawa's presence forthwith.

"Are you sure he has to go this very instant?" Rose asked.

"Well, I suppose we could grant a reprieve of sorts." The chief added that in cases of this nature an endless trail of forms often delayed matters.

Miss McNally clutched onto his cheeks with both hands and planted a firm kiss on his mouth. She swabbed away the lipstick with the soft underside of her gloved forefinger before saying with pointed respect, "Thank you, Mr. Delaney."

"Agent Harris shall, uh, accompany you," the chief added with awkward phrasing, pulling away. "I can give you until noon. Understood?"

"Not to worry, understanding is what I'm all 'bout," she said, flitting her big lashes at him.

Chapter Twenty-six

The sun spilled over the Oakland Hills and fanned itself across the bay to the City. Shadows pooled up behind skyscrapers while an orange salutation filled asphalt canyons.

Down in Little Tokyo, the second of 500 evacuees had arrived at Raphael Weill Grammar School, the order of evacuation predetermined. Households numbered **300-480** circled around to the playground with their meager belongings. A youngster straddled his father's shoulder. His stilled mouth showed below a beanie that read "U.S.A.", stitched in gold against a navy blue crown. Though the boy comprehended little of the day, his father knew the symbolic meaning of the logo—that at this moment, above all others, no one should doubt where their loyalties rest. Nearby, however, a bespectacled twenty-year-old saw no reason to be glad over his forced withdrawal from U.C. Berkeley and expressed his discontent with likeminded souls.

At the front of the line, a Military Reservist inspected suitcases, duffle bags and bulging pillowcases. Occupied with the task at hand, faces of the detainees before him escaped his recognition until a familiar voice rang out.

"How are you, Mr. Klausen?"

"Mishi?" the sergeant said as he looked up.

"You remember my mother, don't you?"

He did not acknowledge her with a shallow "good to see you again", and as a substitute he offered a handshake.

Sato grumbled something in Japanese. Her arms remained folded. Mishi disregarded her mother's rancor and asked Mr. Klausen in a meek tone, "Have you seen my father today?"

He caught her concern and said, "Come with me," and guided both past a pocket of MPs to a fellow State Guard who held a clipboard in his hand.

"Hajime Ishigawa checked in yet?"

The soldier ran down the list with his pencil and returned a negative. Sergeant Klausen signaled his appreciation and ushered mother and daughter away from the assemblage.

The cups of Mishi's eyes welled up. With a delicate stroke, Sato swabbed away the tear and whispered "all rights" into her ear.

Stirred by the moment, doubts entered Elmer. He didn't know if such precautions were necessary—the filing away of so many human beings, their property and personal belongings stored in limbo, an entire culture sold on the cheap. Like everyone else, headlines of the day filled his head. Periodicals preached a wary approach, warning of the destructive potential of aliens and Japanese citizens. Yesterday's *Examiner* released the names of 13,000 "Class 1" individuals, persons suspected of sabotage and espionage. It announced the arrest of George Nakamura of Santa Cruz in possession of sixty-nine crates of fireworks—rockets, flares and torches. As others, Elmer trusted the media to shape his opinions during these conflicting days, but his personal experiences, such as the scene before him, obliged him to listen to his instincts, and he led the pair to the rear of the yard.

"We've lost our place in line," the teenager said. "What are we doing, Mr. Klausen?"

"Doin' nothin'."

"Can't do much with nothing," the mother complained.

*   *   *

A black diagonal mark ran through **416**. Hajime glared at the crossed out number as if it carried an apocalyptic warning, as if the day demanded a final reckoning. Rose, Anne and Agent Harris waited on the porch while Hajime went inside. He stopped next to the tansu cabinet and listened for any telling pronouncements. Nothing. He stepped from room to room calling for wife and child. Aged floorboards underfoot creaked the lone reply. After a failed search of the upstairs, he returned to the others.

"Not here. Suitcases gone." His contemplation took hold of Agent Harris in the hope an answer might volunteer itself.

"Must be over at the boarding depot," Harris suggested. "Best we walk, streets will be jammed."

Hajime held up a finger to request a moment and spun around and dashed back into the building.

"Ain't no time for games," Rose shouted after him.

Hajime returned not sixty seconds later with a threadbare valise.

"Better have a look," the agent said as he rifled through the contents, tossing items aside.

"What you do?" Hajime asked as he stared at a pair of candles, a miniature likeness of Buddha, a praying tatami mattress and two cookbooks lying scattered across the porch.

Harris pushed back the open suitcase. "This is all you'll be needing—change of underwear, socks, toothbrush and razor."

"But…but I lost without Buddha."

"He'll still be here when you get back, I reckon."

The front door thudded shut with a pull. The quartet streamed down the steps and hurried along Webster Street. They turned onto Buchanan where a string of Greyhounds began to roll away. Hajime extended his hand as if to reel back in the train of buses. The outline of a teenage girl was pressed against the rear window of the last transport. Hajime cried out for Mishi but there was no reaction, not even a wave. He slumped to the sidewalk.

Anne knelt beside him, all she could offer. Agent Harris glanced further down the lane to the convoy, which dulled to faint images behind clouds of exhaust.

"All gone," Hajime said.

"We'll get a letter to them," Anne promised and then looked back up over her shoulder. "Do you know where they're headed, Mr. Harris?"

The agent took in his surroundings—something not quite right. He focused on a buzzing in the distance. Heated voices rode the air.

"Let's go," he said and led the way without further explanation.

A ruddy-faced Rose, rouge and mascara all twisted and runny, labored behind. She motioned for them to wait, but her depletion swallowed up her request.

Hidden from view along the street, additional blue and silver shuttles rested atop an asphalt field. A short distance away, younger Nisei argued with their Issei elders. A throng of college-age Orientals quarreled with a wrinkle-faced person. Others came to the rally of the respected senior, reiterating his request for calm.

"*Shigatoa jan-ai* (It cannot be helped)."

The young contingent grew louder, extolling their anti-internment agenda, saying that racism was the driving force behind the government's action.

Within the shrill of whistles, men in different colored uniforms scurried to what was fast building as a skirmish. They wielded their batons in an effort to harness the turmoil, pushing the evacuees backwards against a six-foot picket fence.

Hajime and Anne barreled up an alley along the other side of the wooden barrier. The husband peered between the boards into the melee, spotted a familiar figure under a lanky man's protective frame and shouted his wife's name. A beseeching arm edged forward from the mass as if rising up out of Dante's hell. Anne's gaze slid from Sato to the wrenching face of the Reservist. Anne too called out, but the chaos forced her to give up the effort and she sprinted back around to the entrance, tracing Agent Harris's earlier route.

MPs separated the mob into two groupings—young and old—for that seemed to be the natural way of things. The league of elders assisted with the reorder of the moment while the youthful protestors required greater persuasion. Soldiers encircled the edgy Nisei and hazed them toward a remote corner of the playground. The bunch would be rerouted to Heart Mountain, Wyoming, their files updated, their part in the disturbance recorded.

Sato slithered from the jumble, scampered forward and reached through a slit in the fence to touch her husband's face before gesturing for her daughter to join them. Pressed against the enclosure from either side, a family reunited. They remained there, holding onto each other. Hajime started to explain the reason for his departure last night and his nonproductive visit to *mamasan*'s.

"You here now," Sato said. "All that matter." Then she saw his uneasiness and repeated, "You here, right?"

"Must leave soon," Hajime confessed and provided what few details he possessed of his fate.

She took away her hand, peered at him and pictured a life filled with uncertainties. "You had duty to family. No should have gone back to Music Box."

"I did it for us, for Mishi.   So we have home to come back to."

She lifted up her satchel and pointed to it with her glare. "This our home now. All we have. All we know."

A winded Rose came up from behind and viewed the commotion. "What's all the hubbub?"

"No hubbub," Sato said. "Just old fool who go to boss lady for no favor."

"Now just a damn minute here."

"No reason to swear at time," Sato said. "Hour not to blame for ungrateful woman."

Further away, Anne arrived near the rear of a bus where she saw the features of a balding man. "Has anyone seen a big, ugly Kraut around here?"

At the sound of her voice, Elmer turned and motioned for his daughter. "Get your ballerina butt over here."

She crossed the remaining distance to him. He wore a smile to embrace her with, but instead she swatted it with a straight-arm jab.

"What the hell?"

"Do you have any idea what yesterday was?" Anne asked, the toe of her saddle shoe tapping the ground.

"National Pecan Day?" he said behind his massaging hand.

"No."

"National Donut Day?"

She flexed her hawkish eyes at him, not letting him off the hook.

His look widened with realization. "Your birthday?"

"Unbelievable," and she backed away.

"Eighteenth, isn't it? My baby's a grown woman. Ahh," and he stretched out his arms.

No gift (not even a card) appeared within the space, and she brushed aside the gesture. "You needn't bother. I won't disturb you any longer. I shall seek accommodations elsewhere where I am appreciated, where I don't have to lower myself to the whims of some absent minded fool."

The atmosphere turned acrid, as was their form, and the squabble raged on as Elmer's final notes found her backside thumping to the far end of the yard.

*   *   *

Mishi ran the flat of her hand across her scalp as if searching for something. Her examination found nothing but her raven hair. Where'd it go? She scoured the immediate area. Ruffled clothing poked out from the seams of her suitcase. She sifted through it with frantic swipes. Not there. Her vision roamed the confines as one might in search of lost treasure. Suddenly, the item of her consternation glistened a short ways away. She bounded up and scooted past a burly policeman to a peach-fuzz of a boy who huddled with others.

"That ain't yours," she said to Peach Fuzz, clawing at the feathered headdress sitting atop his cropped hair.

He jerked all about while correcting her with collegiate diction. "Don't you mean *isn't* yours?"

A wisp of air from someone's reach came from his blind side. "Either way you say it, prissy boy, all you got up there now is an empty head." Anne held up the tiara and then fled with a giggling Mishi.

With freed emotions, the teens dashed to a nearby swing set. They swung with their hands clasped together and for an instant the world approached with a more reasonable countenance. Not a word was spoken. What would they say? The next hours had been scripted for Mishi, her path preordained by men she had never met. Anne knew all of this and other kind to be true.

Mishi plucked a roll of rice paper, bound by a red ribbon, from her sweater's pocket. Glad this opportunity presented itself, she told Anne to read the haiku later in private away from the day's bedlam.

Reservists waved their hands in a circular motion for all to get back in line. Anne's smile deflated at the announcement, and she turned to say something to Mishi but didn't know how to arrange the words.

Buses started up their engines. A Reservist came to the cluster near the fence. Of single-minded intent, he eyed the patch on the lady's coat collar and requested that number **416** come with him.

"I not number you add up and toss away," the diminutive lady answered. "I *Mrs. Ishigawa*," and she gave her spouse a knowing glance to confirm that such would always be.

Hajime brushed his hand along the pickets as his wife shuffled toward a waiting transport. With one foot aboard, Sato waved goodbye and perceived a person in a black fedora attached to her husband and knew she would not see him anytime soon. Mishi hurried to a window seat and placed her hands against the barred glass. She exchanged a long distance kiss with her father before sliding her eyes to her friend. She tapped her headdress to show that they would always travel together, that feathers of the same flock flew as one.

Hajime and Anne gestured farewells and stood there long after the Greyhound and its military escort faded down O'Farrell. All disappeared onto Van Ness and headed south toward the Bayshore Highway and San Bruno's Tanforan Racetrack.

Anne unfurled Mishi's haiku—*mono sen surippa wo hakitsubusu hodo no jikan ga tatta.* She turned to Mr. Ishigawa for translation, but his sorrow told her that this was not the right circumstance and she pocketed the bequest.

"We finished here?" Rose said. "Got a business to run."

"You're not such a tough broad," Elmer said with a smirk. "Don't pretend ya are."

"The past is gone. Can't bring it back," and then she made an about-face to Number One to invite him to drop by the Music Box if he had the chance. He didn't know if the people in charge allowed such visits but he'd try. Anne came forward and presented him with a squeeze to which Hajime returned a bow.

"One more bow," Rose blurted, "and I'm gonna shoot myself."

"No objections here," responded Elmer.

Agent Harris took Hajime away while Mr. Klausen offered a ride to Rose. "Can sit next to this old bag of bones. Never know, ya might get lucky."

She glanced at his backside. "Appears there's more than just bones back there."

*   *   *

Klausen pulled the sedan in front of the Music Box and asked Miss McNally if she wanted assistance to the door.

"Do I look like I need any help?"

"Don't look like ya need much of anythin'. That's your problem."

She dismissed the jibe and marched away under a flashing row of bulbs.

"That woman will drive some poor soul to the nuthouse," Elmer said.

"Like her, don't you?" Anne said.

"Like her enough to buy her an early funeral."

"That's a heap of like if you ask me."

"Never asked but didn't know when that stopped your mouth from goin' off."

"Just drive," Anne said.

"How's 'bout takin' a turn at the wheel. Guess you've earned it, seein' as how you're eighteen now."

A grin slid across her face.

The Chevy traveled down Larkin Street, working its way over to the Mission District. The sun dropped below Twin Peaks and pinked up a reef of clouds, a day's length running to its end. Venus appeared in the dusky sky, standing guard over the heavens, waiting to show the path for its celestial cousins.

"Thanks," Anne said from within the stillness.

"What for?"

"Back at the school, watching out for Mishi and her mother like that."

"Just doin' my job as a Reservist."

"Oh, yeah. Heard you Grays had to turn in your uniforms."

"Part of the deal. Under the ultimate authority of the California State Military Reserve now," and he hiked up his shoulders as if it was meant to be.

"Sorry," she said.

"Maybe for the better." A remembrance of a different sort came to him and he said, "Not mad at me anymore?"

She pursed her lips.

"How's the car handle?" Elmer asked.

"This is your birthday gift, a chance to chauffeur you back to the house?"

"Short on cash. 'Sides, you're lucky I don't take that uppity disposition of yours across my knee for not comin' home last night, not even callin'."

"Rose heard through her connections that Mr. Ishigawa was in some trouble and thought I might want to tag along. Our visit to the Hall of Justice took longer than anticipated."

"Interestin'," he said in a doubting way.

"You can believe it or not. It is of no matter to me."

"Givin' out options, are we? Someone's in a generous mood."

Anne could feel the warmth from his sarcasm, could feel the return of normalcy to their relationship. Normal is good, she thought. In the spirit of the moment, she said, "Since you know of my employment at the Music Box, I guess you wouldn't mind if I continued."

"Guessed wrong. Arranged an interview for ya down at a friend's chemical factory. Just so happens he needs a good secretary. Lied and told him ya knew how to do practical things like type and make coffee."

Anne rolled her fingers over the steering wheel, tightening her grip. "That's not going to happen."

They squeezed the quiet out of the car. Back and forth they went when Anne, for no particular reason, glimpsed into the rearview mirror. A burgundy, windowless panel truck came into sight some six cars back. She spotted the vehicle when they crossed Market Street or so she thought. Could've been mistaken.

The light changed and she began to take a right onto Sixteenth when her dad noticed a "Closed" sign on the entrance to the Cigar Box Café. "Heard they got busted by the Health Department for stuffin' their raviolis with dog food. Did ya know that?" and without waiting for a response he moved the conversation to something completely different, rattling on regarding a woman's place in the world.

While presenting a deaf ear, Anne made no sudden motions, kept a light foot on the pedal, eased along. The father stated how France and Switzerland had it right, still refusing to give the weaker sex the right to vote. He included other notions in his rambling as they passed a construction spot where a billboard read: FEDERAL PROJECT / VALENCIA GARDENS.

"Prob'ly intended as affordable housin' for the spillover of Negro workers from the shipyards."

Anne kept a watch on the truck behind, which had mimicked her turn onto Sixteenth. On this side street, however, there was not the cover of traffic to hide.

The Chevy motored to Dolores Street. She could continue on, but the idea of bringing any ill-minded deeds to her doorstep didn't seem wise. While hesitating at the stop sign, the old man glanced sideways. After another minute of no movement, he said, "Intersection ain't gonna get any clearer, not today, not ever."

Without warning, Anne snatched a tire iron from beneath the seat, swung open the door and leaped out. With deliberate strides, she advanced toward the panel truck. The day's last light evaporated within the oncoming night. From inside the cab, murky figures began to take shape when the vehicle made a slow U-turn and withdrew, not with the panic of being discovered but with a disturbing casualness.

Chapter Twenty-seven

Doolittle's Raiders Attack Japan

"Yesterday, Lt. Col. 'Jimmy' Doolittle and a force of sixteen modified B-25 Mitchell bombers struck back at the Imperial Government of Japan. It is reported that the cities of Tokyo, Kobe, Yokohama, Nagoya and Yokosuka sustained heavy damage. There is no word yet on how many of the eighty crewmen survived what is being labeled as a 'suicide mission'. Lieutenant General Wright has put all available West Coast military and civilian units on high alert."

San Francisco *Chronicle*
April 19, 1942

Bunting strung the length of lampposts along Market Street. Miniature Stars and Stripes waved from zealous hands as the financial district shut down for the day to show their support.

Two young WACs led the parade, hoisting a banner—
DOOLITTLE VICTORIOUS. Galileo, Commerce and Mission High School
marching bands followed. Trumpets blared, drums rolled and
trombones bellowed, all in rhythm to high-kicks.

Flanked by color guards, pennants announced different
branches of the service, volunteer organizations and government
agencies. Each heralded a small contingency with the exception of
the 184th Regimental Combat Team who marched with a
compliment of 2500 men, the latest effort to bolster the City's
defenses.

Block Wardens walked with the stride of everyday
pedestrians as they waved to the patriotic crowd. Next followed
the Red Cross equestrian unit, shoed hooves clickety-clacking
across the blacktop. A large chestnut rocked its head and snorted
while trotting sideways. The formidable beast meandered back
and forth, neighing. Brocade on the saddle blanket announced that
the animal belonged to actor Spencer Tracy.

Everyone was getting in on the celebration. Doolittle's
penetration into the heartland of Japan was a quick and decisive
response to Pearl Harbor. Don't mess with the red, white and blue.
While not a major reversal of the war, the raid gave notice that the
United States was back in business. Never again would America
be caught off guard.

*　　　*　　　*

"You jeopardized ship and entire crew by arriving late at
the rendezvous point," Commander Minoru said in Japanese to his
pilot.

"Well, technically my calculations were ..."

"Your *calculations* were the product of a simpleton."

"What's five minutes?"

"Those five minutes resulted in the destruction of your
plane. Do you know how much such negligence has cost the
Emperor?"

"I venture to say approximately..."

"Your family will suffer the consequences of your bumbling, not mine."

The airman's features tensed up. Images of his distraught daughter and embarrassed ancestors gathered before him.

"There is, however, a way you can make amends." The commander left the words hanging.

Nobuo raised his head.

"Not only would you restore honor to the I-25, but you would also leave a handsome endowment for your child." He took it slow to underline the announcement's significance. "Since you can no longer serve your vessel as an aviator, you have been reassigned. Our midget sub's engineer is incapacitated. He suffered a debilitating back injury incurred, I might add, while assisting with the removal of your craft from the deck."

Nobuo quickened his breath.

"You will assist Lieutenant Commander Nasuri Shuno on his quest to avenge Doolittle's attack on our homeland. In exchange the Empire shall reimburse one hundred thousand yen to your survivors."

"*Survivors*? I don't understand."

"Further instructions await." Minoru's attention fell back into a pile of documents on his desk, saying, "That is all."

The pilot lifted a finger to make a point, but his brain malfunctioned and he reshaped his hand into a salute and exited. Upon reaching his cabin, he flopped into his bunk and stared at the ribbed ceiling and thought of his next assignment.

Christened the Heaven Shaker, the minisub was a Type 2 Kaiten, sailored by males between the ages of eighteen to twenty, all volunteers, a mixture of idealists and fatalists. Most did it for the sole honor of serving the Empire. Others envisioned no recovery from the worldwide depression and desired to pass on monetary rewards to their indigent families. They trained near the island of Otsushima, located within the Inland Sea. Fatalities were common. A crazed bunch for sure.

*   *   *

Third Classman Nobuo Akita stood at attention in his Gakuran uniform with fitted black jacket, matching straight leg pants, purple waist sash and jackboots. Lieutenant Nasuri Shuno chose the traditional white robe.

Commander Meiji Minoru hung the Pacific Star around the bowed head of each. "You shall be venerated in the ship's logs. The hearts of your fellow countrymen shall applaud the tendering of this noblest of sacrifices."

But Nobuo couldn't remember tendering anything. His cramped mind thought about putting words to his objection. Then he saw his compatriots swelling with the same adulation as shown on his prior exploits, albeit exploits laced with exaggeration and fantasy. He stood there, snared in a trap of his own making.

"Emperor Hirohito," the captain added, "has sent his personal wishes for a successful journey," and held up a decoded message. "'For His Majesty and for all of Japan, you shall surrender your lives with dignity and grace.'"

In symbolic gestures, the pair offered twin ceremonial urns. A white cloth with the imprint of the Rising Sun was placed across the forehead of each.

The following poem was penned on Nasuri Shuno's band: *What a fine burial place / Will be the clear blue of these waters.* Nobuo Akita had no such sentiments and, instead, placed correspondence and testaments into trusting hands.

"From this moment forward," the commander added, "you will be considered as resting with the gods and will be worshipped as such. We shall all meet again at the Yasukuni Shrine."

*   *   *

At thirty-seven degrees north latitude by one hundred and twenty-three degrees west longitude, the I-25 arrived twelve kilometers from the mainland. Well inside the shipping lane, it remained submerged for an extended period. The sea was rough, and even at a depth of fifty meters the vessel continued to pitch.

She began to feel heavy and the pumps ran for six hours straight to keep her from sinking further. Batteries ran low. The temperature rose and the air became foul. The men grew irritable.

Different versions of victory spun around inside Minoru as he paced the control room. If successful, this day would make amends for his failure at Pearl, not to mention a personal commendation. He gave the order to ascend to periscope depth.

The jagged outline of the Farallon Islands and other sea stacks came into view. Due east rested the Golden Gate Bridge. Yet the ocean lay barren. Another thirty minutes passed and still no suitable sighting. Exasperated, Minoru muttered a curse. Suddenly, a merchant ship appeared under the red leaf flag of Canada and he slapped closed the handles.

"Left five degrees right rudder. Come to course 089."

"Right rudder, five degrees," the coxswain copied. "Course 089er."

"All ahead one-third."

"Ahead one-third."

Nobuo and Shuno wedged their way through an airtight tube, which was matted to the rear hatch of the Kaiten. In actuality, the midget sub was nothing more than a Long Lance torpedo with seats. A suicide craft, Nobuo thought, an express ticket to hell. A different notion came to him, one so divergent from his present state that it provided a sort of calm. Was this to be the grand discovery that he had hoped for? My little Aiko, he thought, there is hope for your future yet.

Once inside, the pair passed a storage of batteries and a diesel engine, which sat above the aft trim tanks. They came to the helm where Shuno charged oxygen bottles for ventilation. He double-checked the knobs and switches that operated the fuel intake as well as the fuses for the 3300 lb. warhead before strapping himself in.

A warrant officer closed the bottom flap and signaled a thumps up. At a bearing of 303 relevant, the captain ordered the opening of outer door number two. Shuno aligned the torpedo's rudder with that of the I-25 and started the engine. Clamps were cast off and the Heaven Shaker shot through the tube.

Not much time had passed when they glided under the freighter like a whale calf hugging its mother's belly. The second high tide of the day occurred at 9:20 P.M., insuring a depth of sixty meters under the Gate, adequate passage through the narrow strait for both minisub and escort. They sailed past the opened steel net as one, continuing under the fortifications of the Presidio and the machine gun pods nesting atop Alcatraz Federal Prison. Within the dredged channel, the Canadians chugged beneath the Bay Bridge and veered east toward the Oakland docks. The Heaven Shaker drifted away, cruising southwest along the San Francisco waterfront where forgotten barges and sooty factories sat atop urban wetlands.

They rounded a bend crowded with war machines. Destroyers, minesweepers, dreadnoughts and a hospital ship napped at fan-shaped piers, which jetted out from a stick of mud. Must be Hunters Point Shipyard, Shuno thought.

Streams of light slanted in from different sectors while an army of workers moved across the landscape. The partial skeletons of eight additional vessels lay exposed. Giant cranes hovered over them like prehistoric creatures, their iron and carbon tentacles reaching out with strapping appetite.

Intelligence from the covert Black Dragon Society had proved reliable. A twenty-thousand-ton behemoth rose sixty-two meters above the waterline with a draft of eleven. A more agreeable target than the U.S.S. *Lexington* could not be imagined.

Within five hundred and fifty meters, Shuno locked in the controls—a running trim of one-degree nose-down, a ramming speed of twenty knots. He patted his death band, hailed his Emperor and pressed forward on the throttle.

"*Yamato Damasshi!*"

Nobuo's mind floated across the heavens as the armored coffin raced toward the stern of the aircraft carrier, toward his destiny. The seat vibrated. His ears hummed. His terror popped wide as he blurted, "*Sen zori! Sen zori!*" And then a great jarring sound of metal crashing and crunching rose up. The bay gushed in from all sides; electrical pops and smoke everywhere.

For a second, Nobuo assumed he had entered the Lotus Sutra, the lowest realm of hell. In short order, he realized, however, that there had been no fireball. The impact fuse must have failed. What about the manual override? He forced his body up and trudged through the rising water to the helm. The control panel pushed washes of colored light across Shuno's lifeless figure. Nobuo felt for a pulse before closing his comrade's lids.

The waterline ascended with eagerness. Never make it, he thought. His desperation flashed all around. An air bottle cropped up and he yanked it from its hold. He waded toward the rear when he eyed his sword and snatched it. Completely submerged now, bubbles ran free from his lungs. He sucked in a load of oxygen from the canister. His waterlogged wools weighed him down, but he forced his way to the surface and muddled the short distance to shore.

Aft of the *Lexington* a mere ripple showed. The collision was so inconsequential, he guessed, as to cause but a dull clunk against the mighty beast. Perhaps for the best.

Raindrops pricked the bay. The smell of a fresh storm bundled with the pungent odor of grease and things in disrepair. Though the hour moved past ten, the shipyard buzzed with activity. Rows of massive bulbs, attached to hundred-foot towers, poured over objects of all sizes to form a myriad of sharp, angular shadows. A whistle's whine announced the arrival of a half-mile-long locomotive. Such sprightliness Nobuo had not witnessed since his country's preparation for Pearl. He feared, after gazing upon the industrialization before him, that perhaps Japan had accomplished little except to awaken a hornet's nest.

Squeezed between cargo containers, Nobuo squatted in a windless rain, which made but a scant impression upon his clothing. The cold caused him to shiver. His chin found warmth under the folds of his jacket. Disconsolate, his nerves began to tug at his mind. Syllables, nonsensical and out of order, sputtered forth. The rambling increased as a familiar edginess approached. He tried once more to find his *gaman*, his levelness. Nothing.

His daze roamed the wet asphalt until coming to a fellow accomplice. The inscription from the blade's handle showed itself—SEN ZORI—and then he recalled gasping these same sentiments during what he thought were his last moments on earth. He repeated the words again in an attempt to sort out a significance that had long eluded him. A childhood prayer from his prefecture loomed up sudden and unexpected.

Mono **sen** *zori wo hakitsubusu hodo no jikan ga tatta*—the bygone wears out a thousand sandals. He nodded the truth of the matter, a truth that had escaped his deeper understanding until this very instant. His journey had indeed shorn him down to the nub— a journey that he alone possessed, to be understood by him and no other.

With this concession, a distraught Nobuo looked toward the heavens where stars studded no more. Mountains of clouds climbed atop one another to bury the last vestiges of the moon. He drew in the earthy smell of the oncoming rain. As a child he remembered that such weather was a harbinger of things to come, that the gods would soon be unhappy, using Mother Nature to deliver their heartache. Sometimes the rain fell with typhoon force, sometimes with the meagerness of this drizzle before him. No matter what form, the message remained the same—peer inside to give meaning to your sadness. And he did. He reflected upon his particular bygone, how his sandals had supported a coward's frame on a thousand different occasions.

Crestfallen, he lifted the sword with the constitution of his forefathers and said, "Your bloodline ends here with me at this blackened spot, cowering from the enemy. Disgraced, we shall enter the Lotus Sutra together as it should be."

He put the tip of his sword to his stomach, applied pressure with his shaking hands. He could feel the tapered steel against his warmth. With a final reverence to his ancestors, he crossed his legs in a solemn pose and tightened his grip for the thrust.

Men, talking behind the skittering beams of their lanterns, approached. His trance broken, Nobuo slipped further back into the tar-black cranny. He ventured a look between lumps of dank cardboard boxes. Another gang of uniforms appeared, MP written upon the face of their white helmets. They passed him and headed toward a clutch of tenements situated atop a nearby knoll.

Discovered his sunken vessel? Searching for conspirators? He dismissed the notion. Too soon, he figured. Waves of soldiers followed, some on foot, others in jeeps. An operation was underway, all right, the nature of which he could not guess.

He shook his head at the irony of it all. Can't even die in peace. Bad Karma. He sheathed his sword as the faint shower matured into a persistent rain. He began to make his way around the knoll while skirting the bay's edge. Storage sheds, bulky hangars and other contrivances provided a cover of knotty shadows.

Behind a cache of lumber, he tracked the movement up at a row of apartments. A chain of Negroes, hunched over, carrying luggage and infants, slugged to a canvas-covered truck. Once loaded, the vehicle motored away down the hill. Identical machines, perhaps two dozen in all, moved forward in orderly fashion to accept the next batch of civilians. No cries of protest could be heard, just the submissive movement of families resigned to their fate.

The activity might serve as a welcomed diversion, he thought. The presence of so many soldiers, however, froze his capabilities. Ribbons of water rushed from the knoll down into a basin where a collection of oil drums now concealed him.

Can't just sit here. The chill penetrated his aching bones. He saw a pair of abandoned overalls lying in a lump upon the seat of a parked forklift, and a plan began to take form inside his twittering skull. A bold plan for sure, perhaps too courageous for the likes of him, but there it was. He stepped into the trousers and hoisted a wooden crate to his shoulder. He loped with measured strides, staying afield of the light towers whenever possible, and cut along a rutted lane toward the motorcade.

Upon reaching the housing projects, a quick surveillance told him that the nearest MP had entered one of the residences. He lowered the container and shimmied his way under the chassis of the last transport. With his belt he fashioned a grip to the rear axle. His feet slid into a nearby metal slot.

A half-hour later, the 2½-ton started up. Defeated voices crowded the compartment above. His body jounced about as yellow hash marks passed underneath. Not more than a mile or two down the road, his arms ached with such misery that he feared his limbs might separate altogether. When they lugged to a stop, he freed his hands and feet and stole away.

Chapter Twenty-eight

The blare of sirens rolled over him. Must've unearthed the Heaven Shaker, Nobuo surmised, and fled from the hustle of Third Street toward a darkened precinct. A handful of shingled shacks with beards of moss appeared. Tattered couches and rockers occupied weathered stoops. Clusters of manufacturing endeavors came next. Abandoned or shut down for the night, chemical factories, scrap metal enterprises, toxic dumps and junkyards became his allies.

The vertical rain reminded him of the monsoon season back home. His voice labored under his melancholy, stranded so far from all that was true and dear. Dejected, thoughts of his daughter, of his favorite cooking recipes, of his other life came to him.

On the far side of a pair of railroad tracks, a series of weedy lots rested. He weaved his way around galvanized pipes, rusty prongs and concrete slabs. With a wan glance, he crossed a barren lane to a depository. Upon closer inspection the warehouse seemed to run out into the bay, its backside supported by aging piers. Pasted against the building's aluminum siding, Nobuo crouched behind a waterfall cascading from a gutter above. Not too far away, on the other side of a patio area, boxes of light pushed out from windows, which tipped at different angles to each other. Cutouts moved across the bubbled glass. Atop the roof of the salt-bitten clapboard ran a sign advertising "Indian Basin Bar & Grill".

A beam shot from the doorway, and a trio of men spilled from the saloon. They waved their pewter mugs in syncopation with their song as they staggered away.

With caution Nobuo moved across the patio between vacant tables of giant wooden spools toward a cement ramp. His jackboots clenched down against the serrated surface at the bay's edge near a scarred Chris-Craft. With elongated steps he lifted a light foot into the water and, after a pause to scan the area, placed another with care into a forward spot before repeating his effort. A blue heron appeared, copying him, loping at decisive intervals on his starboard side. The airman gave the mystical bird's presence little meaning as the weather and distant voices spurred him on.

He hoisted himself onto the deck and sidestepped along the emptiness that shown from portholes. Dry garments and perhaps a meal awaited. Hope entered. A gathering of crows on an overhead wire elected to move on, cawing and crying. The disturbance woke up a Doberman, leashed to a cleat near the stern. The canine lifted his drowsy head and bolted up barking, running out its chain to the jackboots.

Patrons abandoned their celebration and left the tavern to investigate. Nobuo slid overboard and considered swimming further out into the bay but determined that to be a poor choice and sank under the transom.

His cheeks collapsed with the last of his breath. He grabbed his sword and, with the aid of a dim light from a dock lamp above, augured through the rotted chinking of the hull. In the process, a section of the decomposed wood broke apart. Thrusting his head into the cavity, he gulped the musty air.

Upon arriving at the boat, stubbly faces explored the perimeter. Some held pipes and hammers within their calloused hands, others their libation. The heron fell within their inspection. In unison all waved off the insignificance and scolded the

Doberman for calling them out on such a sloppy night and withdrew.

Nobuo's eyes rose just above the waterline. His disquiet probed the confines. Men grew smaller until disappearing altogether behind the pub's door. Confident of his deception, the alien stood to his full height. Instead of retracing his steps across the patio, he elected to plod through shallow water back toward the warehouse, his sword held high. Halfway to his sanctuary, a boot got caught up in the sludge. Anxious, he abandoned his shoe and sloshed toward a group of pilings.

From within this pit, Nobuo looked back to where cheer and song and hardy laughter rang out. His continued survey of the surrounding sector soon took in the realization that the pleasure craft began to list. A grin spread across his face. Perhaps the news would bring cheer to his ancestors. After all, how many had ever brought down a monster this size with a single stab of their blade? Few, he guessed, and puffed up with pride.

From under the pier, he emerged with half the bog on his frame and sprinted to beneath a familiar eave, hiding behind a sheet of falling rain. It was during this intermission from the war that the heron reappeared. Light from the saloon cast the critter in a silhouette as big as a man's. A streak of yellow appeared whenever its head tilted a notch off level. Tufted wings threw off a bluish sheen, the tips of which were as black as the mud flats the animal pecked food from.

"What are you doing here?" Nobuo said.

A keepsake from his previous world came to him, a bedtime poem he recited often to his Aiko: *blue heron gliding upon evening waves / on the Omi Sea to my Hokkaidō Island / when you cry, so my heart trails / like dwarf bamboo down to the past.*

While studying the movements of this grand creation, he noticed that the storm had abated. Ignited pinpricks showed between racing clouds. A coincidence? Nobuo did not think so.

He tracked the feathered creature, certain that deliverance was soon at hand. The heron passed under the rear of the aluminum structure while Nobuo, limping on a single jackboot, hurried around the front along the puddled street as jangled speech faded to nothing behind him.

The bird moved as if on broken hinges, as if attached to lifters and spindles and pulleys and all manner of mechanical doings. With little effort, the regal fowl lifted skyward. Nobuo felt the sweep of its shadow across his skin. The heron glided low over the flats until settling upon the peak of a solitary dwelling not far away. A one-room cabin of squared-off timbers sat atop a grounded barge. Thin curls of smoke whipped upwards from its smokestack.

Tchaikovsky rode the delicate hum of a violin. With his curiosity Nobuo hobbled up a wooden plank. To his surprise the brass knob received his gentle twist, and the door swung free. The ragged flames of a hearth's fire whooshed up with the incoming rush of air.

"Who's there?" said a kind voice from inside. "Benny, is that you?"

No response except for the sound of the latch catching the bolt.

"Well, whoever it is, come forward. Don't make an old man leave his comfort." A wrinkled white shirt with black vest covered a substantial paunch. The senior gnawed on the end of an unlit cigar while a bead of juice formed on his chin.

As the intruder approached with his raised sword, the pudgy man cocked his head in a peculiar way, guiding his ear sideways as if the lobed organ was designed to do both hearing and seeing. There was no reflection in his eyes, which were set above leathery seams.

"Join me for a spot of whiskey?"

The interloper's hands quivered as the sharp edge of his blade hovered over the blindman. A black lab left his spot and gamboled over and rubbed his snout over a single bare foot.

"Gaspar, don't bother the gentleman," and he shifted his attention upward. "You'll have to pardon him. We don't get many visitors out this way." He paused to allow space for an acknowledgment. None forthcoming he suggested that the caller come closer.

With no sign of ill will forming, the outsider put away his weapon.

"Now kneel so I can get a sense of you."

The stranger bent before the rocker. Mud caked his feet and legs, wafting up a powerful reek.

"Whew, what in the Lord's name?" The old man reached out to identify the source of the foul smelling bouquet. He felt the smallish head, the thin line of a mustache and then measured the man's length along a pair of overalls, which were drenched through and through. "This won't do."

The eyeless one made his way to a dresser, yanked on a handle and felt inside. He soon selected a workingman's ensemble and brought it over and held it against the diminutive frame. The newcomer stood rigid and stretched out his arms as if at a tailor's shop. He did not understand every word coming from the mouth of his gifter but knew that a gentle soul was present.

"Could fit three of you in there. If you were to roll up the cuffs, I suspect you'd still trip over yourself. Can't do much as regards the waistline, either. I'm afraid the missus, God rest her soul, made sure I ate well. The habit took hold, I guess," and patted his stomach with meaning.

The householder fumbled back across the room to return to his hunt. "Got to be a better fit for you in here somewhere." He soon extricated a flower print nightgown. He held the cotton fabric to his nose and inhaled slow, saying, "She's still here." Another whiff. "Can't seem to grasp the notion that the wife's gone. Like to keep a part of her around. I suppose that sounds a little creepy, huh? Anyways, she was around your size." Upon returning he said, "Now get out of those garbs before you meet her personal like."

The transient did as he was told and began to undress. To no avail he turned his frame away from the searing glare of the dog. Onyx-black pupils followed him as a faint steam swelled from the clump of trousers and a uniform that collected at his feet. After hopping into the pajamas, he took in his surroundings. The place was sparse of furniture, but the craftsmanship that went into making the few pieces on display appeared worthy. A whittled figure attached to a cross decorated the space above a handmade, leather couch. A painting of a woman with a soft circle of light over her head rested atop a cramped bookcase. Must be his deceased wife, he guessed, and reflected on her soft demeanor and conjectured that she and his host were probably a good match for each other. Another thought came alive and he said in clipped fashion, "Tchaikovsky's 'Violin Concerto in D major'."

"Say again?"

"Outside, heard you playing Tchaikovsky, yes?"

"Yes, absolutely yes. You're an appreciator of the arts, are you?"

No response.

"Excuse me, where are my manners? I'm Harry Mitchum," and stuck out his hand but in the wrong direction.

"Nobuo, Nobuo Akita," and came sideways to accept the offering.

Harry, after withdrawing from the formal introduction, smoothed out the wrinkles of his deceased spouse's nightwear, which now rested upon his guest. "Fits okay?"

"Okay," Nobuo said while hiding any judgments regarding the floral pattern or the odor of mothballs.

Harry clapped his hands, did a small jig and said, "Let's have some music."

A jazzy piece fought its way through a radio's speaker. Nobuo guessed George Gershwin.

"Right again."

"Saw movie, *Shall We Dance*, in thirty-seven. Like American movies, like Hollywood."

The lab wagged its tail with expectation of play. Harry obliged and lifted the critter's front paws. The pair waltzed around the room when the old man motioned for his new arrival to join them. Not wanting to be disrespectful, he hooked on. With paw to hand and hand to paw, the trio skipped in circles. Objects passed by Nobuo as if spinning on a merry-go-round. Lamps and chairs and tables and pictures blurred together in a twirl of color and fuzzy shapes, reminding him of a similar scene from the *Wizard of Oz*. Or so he thought.

Soon, however, the merriment caught up with the senior, and he collapsed into his rocker. With restored calm, he placed a snipped cigar into his mouth and began to chew while tendering an offering of like kind.

Nobuo waved off the overture. His captain's smoking habit had offended his delicate senses, but this, this nauseous display of the most grotesque sort, disgusted him. A strange land indeed, he thought—dog and man prancing around together, the loaning of dead people's apparel, the tasting of tobacco as if a dessert.

The pair settled in and shared their mutual fondness for musicals. Spittle clanged against a copper spittoon at each recollection from *Two for the Show* or *Porgy and Bess* or the *Ziegfell Follies*. Nobuo's loathing increased with each discharge. This uneven rhythm formed a ragged coexistence when, without warning, a siren pierced the conversation. Nobuo knocked over an empty whiskey glass.

"No need to get all twisted up, my friend," Harry said. "Relax, most likely just another drill." But the knotty pause defined the tension aboard his visitor. "Strayed from Little Tokyo, did we? Not to worry. I'll have you back home quicker than a hummingbird can flap its wings."

With that promise, a bite to eat was suggested as a proper distraction. The horn's continued cry, however, widened Nobuo's paranoia. He entertained the notion of fleeing when a curious sight captured his attention. Rolled rice paper, tied in red ribbon, lay on the kitchen counter. With images of something familiar, as if this may be the reason why the mystical bird led him to this place, he brought the item to his inspection. He unwrapped it with hurried motions and read the Japanese characters in silence: *mono sen surippa wo hakitsubusu hodo no jikan ga tatta.* To his astonishment it was nearly an exact replica of the proverb he had recalled not more than two hours previous.

In disbelief he said, "Where you get this?"

"Get what?"

"This," and held up the haiku in presentation.

Harry, hearing the jostling of curled paper, identified it with his touch. "This belongs to Annie. Nice girl, wants to be a ballerina, but her father…"

"She Japanese?"

"Japanese? Why, no, she's American."

"Where she get this?"

"What's with all the…"

"Where she get this?"

"Well, I think…," and Harry stalled out under this persistence before collecting himself. "Believe it was a going-away gift from her friend Mishi. Annie must've left it here last night by mistake." Her visit rekindled his memory and he added, "She hadn't found anyone to decipher it. You'll have to stick around and…"

"Who this Mishi?"

"Huh?"

And the stranger repeated his question.

"I think her last name is 'Ishigawa'. Not sure. I do know that she worked with her father and mother over at the Music Box, at least ways 'till the evacuation started. Why?"

Nobuo, knowing he couldn't answer the one-word question within a single lifetime, returned paper and ribbon to the counter and became unsettled.

In an attempt to ring out the stress from the moment, Harry said, "Let's get that meal going."

Silence.

Harry began to slice away at a pile of red potatoes upon the butcher-block in a slow and tedious fashion. Nobuo nudged him aside, took the knife and unleashed his frustration upon the vegetable. The straight edge worked to the pulse of a seasoned chef. Harry stood back in surprise.

The sound of cutting steel rose up singular and crisp until Nobuo said with unexplained perfunctory, "I be back," and cloaked himself in a borrowed coat and exited.

"Curious little fellow," Harry said to himself as he snapped peas.

Outside, Nobuo's vision came across the houseboat's gabled roof. It was here that he last saw the heron. As if the space was still occupied, he said aloud, "You've done enough. You've led me to this serene individual. I thank you."

With different intentions he proceeded to the nearby mudflats. His hand raked the volcano-shaped welts where bubbles pushed up. The bottom of a galvanized bucket clanged with the tinny echo of his first finds until giving way to the clunk of shell against shell.

In the distance specks of light showed. Mechanical rumblings expanded into growls as beams grew closer. He prattled nonsensical gibberish until he fathomed the emergency and flattened to the ground.

Chapter Twenty-nine

Persons emptied from a civilian vehicle and marched up the plank and rapped on the door.

"This night is showing promise," Harry said to Gaspar as he went to the entrance. After exchanging introductions, however, he concluded that this was no social visit. "Fredericks, to what do I owe the dishonor?"

The major skirted the attitude and said straightaway, "A Japanese force of some magnitude has landed at Hunters Point."

"Heard the sirens."

"Apparently they have scattered into the City." Fredericks's vision fanned the room. "By chance, have you seen anything out of the ordinary?"

"Other than dim-witted vigilantes roaming the neighborhood, scaring people half to death with their wild stories? Nope, guess not."

"I would advise you to mind your tone, sir."

"Yeah, wa-watch your tone," another copied as he entered on the heels of his superior.

"Sounds like you brought your henchman with you," Harry said. "Why don't you two go harass someone else and leave me be?"

Jones noticed the large portion of food on the kitchen counter, the muddy tracks on the floor and asked Harry if he was alone.

"Just me and a friend whom I expect back momentarily," Harry said with caution. While arrest or something worse awaited those who ventured from Little Tokyo, he had no intention of assisting the Grays with either.

Fredericks came across a black jacket and matching pants and yelled back from the bathroom, "There is a military uniform of unknown origin draped over the shower curtain."

With this unexpected discovery, questions stumbled across Harry's brain. Filled with uncertainties, he tossed out the first thing that came to him. "Uh, I pick up a little extra scratch cleaning and mending costumes for the Music Box." He didn't know why he should defend the one who calls himself Nobuo, but there was something endearing about the man. Hearing the doubt in the other's voice, he embellished, "The theater is working on a skit where this American tourist falls in love with a Japanese officer. The love doesn't last, I'm afraid, as the girl realizes..."

"You sure like to babble, don't you?" Jones interrupted.

"My bride believed that it was impolite not to share conversation."

"Some-someone should tell her that a little quiet goes a long ways."

"I'm afraid she has departed this earth."

"Guess you can tell her yourself soon enough."

"If you observe any irregularities in the neighborhood," Fredericks said, "you can acquire my services at this number," and left his card.

"You'll be the first I call, rest assured of that," Harry answered with a fake grin.

At the exit Jones poked the blindman in the chest with a forefinger. "I'm gon-gonna keep an eye on you."

"Wish I could say the same," and Harry closed shut the door.

After the uniformed men had departed from the block, Nobuo returned. He peered into a wicker stand. His sword still lay hidden amongst walking sticks and umbrellas. A flush of toilet water told him that his host would soon reappear.

"Is that you, Nobuo? I was starting to worry. Thought you might've received a better invitation." Partway into the living room, Harry tripped over a metal container of some sort. "What's this?" and dropped to a knee and pawed over the shells. "Mussels?"

Why does he not speak of the soldiers? Nobuo thought. What is he not telling?

"Clams?"

No response.

"Speak up, man. Are...they...clams?" and drew out his words to insure their delivery.

With doubts on how to navigate his newfound concerns, Nobuo said, "So sorry. You guess good."

"Where in God's name did you find these?"

"Huh?"

"The clams."

"From mudflats." Nobuo guided Harry to his rocker and stoked the fire before retreating to the kitchen to pour the crustaceans onto the counter.

Garlic and butter soon came to a sizzling tan inside a hot wok. Nobuo threw in the shells and added a cup of white wine. The industry, however, failed to smooth the turns in his head. His taut muscles mirrored his fears. Unsettled as to the whereabouts of another sanctuary, his brain muddled out. He finished the task with robotic motions and waited another few minutes for the clams to open up to release their juices.

*　　　*　　　*

The main course completed, Harry said with delight, "Best fettuccini that's ever graced this table.　An absolute truth."

222

He patted his lips with a napkin. "How'd you learn to cook like that?"

"Went to school before war, wanted to be sushi chef at Shinjuku Hotel in Tokyo." Stunned by his gaffe, he sat still over his plate.

Within the ensuing lull, Nobuo gathered up the dirty dishes and quick-stepped away. Need to be more careful, he thought, need plan.

A sweet scent circulated the room. A short time later, an orange pastry rested before Harry. He fanned the bouquet to his nose. "You have a gift. Yes, sir, you certainly do."

After satisfying himself on sponge cake, the old man latched onto his violin. "Here, try it," and held out the instrument with his upturned hands.

The visitor's own musical gifts were not without merit. Back in the day, before evil went on a rampage, he toyed with the Biwa, a 5-string short-neck lute, playing background music at Aiko's neighborhood puppet shows.

He fingered the fiddle, admiring the symmetry of its round parts, its fine mellow tone. Lessons followed: how to twist the pegs for tuning, how to frail with thumb and forefinger, how to strum with bow. Soon he scratched out a series of chiming phrases. The scraping sounds, chiefly of middling tempo, began to make sense. Nobuo soon forgot his dilemma and began to add little runs and fills.

In the middle of such trial and error, Harry said, "The soldiers, well, not really soldiers—more like half-wits with weapons—anyways, one of them found a military outfit in the bathroom."

The bow slid off the gut-strings with an ear-awful screech.

"I figured you for a man of gentle tastes," Harry said. "Most likely a victim in your own right, forced to do the will of corrupt men." He flicked the nub of his cigar into the flames, adding, "Seems to be a lot of that going around these days."

Silence.

The room began to burst with color. Harry felt the warmth and walked to the window. "Is that the day trying to break in?"

"Time to go," Nobuo added.

"Time to rest, you mean." Gaps of their conversation needed to be filled, but the long night weighed on Harry and he excused himself to his Murphy bed. "We'll talk later."

With still no escape plan, the outlander found this logic as sound as any and retreated to a corner and rolled up inside a tendered blanket. Unhinged, he pitched from side to side, cataloging all that had come and gone. Thoughts pulled on him. His mind soon became a collection point of that infectious day— the failed mission, the heron's mysterious visit, the haiku. Exhaustion soon introduced itself and he meandered off into a fitful sleep.

Chapter Thirty

Nobuo jerked awake as a bad dream tried to hold on. Ramrod, he gathered in the fuzzy outline of someone standing over the stove.

Harry heard the stirring and said, "Morning, or should I say good afternoon?" He moved from one pot to another. Bacon popped in the frying pan. Water gurgled and spat.

A caustic aroma assailed Nobuo. "What you make?"

"Call it the Mitchum Benedict." Then honesty took hold and he said, "Have to confess. Borrowed the recipe from a Negro up at the shipyard. Most of them folk arrived from the South during the Great Migration of the thirties in search of work. Now the U.S. Navy has confiscated their homes…,"

Nobuo tipped his head to the side like a cocker spaniel.

"…eighty-six residences and twenty-three enterprises, worth almost two hundred and fifty thousand, I'm told. Poof, gone just like that," and snapped his fingers.

Must have been that commotion yesterday with the caravan of army trucks, Nobuo guessed, and then he coughed to get his host back on track.

The blindman drifted for a minute before coming back to his creation. "Well, it's a mixture of eggplant and poached eggs served over a bed of grits."

"Grits?"

"Common in Louisiana, Mississippi. Ground hominy."

The guest moved to the table as the smell of boiled corn puckered his expression. There is so much to teach these people, he thought, but his hunger didn't care about such enlightenment.

Harry slipped a spatula under the fare. "This should quiet that belly of yours."

Nobuo waffled it down, all the while spinning variations of the meal in his head.

Due to their late start on the day, the evening hour hurtled upon them. The storm had moved east into the Sierras. Cumulus clouds trailed and dotted the skyway. The whirlwind of activity blurred the foreigner's clock. Sleep past noon? Breakfast at suppertime?

"Up for a little mischief?" Harry had decided that he needed the advice of others and added with a lie, "We'll trip the town fantastic."

"No trip. Stay here."

"You're going to refuse a handicap person his weekly diversion?"

A strange sensation fell upon Nobuo, and he grappled with an answer. In Buddhism guilt was the way of the self-absorbed, which led to loneliness and a cluttered mind. Footsteps on the wooden walkway rattled him. Could be more soldiers, he thought, and he dashed to the umbrella stand before fleeing into the bathroom.

"Hello, anybody home?" a familiar voice called with a knock.

"Annie," Harry responded as he made his way to the door. He opened it and said, "You're just in time for breakfast. Made my specialty," and he started back to the kitchen.

"Be right there," she said with a hurry in her step. "Gotta use the facility."

"No, someone's...," but he was too late. A wrenching scream bolted through the residence.

Anne shrunk beside the porcelain sink. A blade showed from the sleeve of a floral nightgown.

"I not go to prison. I go home," the alien declared.

Harry approached with care. He slinked past Anne and placed a palm upon Nobuo, saying, "It's okay."

"She not take me away," he said, eyeing her uniform.

"*She* is not a soldier. *She* is a famous ballerina," Harry said in an even way.

"Well, I don't know about *famous*," she answered as flattery replaced fright. "While the Music Box is not the Opera House, I must confess that…"

"Hush!"

"No," the blindman persisted, "she speaks the truth," and he felt for a periodical from a small rack nearby and held up last October's issue of *Life*.

Nobuo peered into the glossy photo, back to the auburn haired girl, back to the magazine. "You her?"

"Yes."

"Not soldier?"

"Not a soldier." To prove her claim she rummaged through her carrying bag and yanked out a white tutu. She held the outfit up against her Block Warden suit and sculpted as best she could a dancing pose.

Harry could sense that this did not pacify his visitor and added, "This is the person whom we discussed earlier."

"This Annie? One with haiku?"

"Yes," Harry said and eased the sword to the floor.

"*Mono sen surippa wo hakitsubusu hodo no jikan ga tatta,*" the stranger said.

"Sorry?" Anne said.

"Nobuo here has deciphered Mishi's parting message," Harry interjected.

"How wonderful," she said with delight as if the recent threat on her life was nothing more than an inconvenience. "What does it mean?"

"The bygone wears out a thousand slippers. Means the past burdens you, too much for your shoes to carry."

"Nothing I can't handle." Her pride blinded her from the proverb's deeper implication.

The alien pointed at her swollen feet. "Let me see."

"My feet are none of your concern."

"They have much to say."

"What's the harm?" Harry said.

"For heaven's sake." She sat Indian style and removed her saddles and bobby socks, thinking this was as strange an introduction as one could design.

At the sight of scar tissue and mustard colored contusions, Nobuo said, "Not sandals nor slippers nor footwear of anyone's making can hide such hideousness."

Embarrassed, the dancer withdrew her bruises further under her legs.

"You own your feet," the foreigner said.

"Well, of course I do. Who else would?"

*   *   *

The industrialized area teemed with a buzz. Vehicles of every size motored by with purpose. Hardhats advanced from all directions.

Nobuo stooped beneath the spacious hood of a sweatshirt. The emblem on its front read SAN FRANCISCO SEALS. These Americans are a sensitive lot, he thought, carrying enough for the beasts of this world to wear them wherever they go.

"Here he comes," Harry said at the sound of a husky drone from up the street. His left hand fanned out his cane in search of the curb while the other hooked onto the crook of the mystery man's arm.

A blow of air billowed from squealing brakes. An accordion door opened to reveal a man in a brown uniform.

"Sorry, Harry, out of service," the driver said.

"What seems to be the problem, Benny?"

"Some sort of fracas over at the shipyard. All lines have been rerouted back to the barn."

"I'm not in the mood for trivialities," Harry said, continuing his fib. "My friends and I are all set for a bit of cheer and we're not going to let a little disturbance stand in our way," and before the civil servant could revisit company policy, the blindman stepped up, blocked the door and called for the others.

"They could put me on suspension for this," Benny said. "You know that, don't you?"

"Nobody's going to punish you for helping the disabled."

"Good afternoon, Benny," Anne said as she boarded.

"Afternoon, ma'am," and he pinched the glossy bill of his hat.

The door closed and the muni rolled down Third Street toward the financial district. "Who's the little guy?" the driver asked.

"My name Nobuo. You Benny."

"I know my name, but what are you doing outside Little Tokyo? Thought all you were suppose to stay put."

"I no hurt anybody."

"Damn straights, not on my bus. Now stay to the back."

The trio moved beyond the empty seats to the last row, a synthetic covered bench that ran from window to window. Nobuo slid over to the far side. With his eyes perched just above the sill, he studied the foreign landscape. An embarcadero whizzed past with slips that occupied ships of war. He remembered Pearl Harbor, but it was not the image of victory that rose up. Instead, he saw the downcast expressions of mothers and wives that would bury their men, men not unlike Harry and Benny, simple men who before the war were blue-collar workers or just made do. He became sad at the thought of an Imperial officer approaching his Aiko to tell her that she would be without a father as well.

A motorcade rolled past them and veered off in another direction. From the rear opening of the last truck, a clump of

Negroes peered out. Nobuo guessed that their emptiness was twin to his.

Anne, sitting at the opposite end of the seat, tugged at Harry's coat sleeve. In soft speech she asked what they were going to do with this interloper.

"Can't turn him over to the Grays," Harry whispered to an agreeing Anne. "No telling what they'd do." With remembrances of a comradeship the previous night, he offered, "He can stay with me for a little while or until the end of the war, whichever comes first."

"Are you insane?"

"That's a possibility."

"He's not some tourist who strolled into town," her whispers getting louder. "He's the enemy."

"Shhh, keep your voice down," and Harry leaned his ear toward the far window before returning to Anne, saying, "Seems harmless enough."

With finality she exhaled, "We'll surrender him directly into Lieutenant General Wright's charge. Perhaps we can use Rose's influence to insure proper treatment."

"Heard the Grays did the bidding of Wright."

"Well, what the heck are we..."

"Where parents of Mishi Ishigawa from?" Nobuo interrupted as he crept to them, crowding in.

"Do you mind?" Anne said as she gestured for him to back off.

"Where her parents from?"

"Mishi's parents?"

Nobuo threw a glare at Anne. How many times did he have to ask?

"Hajime and Sato were born in Japan."

"Which prefecture?"

"Well, I..."

"Which prefecture?"

"I don't think I care for your tone," Anne said.

A thin line sealed Nobuo's lips in annoyance. A new tactic came to him and he reached into the sweatshirt's front pocket under the seal's rump.

"This yours?" He dangled the rolled-up haiku before her.

"Give that to me."

"This important, yes?" The personal item was withdrawn with a tease. "Where I find family of Mishi?"

"That is none of your business," and she lunged at her memento.

Ribbon and rice paper traveled from one hand to another, speeding above his head, behind his back in a game of cat-and-mouse. "Tell me and I return it, deal?"

"I don't bargain with our adversaries." She clenched her teeth and went after her possession with renewed determination.

"What in the name of Jesus Hilary Christmas is goin' on back there?" an imperious voice said from up front.

Harry struggled to separate the combatants as arms whizzed past. He called back over his shoulder, "Not to worry, Benny, got it under control."

As the quarrel grew, the transport jerked to a halt at the intersection of Third and Brannan. Heavy footsteps marched back down the aisle.

"That's it, everybody out," Benny said.

Nobuo and Anne untangled themselves, adjusted their attire and presented themselves with nervous twitches.

"Sorry," she said. "It won't happen again."

"You got that right. Out." A knotty finger pointed toward the exit.

"But..."

"Now."

Someone from the front door called out, "Everything all right in here?"

The civil servant turned his large frame around, blocking a clear view of the rear seat. "Happy to see that the Republican Grays are on the job," and he started to walk toward the soldier.

"What happening?" Nobuo murmured.

Harry didn't have time to explain and told his friend to hide. The militiaman asked the driver if he had come across any Nips during his travels to which Benny gave a hesitant no. Undefined movement toward the back, however, drew the Gray down the aisle to the young lady.

"Well, hello there." With a wicked smile, he sized up her chiffon tutu, which was displayed across her khaki jacket and pants like meringue on pie. "Nice." He was a crooked wire of a man with a jagged line of stained teeth that punctuated his greeting. A pair of stiff hairs sprung from a spidery wart.

Anne blinked away the grotesqueness and ruffled up her costume. "Just repairing a tear," and she began to thread a sewing needle. "I perform at the Music Box. Have you heard of it?"

"Who hasn't?" His inspection poured over her in earnest.

She started to raise the skirt to cover herself when a pull from the other end brought it back down. Anne smiled with a quiver and said, "It seems to have a mind of its own," and kicked the source of her resistance. A complaint sounded from below, but Harry masked the slip-up with a sneeze.

The strangeness before the Gray went undetected as the lusty image of dancing girls dominated his testosterone-laden mind. "Okay if I drop backstage sometime and say hello?"

"Not at all, officer."

"*Officer*. I like that."

She picked a ticket from her pocket. "Please, come as my guest. I insist."

He brushed across the gifting hand with his own, lifting the corner of his mouth in a sinister grin.

Her earlier confidence waned, and she manufactured an awkward compliance. "See you then, I guess."

"Count on it." He gestured goodbye with a wave of the voucher and retreated to the street.

The bus started up again and rolled through the checkpoint. A moment later a hooded head popped up from under the lacy mound.

"What you kick for?"

"Stop your whimpering," and she gathered up her dress and bundled it back into her bag.

"All Americans mean like you?" Nobuo said as he climbed up from his hiding place.

"Just the ones that count for something."

"Buddha have much work to do," and he slumped into the small cavity between girl and old man and sat stiff.

Harry leaned over him to Anne and said, "You're pretty free with those passes."

"Works every time." Underneath her stalwart demeanor, her heart throbbed.

At Third and Market, the soul of the financial district showed itself, and Benny steered to a stop and swung free the door.

"Meet up with us later?" Harry asked.

"Got enough trouble waitin' for me at home. Don't need to ask for more."

"Missus been acting strange again?"

"Something like that. One moment she's happy as can be, the next she's moody as all get-out."

"Goodbye, Mr. Benny," Nobuo said and took a step down before he stopped and turned back around. "You buy medicine for wife. Drive torture from body." He asked for pen and paper and wrote down the Latin names of a few roots and herbs.

The driver accepted the list and glanced at it with a puzzled grunt. He'd let the wife make sense of it. "Thanks, Little Guy." Another thought came to him and he said, "Better hightail it back to Japantown before those vigilantes catch up with you."

Nobuo saw no reason to enlighten the man on his true address and bowed in agreement. Anne pursed her lips at the performance and snatched onto THE SAN FRANCISCO SEALS and gave all a heave.

*   *   *

He brightened at the sound of brass horns and singing and laughter. Thinly clad dancers pranced past him.

"Most beautiful women," Nobuo said to Anne, noticing a flock of ostrich feathers in the grips of the performers. "Fan dance began centuries ago during reign of Emperor Jimmu. For aristocrats only."

"You won't find any such fuddy-duddies at the Music Box," she said. "Mostly just your average wham-bam, thank-you-ma'am types."

"No understand."

"You don't have a need to know such things."

"I know why Mishi wrote you haiku."

Anne stopped and whirled around to him. "Her message is for me, not you."

"Now you get closer."

A knot of patrons in their navy whites entered Nobuo's consciousness and he vanished under his pullover. Bounded by the walking tandem of Anne and Harry, he traveled down the side aisle of the main hall to the safety of backstage where a voice echoed off the brick walls.

"Fifi, get the snags out of your stockings." Rose paced from one entertainer to the next, extolling attention to detail. She pointed to Dirty Martini's boas and said, "If you're aimin' to be some two-bit harlot in a flea circus, arrangements can be made." The owner pivoted from her preoccupation and bumped into a clump of people. "What're all you folks doin' back here?"

"I'd like to introduce you to Nobuo," Anne said. "Unfortunately, he happens to be a foreigner. Actually, he's more than that. You see…"

"Lollipop," the owner interrupted, "scoot up that hosiery. Look like a bed-wetting senior with her drawers down," and then she turned back to Anne. "You still here?" and she started to move away when a white cane halted her.

"As Miss Anne started to say," Harry interjected, "Nobuo studied at a culinary academy. One fine cook."

"No," Anne said in a loud voice, angry at Harry's gamesmanship, "that's not it at all. Like I was trying to…"

"A cook you say?" With the absence of Hajime, Rose was desperate as Number Four continued to struggle with his new responsibilities as head chef.

"Yes, indeed, a fine good cook," Harry repeated.

"*Good* helps."

"Miss McNally?" Anne said.

The boss cut her short with a glare before lifting the Oriental's chin. "You Japanese or Chinese?" She dismissed the notion away with a toss of her hand, saying, "No matter."

"Well, actually it does," Anne said. "You see, this person has a very different slant on the war than you or me. In fact, you could say that…"

"Don't care much 'bout the war or anyone's *slant* on it as far as that's concerned."

"No," Anne pleaded, "you don't understand. He's a…"

"For cryin' out loud, not that again," the owner said before adding in a maternal style, "Now go on and get. You *are* working tonight, correct?"

"Yes, but…"

"Honey, it wasn't a request," and cajoled Anne away with a pat on her rump.

Rose guided Nobuo toward the kitchen, saying, "We'll put you on a trial basis as our sous-chef, see how things work out."

He thought that this offer of employment was a much better idea than prison. In a low voice he was saying as much to Harry when an aluminum door swung out at them.

"Excuse very much. Trouble with sashimi at Table Twelve," said an employee.

"Whoa there," Rose said, raising her hand like a traffic cop. "Want you to meet someone."

Four appeared frazzled.

"This is the new help," Rose said. "I'm told he comes from an excellent background."

"That nice," and he sped off toward the dining hall without a look.

Rose demanded that Four return, but he kept on going with his original purpose. Nobuo put on a sappy face, not knowing what else to do.

"First rule," Rose said, "don't get in a fight with your co-workers, understand?"

A nod and then another.

"From now on you'll go by Six. Hajime was One. Can't give that number away. Figured I'd retire it. I was able to fill the vacancies left by his wife and daughter with a couple of Chinamen. Everyone in the kitchen is a number. Don't want any trouble with the authorities, got it?"

"No make trouble no more."

Rose instructed Six to wait for his fellow servant after which she escorted Harry to his seat out front. Four soon came back with a rejected meal whereupon Nobuo tasted a sample and said, "No fresh ginger?"

"Who you?"

"New assistant. My name Number Six," and Nobuo presented his hand.

Suspicious, Four studied the stranger. "Never seen you 'round before."

"Not from here, from far away," arm still extended. "Call me Six if like."

"Number don't make you Chinese. Everyone else Chinese now." Four glared down at the offering, huffed and sauntered away.

At that moment a curvaceous entertainer in a skimpy top, unbuttoned to mid bosom, sashayed by and took hold of the outstretched limb. "Hi, I'm Dirty Martini. It's very nice to meet you."

He ogled at the cranny of her bosom, his concerns of a moment ago muddled within her bewitching folds. Fleshy lines showed in pleasing arcs while ample thighs were on full display where a dress's hem split away. With effort, he lifted his stare, afraid of being too obvious, but his thoughts strayed back to the cleft of her breasts. Dazed with disbelief, he blurted out the only thing that came to his rattled mind. "I no kill anyone."

"You're cute," and she cupped his cheeks within her hands and stamped a kiss upon his forehead.

Chapter Thirty-one

Gyozas rested upon dinnerware near the pickup counter. Whiffs of warm pork and cabbage and spices lured a pair from their chores. Doubt dictated their movements as they dried their hands, sniffing the air, stepping closer toward the efforts of the newest staff member.

Number Six pinched off a section of the doughy dish and plopped it into his mouth. With a satisfying grin, he circled his hand over his stomach as if to reassure them that all was right.

In Cantonese Number Four beckoned another to test the appetizer, but Number Five crisscrossed his hands in syncopation with several no's. "A potsticker?" Number Five said to Six. "You make joke, right?"

Over Five's lifespan, thousands of the tasty morsels had passed through his gastronomical gate. What emboldens this foreigner, he thought, to think he can cook up a surprise when dealing with one of China's national treasures?

Enwrapped by the scents, the duo broke out in animated exchange of half-whispers. Four, as was his privilege by rank, nudged Five forward again but this time with a command. Five held the pastry with thumb and forefinger, peered back at his counterpart and knifed off a section with a mousy bite. The whole of the dumpling soon filled his smile.

They quizzed each other on the treat's makeup, unsure how to label the piquancy before them. A mysterious essence circulated their culinary tracts as stupefaction settled upon their faces. Number Five insisted that the enticing ingredient in question was leek. Number Four retorted, saying that the riddle belonged to a spice, perhaps sesame oil.

"Even monkey fall from tree," Six said. "Everyone make mistake sometime." A child-like simper rolled up in play. "Marinate in saké with clove of garlic."

A chorus of "ahhs" sounded in unison from the Chinese as if they should've known. They signaled their approval and, after some hesitation, requested another.

While the trio were bantering the pros and cons of Japanese cooking, Rose pushed through the swinging door with her elbows. A pile of dirty dishes teetered within the cradle of her arms.

"Why you clean tables?" Number Four inquired.

"'Cause I got nothin' better to do."

"Thought we busy?"

She released a note of exasperation before transferring her load to the counter. "Why's everyone standin' around?"

"I make dumplings," Six interjected as he tendered up a sample.

Her nostrils sucked in the aroma, and with nonchalance she pitched the potsticker into her lipstick-framed aperture. She licked the tasty coating from her fingers. "Not bad, not bad at all," and asked, "Goin' okay in here?"

Number Four growled, more for show than anger. He couldn't let Six think that a reformed League of Nations had taken shape within the kitchen.

Yet Rose took the disdain aboard Four in seriousness. "Don't forget, all worked well enough before. It will again." If truth were known, she preferred the old ways—a civilized standoff between China and Japan, a détente introduced years previous by Hajime. Borders were established, delineating duties, stations and schedules. A certain amount of tension kept everyone sharp.

The boss bent into Six. "Can't give out a higher number just 'cause ya can cook. Life's confusin' enough around here," and started to leave when she said, "Got patrols all over the place."

Expressions darted back and forth.

"A commotion over at the shipyard."

"Commotion?" Five asked.

"They say a battalion of Japanese commandos have landed."

Battalion? Nobuo thought. That would be a grand accomplishment for a minisub.

"Not to worry," Rose continued. "Wright and the Fourth Army will have them penned up in the short run of things. In the meantime, no tellin' what crazies are out there wantin' trouble and such. Chinese, Japanese, Mexican—don't make no mind to certain folk what shade of brown ya are," and she exited with a warning that everyone should watch their backs.

Nobuo didn't know how to watch his back. Besides, he never thought there was much there worth looking at and gestured with a shrug.

*   *   *

Number Six made every effort to insure a productive night. Food requests found completion as fast as they appeared. Favorable reviews journeyed from the dining room. Rose, delighted with the feedback, heaped a good deal of praise upon her latest hire, all of which he shared with the rest of the kitchen staff. Around midnight, Six put his apron to rest and spooned up a few goodies onto a platter and left.

Dirty Martini and Fifi, festooned with hair papers, lazed on a chaise lounge of red damask. Robes dangled untied from diaphanous clad frames. The sous-chef took a seat and offered a thorny treat, saying, "Tender artichoke reveals its succulent heart to prying, fleshy digits."

The ladies brought him into their huddle and ladled up the snack with their fingers to each other's lips. A ropy curl pushed up his pencil-thin mustache. The grin widened when bookends of fleshy pendulums—as if pushing free from their lacy riggings—pressed against his cheeks.

Further down the hall, Anne tried to ignore the noise. Irritated, she mouthed a protest to the space before her when she felt the moistened tip of some creature at her ankle. She gathered in the inquisitive stare of the uninvited and said, "What are you looking at?"

"Not the dog's fault," Harry said at the sound of a whine.

Anne went back to her makeup and said to the image behind her in the mirror, "Do you have to bring that *thing* with you? Aren't there health laws regulating the comings and goings of such beasts?"

"Well, Gaspar'd appreciate the reference to *beast*. I think he's been questioning his manhood lately."

"And that inferno clatter down the hall." In her attempt to brush on an application of rouge to her cheekbone, the bristles found her iris instead.

"Damn," and she banged the tool off her chromed makeup case and started to rise when Harry said, "You stay put and get ready for your number. I'll see to the trouble," and he felt for the exit.

Minutes passed but the uproar continued. Anne, unable to ease herself, snarled and bounded from her dressing room. She arrived at the disturbance and wedged her way between body parts and peeked into the stall. The scene promoted itself similar to the mayhem at Santa's village inside Union Square's City of Paris. But instead of a plump, full bearded man, a peach-fuzz of a stick figure sat there in merriment.

"Having fun?" Anne said.

Number Six failed to catch the gibe in her speech and responded in all sincerity, "Yes, most kind to ask."

"And you," Anne said to Harry, "I was under the distinct impression that you were going to do something regarding this..." and she scanned the scene, "...this circus."

A small taste lingered at the bottom of a bottle and Harry presented a sip as a peace offering, but Anne would have none of it. "You ought to be ashamed of yourselves, consorting with the likes of this foreigner. Disgraceful."

"I didn't take you for a bigot," Fifi interjected before sampling another treat.

"Yeah," agreed Dirty Martini. "Six is just trying to make acquaintances. He doesn't mean any harm." She brought his chin around and said, "Do you, darling?"

Determined to lighten the moment, Six submitted another culinary quip: "Artichoke hides its tender heart under pricks. In my bed, the same," and his cheeks became flush with laughter.

"Isn't he just the most adorable thing?" Dirty Martini said.

With agitation chiseled onto her phrasing, Anne reminded the alien of his precarious position in life. With the realization that perhaps he had become too comfortable within his surroundings, Nobuo excused himself and started to peel away from the throng.

In the hallway, Anne pulled him aside. "Listen," and then she noticed the glances that followed and steered him further down the corridor toward the rear exit.

"I don't know what to do with you. Perhaps we should..."

"Make Nobuo your choreographer?" he suggested in anticipation.

"What? No."

"Use feathers all wrong."

"This isn't about me or my..." She halted in mid sentence as if his critique had just registered and said, "Well, excuse me, Mr. Fred Astaire, but it just so happens that I learned the fan dance from the inventor herself, one Rose McNally."

"Yes, Rose Number One. I Number Six."

"No, Hajime was Number One but he's gone. I suppose Rose should be...," and she brushed back her hanging hair with the flat of her hand. Flustered, she started to fumble over her words again before quitting the effort altogether and left to repaint her face.

*   *   *

At closing hour, Six escorted a group to the exit. In the foyer he climbed on his tiptoes with a kiss for the ladies, appreciating each in turn, before giving Harry a hug.

The blindman pried the embrace from his frame only to witness the rejoinder of another. "All right, that's enough. Don't want to give these folks the wrong impression, do we?"

"Nobuo has American friend, correct?"

"Sure," Harry said when another thought came t o him. "You gonna be okay?"

"I work out arrangement with Rose. That how you say it, *ar-range-ment*? What mean *arrangement*?" Before his new ally could answer, Six volunteered, "It mean marriage?"

"I don't think she intended anything permanent by it. Probably just offering a place to bed down. In any case, don't you go hurting anyone, you hear?"

"Six a chef now," and Nobuo swept his hand over his white hat and apron, thinking that this uniform was a better fit for him than his old one. He rendered another thank you and said goodnight and secured the doors.

Bands of light cut to blackness as Nobuo flicked off switches along the length of the hallway. Backstage, near the rear exit, he followed a circular staircase to the boiler room. Mortar dripped between cockeyed rows of bricks. Concrete lay underfoot while a naked bulb hung loose from the battened ceiling. A rusty shower stall, corroded sink and a part-time working toilet rested near a floor drain. A haggard rug served as the lone wall ornamentation. He pounded the carpet. Dust motes reeled and skittered within the suspended glow. Rather than endure the unseemliness, he lifted the tapestry from its hooks when a human-size hole introduced itself. Down the tunnel ran the bulb's weak glimmer until fading to nothing. Interesting, he thought. The draft of cold air, however, did answer the rug's purpose and he rehung it.

Chapter Thirty-two

With her mouth fixed to the waxy tip of her lipstick, Anne sounded stilted and stiff as she complained to her image in the mirror. "Caribbean slut," and slipped a gold one-piece, tie-down bra over her breasts. A multi-colored ruffled skirt came next. Bangle bracelets slid onto her arms while a black wig, replete with orange turban, fit snuggly atop her head.

A diminutive man leaned into the cubicle, wearing a matching calypso outfit. "You ready?"

Anne glanced up to acknowledge the announcement when she realized that the man before her was not her regular dance partner but an imposter. "Nobuo, please tell me this is just more of your sick humor."

"Regular guy sick. Not from humor. Sick of wife." He puffed up and added, "I not sick. I no have wife."

"You expect me to perform with you on a stage reserved for those very souls you tried to destroy?"

"Tried to take pictures only."

"You should be in handcuffs awaiting a firing squad."

His grin collapsed. "You wish Nobuo dead?"

Anne hauled in her anger. "Maybe I was a bit hasty as regards to the firing squad part, but you do belong behind bars."

"You no let me dance?"

"What?" and she scrunched up her face at the difficulty of trying to convey a simple truth. "No, like I said, you..."

"Everyone," he interrupted, "inhabits earth with telling. Be careful or soon you tell anyone. Or perhaps one day no one to tell."

"Would you stop doing that? Just say what it is that you want to say instead of..."

Rose pushed open the curtain and entered. "Mind explainin' what's goin' on in here?"

They started at the same instant to describe their separate and quite different versions when the owner shushed them. Within the moment that followed, she loosened her jaw as if trying to shake the tension from her skull before saying, "Anne, on in fifteen. Six, need ya to sort out what's wrong with Five. Let's get back to doin' what I pay ya for, okay?"

Grumbling crossed each other.

"Can't hear you."

"Yes, ma'am," Anne said.

"Got to be a better way to make a livin'," Rose said beneath her annoyance and turned to Six, repeating herself, "Kitchen's waitin', let's get crackin'," and the pair departed together.

Anne stared at the exit long after they had left, pondering the dilemma this foreigner presented. Perplexed, she sought solitude and went to the back alley.

*   *   *

A bottle whooshed past Number Four's ear. He bolted around, snared at his attacker. "You got problem for me?"

Number Five looked for more ammunition, saying, "You forget to buy sweet saké for teriyaki sauce again."

From behind, someone blocked Five's next attempt. "You brothers of same nation," Six said. "Should harmonize."

A string of Cantonese curses followed—or at least Six thought they were by their inflection. Couldn't be certain. The harangue summoned a group from the hallway. Dirty Martini, Fifi and Lollipop clogged the kitchen's glass portal.

Unawares that they were the main attraction, the pair of Chinese ratcheted up their debate while circling Six. Swats, thwacks and swings found their way with such insignificance as to barely wrinkle uniforms. To the ears of their audience, however, the complaints carried the potential for some entertainment.

"I own higher number," Four said to Five, poking the air with his fist. "You must obey superior."

"My superior owns brains of dung-eating horsefly." Then Five kicked Six by mistake, apologized and took another try at his countryman.

The sound of girlish excitement came to them from the other side of the kitchen door. Jabs stopped in mid flight as the kitchen staff swiveled in unison to the giggles that entered. The ladies drew near, poking the Chinamen in fun, stirring things up.

"Are those aprons...or skirts you're wearing?" Fifi said.

"C'mon boys, you can give us somethin' better than that," Dirty Martini added as the dancers spurred them on with dares and backslaps and hisses.

A soldier in his pressed uniform stood within the entrance and said to his former co-workers, "You still cook up trouble, I see."

They inspected the man before them with awe.

"You must be Caucasian now. Only Caucasian get into U.S. Army," Four said. "How you do this thing?"

"Somebody did it for me." Hajime told the tale of Lieutenant General Wright "volunteering" him to be a code breaker, of Rose brokering the deal in lieu of a Montana internment camp. A calypso outfit suddenly latched onto his awareness and he said, "What are you?"

"I performer *and* sous-chef." A head full of teeth showed below a pencil mustache. "I Number Six."

"You don't look Chinese," Hajime said.

"I could be," and pivoted toward others for affirmation, which they freely gave.

Puzzled by this person's presence in a nearly Japanese-free city, the former cook examined the stranger, touring him as one might a car for purchase. With a hooked finger, Hajime splayed out the foreigner's neckband and gawked at a Rising Sun with wings. At the realization of its meaning, the soldier took a step back and said in clipped tone, "Everyone leave, except you," and pointed to the enemy.

All but the two Japanese exited to the hallway. The alien sensed his vulnerability and searched for a weapon.

"I advise strongly that you don't try anything foolish," Hajime said in his native tongue, patting his holstered revolver.

"Who are you to give orders?"

"I am Private Hajime Ishigawa of United States Army."

"Mishi's father?"

Hajime assumed that such knowledge came from fellow workers and swept it aside. "Your tattoo like roadmap. Tells where you have been, where you will go. You are member of Japanese Imperial Navy Air Force. Do not deny."

"Not a fighter pilot," the former aviator said. "Reconnaissance," and mimed the clicking of a camera with his hands.

*　　*　　*

Anne paced the alley with her haiku—*The bygone wears out a thousand slippers.* She tried to fit the message's meaning with Nobuo's words. A vague notion ping-ponged inside her head when, without warning, someone snuck up from behind and shut her mouth with his palm.

"Hello, darlin', remember me?" and he slid his other hand along the inside of her skirt.

The bitter taste of his sweat settled upon her in league with his boozy breath. She kicked and then kicked some more.

"Got ourselves a wildcat, do we?" and he spun her around, spread out her arms and pinioned her against the brick wall.

"Get your filth off me!" Anne squirmed under the fleshy restraints as she glanced at his features. A warty nose and jagged stained teeth brought a previous encounter to her. Bastard. She scoured the passageway for help. A sound, not too distant away, came to her. Her eyes popped wide with hope, but the fracas was nothing more than a rat slinking scared from its hiding place. Brass and cymbals and drum rolls jangled alongside the distant howls of excited men from inside. She thought of calling out, but what would be the point?

Her attacker's tongue traveled down her neck. She twisted away.

A moan drew out from rusty hinges. A French sconce put details to a man near the rear exit. At first Anne thought the features might be attached to a fellow performer. Upon closer inspection, however, the rusty-colored hair and freckles belonged to a singular person. A waft of rotten bananas confirmed his identity and she yelled his name.

Curly studied the broken scene. "Hello, sweetcakes." He worked up a jeer before disappearing back behind the closing door.

Damn. Enraged, she jerked up a knee and caught her abductor in the crotch. The Gray groaned, folded over. She started to untangle herself, but he snatched onto her arm, swung her around and slapped her full across the jaw. Her head jerked sideways. Comprehension returned in steps. Pieces of her surroundings slowly floated back into their slots.

She set aside her dread with a brash grin. "Is that all you got?"

The Gray flinched. His countenance hung in suspension unable to fathom the stubbornness before him. Anne shouted a mighty roar and lunged. Sharpened fingernails clawed away, scooping up tissue.

*   *   *

Within the muted hum of an intermission, screams traveled from the alley to the backstage to the kitchen. Number Six, recognizing the outcry's owner, dashed from Hajime's hold but not before snatching up a lengthy blade from beneath the stove.

*　　*　　*

"Bitch." With his freed hand, the Gray swabbed blood from his facial wound. A malevolent sneer appeared and he said, "So that's how were gonna play it, huh?" and balled up his hand into a fist.

The alley door thudded open against the red clay façade. A calypso-clothed figure jumped into a fighting stance, knees bent. The Gray voiced his disbelief at the ruffled costume and flipped open a switchblade. He clutched onto Anne's hair, snorted and dragged her forward to capture a better glimpse of his challenger.

"Appears some chi chi man has come to rescue the fair maiden." The Gray appraised the glint rising in broken bands from an unknown instrument half-hidden behind the Lilliputian head. "Whaddya got there, fully loaded mariachis?"

Six brought a sword around. The Gray balked at the sudden emergence of the much larger blade. The alien slid his left foot forward while bringing the steel across his chest, ready for a backhanded lethal strike. At that instant Hajime dove into the alley, landing flush on Six. The pair crashed to the ground. The samurai weapon clanged forward to the foot of Anne's assailant. Six stood up and cursed in Japanese at Hajime, who leaned forward and replied in kind.

"Hello," Anne said to the quarreling twosome. "I'm over here next to the bad guy. Remember me?"

The Gray told her to shut up. His glare took on a hawkish shape, weapons of different lengths in each hand now.

Hajime reached for his side arm but his holster rested vacant. He searched the area. Nothing. From the exit poured out Rose as well as Numbers Four and Five.

Rose brought up a FP-45 from her garter strap and took aim. "Can't take us all on."

The Gray sized up the peashooter and laughed even as the Chinamen presented a butcher knife and a frying pan. Six, glad they didn't bring tongs and ladles to the fight, pushed a hello to the Orientals. A demonic grin appeared below the Gray's hairy wart as if he didn't care.

Rose saw the recklessness and waved him on, saying, "If you're comin', then get started."

Within a second canvassing of his opposition, however, the Gray released Anne, tucked the sword under his belt and sauntered away.

"And don't return," the owner yelled after him, "unless you're wishin' to be dismantled from head to toe."

"Yeah," agreed Four. "Best not show ugliness in Chinatown either. We hang you out to dry with pigs and chickens and monkeys."

Howls sounded in acknowledgement as Anne stepped to Six and Hajime to thank them. Newly arrived musicians and stagehands crowded the exit. Excited talk spewed forward. After satisfaction settled upon everyone's many questions, the alley began to thin out.

Miss McNally motioned for Dirty Martini and Lollipop to escort Anne back to her dressing room. Number Six retrieved a .45 from behind a crate and presented it, grip first, to Hajime who took his revolver without gratitude. Another concern occurred to the soldier and he said, "Where'd you get the sword?"

"No matter now. Gone with ugly guy."

The boss interrupted their parlay, saying, "Guess we better all get back before our customers run out on us."

Six jerked away from Hajime's hold and took advantage of the opportunity for a quick retreat. Hajime started to follow, but his former employer caught his arm.

"He needs to come with me," Hajime said to Rose.

"He needs to get back to work is what he needs to do." She released her hold on him, saying, "So, where ya been keepin' yourself?"

Distracted, he did not hear the question. "So sorry, what did you say?"

"Whaddya been doin'? Haven't seen you in a month."

"Been training."

"What kind of trainin'?"

"Intelligence kind of training," Hajime said as his absorption flitted back and forth between Rose and the rear of the Music Box.

She stationed her hands on her hips and pursed her lips.

Hajime, seeing her impatience, apologized once again, decided to let the matter with this saboteur rest for the moment and said, "Commander Wright placed me and others from Little Tokyo into Military Intelligence Service—M.I.S." Uneasy, he continued, rendering a shortened version of his future. "Anti-Japanese...," and he paused in search of a term.

"*Emotions?*" she guessed, trying to help. "*Sentiment? Suspicion?*"

"*Feelings,*" Hajime blurted, proud. "Anti-Japanese *feelings* will send unit east to Camp Savage Language School in Minnesota next week."

She threw her head back in surprise. "Your English is better than mine. They taught ya good."

A bow.

"Come back tomorrow night for a proper visit."

"Yes, I be most happy."

On the way out he searched for his rival. He found him in the kitchen filling out a stream of food orders in accomplished fashion. With anticipation of formidable resistance from the Music Box regarding any arrest, Hajime decided to elicit the assistance of the Presidio and left.

* * *

In his pajamas Elmer sat at the Formica table with his *Chronicle*. Within the unusual presence of silence, he said to his daughter at the sink, "Good mornin'."

When there was no reply, he left his chair and went to her and guided her around. Her bruised chin showed before him. "What happened here?" He leaned her hurt into the overhead light. "Did ya hear me? Who did this?"

"One of your militia buddies."

"What'd he look like?"

"A thin, crooked man with a hairy wart."

"Could be Hansen. Maybe Wheeler." He paced the room in thought. With his head fixed upon his steps below, he said, "Knew it wasn't safe. Told Rose that her strip joint was no place for a teenager..."

"It's not a *strip joint*. It's a..."

""But, oh no," he interrupted, "she convinced me that everyone would protect ya." Back and forth he went, head down, finger coming up with each new thought. "Even went so far as to say that the change might be good, give ya some *character*."

"Listen, dad, I know I was wrong sneaking behind your back, dancing at the Music Box, the whole Curly-charade and all..."

"Well, that's more like it," he said, halting, coming around to her. ""Bout time I heard an apology."

"That's the thing, no apology should be necessary."

The father crinkled up his brow, curious as to where this was going.

"If I thought performing at the Music Box was best for my career, so be it."

"Not sure I..."

"Please, let me finish."

He huffed.

"Truth is, I probably sought the job in part to hurt you, but in the end that was all wasted energy. I've got to account to myself, nobody else. Not even you. Especially you. You may not agree with my choice of professions, but it is *my* choice." Anne wetted the tension from her lips. "I tell these things to you, my family, in the hopes that an understanding will come forth, but not with the requirement or expectation that a blessing join it." She raised her shoulders as if to say that was all.

Elmer weaved his hand through his comb-over. "Who've ya been talkin' to, some back-street-word-junkie?" He would've been more comfortable had they settled into their usual tit-for-tat bickering. That he knew how to deal with, but this, this philosophical mumbo jumbo, felt awkward.

"See you're still wearin' the Civil Servant getup," he said in search of some positive. "Guess that's somethin'."

"That *something* has nothing to do with you or your demands. I simply thought I'd try to do right by it this time around."

He pushed his eyebrows down in question.

"And just so that you know, I've decided to reapply for that ballet scholarship in L.A."

"Don't push it, missy."

"Dad, you have to figure out the real reason why you don't want me to leave home." She went to him, held his hand. "You'll be fine."

Chapter Thirty-three

He asked the MPs to wait in the hallway before marching into the kitchen where he snatched onto a pair of apron strings. "Go," Hajime said in Japanese to Number Six and pushed him toward the walk-in pantry.

Once inside, Six pitched Hajime's grasp from him, and they separated themselves. At first, the dialogue went one way as Hajime's voice peaked at the discovery of a second tattoo on the foreigner's forearm.

"A red roundel resting on a single black bar. This is the mark of Imperial Air Defenses."

"You and I are of the same skin," Six said.

"My skin belongs to the land under my feet," Hajime retorted.

Numbers Four and Five leaned an ear against the sliding door, commenting on the rabble as if describing the blow-by-blow of a prizefight.

"Dollar on Hajime," Four said in Cantonese.

"You on," responded Five. "Number Six take his head off."

Hajime backed Six against rattling tins, pressing on. The enemy's body drooped along with his expression. Deteriorated from his deception, from the weight of his bygone, he broke loose with a confession.

"I am Airman Third Class Nobuo Akita, reconnaissance officer for submarine I-25." He admitted that he was most likely responsible for the death of an Oregonian, a girl believed to be younger than his own daughter. He rambled on in spurts, speaking of whichever topic entered his mind first. He told of Aiko's many talents, of their common love for American movies. They were of things no man would label a crime, things far removed from zealotry and war and death.

"I no longer do these things," Nobuo added, his head lowered.

Hajime stretched for a can of peas and cocked his arm to strike. Instead, he unloaded a frustrated cry and returned the object with a bang to its dust-free circle. This person now possessed a name and a face, a family man no less. Hajime's thoughts strayed to Mishi. A melancholy buried him under the realization that each had been displaced from his child.

Hajime wanted the enemy to be heartless and unremorseful, a paragon of hell. Infuriated that such dilemmas were not clearly defined, he roamed the small space with the knowledge that the edges of right and wrong were often discolored with ill choices, that these thin peninsulas of gray worked men old before their time.

"*Ga aruga, shinjitsu no megumi ga iku no* (There but for the grace of truth go I)," Hajime muttered, his back to his captive. He felt his mind weakening.

Distraught, Nobuo said, "*The bygone wears out…*"

"*…wears out a thousand sandals,*" Hajime finished.

"This proverb is a symbol of our beginnings." Nobuo went on to remind him how each prefecture in their homeland had adopted a saying that typified their local way of life, how this particular truism had belonged to the Hokkaidō region for centuries.

"Your family is from this island?" Hajime asked.

"My father worked as sushi chef at the Kawayu Hotel."

"In Akan National Park?"

256

"Most certainly," Nobuo said.

"My father worked there as well."

They confirmed the summers spent, the bonding of workers' children and the punishment attached for infiltrating the upper class. The maze of hallways served as a playground while romps through the lodge invited complaints from well-to-do patrons. Neither, however, could recall being in the presence of the other.

"Time has a way of changing one's appearance," Hajime said.

"As a six-year-old, things came and went with such hurry. So many adventures, so many faces."

"This is true."

"Now our bygones intersect when we both suffer similar sadness," Nobuo said. "At this juncture, I would ask a favor."

"You are a fool to think that..."

"You mail letter to my Aiko for me. Please tell her that I am still alive, that I come home to her soon."

Even prisoners of war are allowed such requests, Hajime guessed. Another consideration came to him within the stalemate that followed. Thoughts spun inside his head before putting forth a proposition, which by his own admission was fraught with uncertainties but one that held promise for both concerned. The two shared opinions on the topic, giving and taking, ideas spilling over each other.

Rose barged into the kitchen with a tight expression. "What're the MPs doin' here?"

The Chinese had never before lied to their employer and Number Four said, "No know a Mr. MP."

She started to rephrase her request when an urgent call came to her from somewhere else and she stormed out.

"You do good," Five said to Four.

"Well, I just do what superior number should..."

"Wait," Five interrupted as he bent an ear back toward the storage room. "You hear that?"

"Hear what?"

"Hear nothing, that what."

Alarmed that corporal harm may have taken up residence inside the pantry, they eased closer until their heads, piled atop one other, were pressed against the slider once again. With an unexpected burst, Hajime and Nobuo spilled out into the tilted frames. Four and Five jerked back, shrouded their embarrassment with wild gestures and started pointing toward where the other pair had just been.

"Uh, we need spices," Four insisted.

"Have soup emergency," Five agreed in clumsy fashion.

"We enter now," Four said as he nudged his partner along with sharp pokes.

"We no drop eaves on your conversation," Five said over his shoulder.

Nobuo brushed the spectacle aside and turned back around to Hajime, saying in Japanese, "We have agreement?"

"Your continued existence depends on it."

Nobuo returned to his kitchen duties while Hajime walked away with the MPs. In the foyer the soldiers approached the exit when another uniform came swinging in.

Elmer noticed the other's attire, paused to digest the image before him and said, "Guess we're fightin' on the same side now."

"Always were," Hajime responded.

"What's this?" Sergeant Klausen said, spotting a patch stitched onto the other's coat sleeve.

"Golden compass with sword, symbol of M.I.S., Military Intelligence Service."

"Didn't know we had to import intelligence. Thought there was plenty enough within our own kind."

"We same kind, both residents of United States."

Elmer gestured his approval with a grunt. "Huh, who would've thought?"

"Group of Hawaiians have formed military unit, the 442nd Infantry Battalion." With deeper inflection, Hajime said, "I join up later."

Elmer's eyes showed his surprise and he said, "Well, I'll be, Japs fighting Japs."

"Americans fighting Japanese," Hajime corrected.

*   *   *

"You're a fright, girl," Benny said.

The dressing room's mirror confirmed the horror as Anne said, "You wouldn't look so pretty either if someone used your chin as a punching bag."

"I have to know every detail," Harry said.

Anne was tired of listening to her own complaints and asked, "How're you boys doing?"

"Wife's due soon," Benny said. The advent of his fourth daughter seemed a complexity that was fast rising to a burden. "Don't know how I'm gonna cope in that two-bedroom chicken coop of ours. No place to hide."

"Is the little woman feeling better?" Harry asked.

"Got to admit, Little Guy came to the rescue with those herbs. Calmed my beloved down to an F-2."

"What I wouldn't give for a little disturbance now and then." Harry's milky stare moved in the direction of Anne. "Where've you been? I've missed your visits."

"My life has been on a crazy ride as of late."

"Hello, my friend," a jubilant Nobuo said to Harry upon entering.

"Ah, there you are. I've brought you something." The blindman fanned a hand across the carpet beneath him and hoisted up a rectangular package bundled in twine and newspaper.

"You so kind." Nobuo unwrapped the present and inspected its contents. His uniform stared back. "The past seems to follow closely."

"As close as your shadow," Harry said.

Remembering the purpose of his visit, Nobuo returned to Anne and said, "Almost forgot. This yours, I believe," and handed over a note wrapped in red ribbon. "Maybe you tie around neck. Not lose so much."

"Where'd you find my haiku?"

"Out back."

"Must've dropped it last night during the attack."

When no further response filled the void, Nobuo said to Anne, "You're welcome. No reason to thank me. No reason at all."

"Actually, I am grateful. Wanted you to know that my feet feel much better."

"Care for them. They still have long journey."

At that moment Elmer walked in. Anne collected herself and began dispensing introductions when her father said that such formalities weren't necessary, his vision resting upon Harry and Benny.

"Know your names as well as your part in my daughter's lamebrain scheme."

Everyone seemed relieved. No more conspiracies. No more fear of forgetting one's lines, which parts of discussions were sacrosanct, which were free for the taking.

Elmer switched his attention to the slender Oriental. "Know my daughter?"

"Yes, I crawl under her dress."

"Beg your pardon?"

"Dad, this is Number Six," Anne said. "The one who came to my rescue last night."

"Oh, yeah, in the alley." The father, as if a past remembrance just registered, swiveled back around to the Oriental. "Whaddya mean *crawled under her dress*? Can't say I care much for strangers snoopin' around my child's drawers."

"Only place to hide."

The father gestured with a scowl to Anne who struggled with an explanation. "Well, you see, he...," and she petered out.

Elmer crossed his arms, waiting.

"Mr. Klausen," Harry interjected, "if I may."

"May not," and the father returned his intent to his daughter.

"He, uh," and she pointed to Nobuo with her look, "he wandered out of Little Tokyo." She offered up the fib to protect a future plot.

"Suppose that explains everything," Elmer said.

His persistence rankled her, a reminder of her continuous struggle to discover an alignment with the world, to assert a newfound independence. She stiffened with plucky grit.

Elmer caught her meaning and with some effort he said, "All right, I get it. None of my business." Not convinced of his own phrasing, he added, "I guess."

Anne shot him a smile and mouthed a thank you. He fanned the crown of her head with a kiss, trying on a different attitude.

"Now, if you will excuse me, I have a show to prepare for," she said.

"Let's depart, gentlemen," Elmer said. "Lady needs to fix herself." He started to shepherd the throng from the cubicle when he turned back around. "Drive home together after the show?"

"Yes, I'd like that."

"Good," and he repeated the word, pleased with the way things had gone during this brief exchange.

Anne's grin shrunk into a tight line as she leaned around her dad and bellowed, "You," motioning to the Oriental, "get back here."

Nobuo, as requested, drew the curtain closed behind the retreating party and took a step closer toward Anne.

"You are no longer safe here," she said. "Since that little incident in the alley, the Grays are suspicious. I'm not sure where Commander Wright's allegiance is with regard to my dad's old outfit either. The only plan I see for you is under the authority of Chief Delaney."

"Mr. Hajime Ishigawa and I already have plan."

"Care to share?"

"No can do. Private."

"Privacy belongs to those who have fought for it, not to those who have tried to destroy it," Anne said. "This cannot continue. I'm calling the police," and she rose.

He brought her back around, his hands clasped onto hers. "Give Hajime's idea chance. You said I helped with haiku, yes?"

"Yes, but that doesn't..."

Without warning, the distant sound of angry men unhinged them. Anne joined her dad and others in the hallway while Nobuo fled to the kitchen.

By the time the disturbance arrived in the ballroom, Rose was yelling at a gang of Grays. "It's Sunday. Ain't you got any respect for the Sabbath?"

"Cannot shield Satan behind the words of the Lord," Fredericks said. "Where is he?"

"Don't know who you're...," Rose started to say but he pushed her aside. "You hoodlums got no right barging in here like this, knocking over furniture and things."

Elmer wrapped his arms around his daughter and studied the dozen or so men he once claimed as brothers.

All of the kitchen help, numbers Two thru Six, glanced at the flapping of the kitchen door. At the presence of raised rifles, they withdrew into a tight huddle. With their frames clothed in white, their features were indistinguishable from each other, as if the head of one might belong atop the shoulders of another.

"Who is the owner of this contrivance?" Fredericks demanded as he held up a curved sword.

Number Four exhaled his awe and said in hushed tones, "Most beautiful weapon."

Fredericks dragged the emboldened one from the gaggle, lurched him around by the collar to another. "Is this the miscreant?"

A warty-nose of a man snarled, showing off his stained teeth before answering in the negative.

Elmer shoved his way through the clump and said to Fredericks, "There is no one of interest for you here." He chose his words with care, aware of what this man was capable of.

"Klausen, you are a traitor to the cause just like your other Kraut friend Schmidt."

The sergeant shot a tsk-tsk, saying, "Best you and your fellow varmints crawl back underground."

Aft of the pack, a young man maneuvered forward with stealth. Physical features showed themselves in bits. A mop of red curls weaved in between men of like uniform toward the front. In a sudden motion he lifted the butt of his Springfield to Klausen's backside.

"*Ki o tsuke!*" another shouted in alarm.

Klausen whirled around, snatched onto the weapon and snapped it back into the boy's throat. Curly wilted and slumped to the floor.

At hearing the foreign words, at spying the one who gave the warning, Wart-Nose gestured with his hand and wailed, "That's him, that's the Jap who flashed the sword in the alley."

With this injunction the very core of the earth broke loose. Battle cries bellowed forth from liquored thugs as they charged the Orientals. Four and Five, armed with nothing but their teeth, bit into anything gray. Wart-Nose and others tossed the infidels aside only to witness the rejoining of them in battle, now armed with a saucepan or a rolling pin or a pair of lethal tongs. Rose, Dirty Martini and others brought out their claws. A man yelped at the inclusion of women into the brawl but didn't know which articles of war to recite. At the utterance of the complaint, Fifi whacked him unconscious.

Elmer bulldozed Fredericks into a stand where cutlery and utensils clanged a discord. While father pinned the Gray to the concrete, daughter served up a volley of rounders. Then she looked up and saw a helpless Nobuo at the bottom of another pile. She left the major to her dad and zigzagged around and in-between the swings of combatants, latching onto a bludgeon along the way.

The flat of a frying pan landed flush on a cavalry hat. Its owner fell atop another.

"Remember the bus?" Anne said looking down at Nobuo.

He nodded his understanding as a dizzying ceiling bowled over him. Anne pulled him out from under the Gray's dead weight, and they rushed to the hallway where the mayhem rolled up to greet them once more. Stage crew and performers banged and punched and kicked at the intruders. Spotlights, wooden stools and other makeshift missiles carved out a path to various targets. Anne sidestepped along the wall in awkward fashion, fanning out her tutu like a matador with his cape. A vigilante thought he detected more than one pair of limbs sashaying beneath the ballerina's costume. Before he could investigate, a stanchion landed on his nose.

Nobuo crawled out from under the lacy hideaway and the pair sprinted to the rear exit. But the sound of angry raps on the other side of the alley door caused Anne to hesitate. She gazed back down the main corridor where the disturbance had erupted into a riot. Low on options, Nobuo said, "This way," and they raced toward the belly of the theater.

The outcome was no more settled when the shrill of whistles sounded from the main hall. Fredericks, still restrained by Klausen's meaty paws, heard the demands of the local police. He pleaded to his lieutenant for assistance. Jones, after fingering a brass button and straightening his lapels, gave his superior a leer as if that was all he could spare and called out to Wart-Nose and Curly.

The trio banged out of the kitchen and dispatched frilly dressed dancers with swats and slaps, as men-in-blue grew closer. The militiamen fled out the back and into the alley, strong-arming their way past their own kind, and disappeared into the darkness.

A phalanx of lawmen reached backstage and marched the disturbance into a corner, separating Grays from Music Box employees. Agent Harris directed a pocket of MPs into the kitchen where armaments of any definition were tossed into the pantry. Orientals climbed strung out from a nearby knotty mass.

"Didn't know you were open on Sunday afternoons?" Harris said to Rose.

With unfinished business on her mind, she turned away and sucker punched a vigilante leaning rubber-like against the counter. "That's better," and pushed up her bra before returning to the agent. "Sorry, what were ya sayin'?"

"Hope I'm not intruding."

"Kind of, fun was just startin'."

Harris dismissed any further pleasantries and ordered the cuffing of the rogue band and sent them away except one. He strolled the short distance to Fredericks and said, "A sad ending to an otherwise inglorious career." Wisps of smoke lazed above.

"You do not comprehend the enormity of your blunder," Fredericks insisted, flush with anger. He jerked from an MP's grasp and pushed forward. "The enemy is here. Are you obtuse?" and spat his disgust at the toe of the FBI.

"Nifty word—*obtuse*. Probably worth a truckload of points in Scrabble. Counterproductive here, I'm afraid." The agent peered down at the spittle upon his Oxford before looking back up. "You couldn't stay within the confines of your assignment, could you? Had to take matters into your own hands."

"We did the task that nobody else dared to want." Defeat entered Fredericks's expression. "Wright left us twisting in the wind once he no longer required our services."

Without any reason to further the debate, the agent said to the MP, "Take him away."

The militia leader continued to spew venom as he passed from backstage to the lobby and outside. Harris drew on his cigarette within the ensuing silence. All stood at a distance from this man who was in the throngs of deep thought.

The Fed tapped the hanging ash of his Chesterfield into the cup of his hand. "You start to lose track of where to put good and evil. Sometimes they seem to travel together like Cain and Abel."

Rose hadn't been to church in quite a while, figuring this as good a time as any for a sermon. Even the Orientals, unfamiliar as they were with these Cain and Abel people, felt something of import rising before them.

"Now while I don't figure that God takes kindly to those who assume His rightful seat of judgment, I'm not so sure that some truth doesn't reside with our Mr. Fredericks."

Harris flicked his smoke to the ground and stubbed it out when he detected a sword that glistened alongside misplaced pots and pans. He retrieved the venerable blade and studied it as might a jeweler of a fine gem, admiring the complexity of its construction. With the recent warnings of the Gray on his mind, he examined four brown-skinned faces.

At that moment a call could be heard traveling down the hall from one patrolman to the next until it arrived at the swinging doors. An officer entered the kitchen and said, "Sir, you better come and take a look at this."

"One moment." Harris kept his attention arranged upon the aproned employees until the policeman insisted that the matter couldn't wait. The agent stationed an MP at the kitchen entrance and strutted toward the rear exit before veering left and descending a spiral staircase. Bare bulbs hung by their cords to illuminate a narrow lane to the boiler room. Harris surveyed the musky confines. A cot with its blankets folded part way back as well as a standing locker filled with clothes fell under his scrutiny.

Someone pulled off a rug from a wall to reveal a gaping hole. Harris crimped into the pit to study its depth with a borrowed flashlight. Fresh hand prints and scuff marks led down the tunnel until they dissolved within the distance. Must be the tracks of at least two, the agent surmised. Next, he moved toward the closet when a newspaper-wrapped package peeked from a nearby stack of laundry, which was sorted and neatly folded.

Outside the galley, ladies entertained the soldier on watch. Dancing fingers massaged his uniform. At the return of the FBI, the MP came to attention. Harris shot him a disapproving glare before passing to the theater's owner.

"Miss McNally, I…"

"No need to be formal here, sugar pie. Call me Rose."

Harris started over and said, "Miss McNally, I was curious about the tunnel down in the basement."

"Ah, well that surely is an interesting tale," and she took a stride toward her office, saying, "Care to hear it over a spot of whiskey?"

If he didn't know any better, he'd suspect her of stalling, but for what purpose? "No, thank you."

"Very well." Rose gathered herself and said in a docent's voice, "Prior to the building's present fame as a theater of burlesque and even earlier as a brothel of some distinction, the structure housed a sanctuary for young women caught up in an East-West slave trade. Angry owners, armed with search warrants, came to claim their chattel."

The Fed's vision roamed along the walls.

"Connected to the main sewer line, the tunnel was built as an escape route and served the females well. Never bothered to plug it up. Didn't want to be disrespectful of the place's heritage and all."

"Hmm, of course not," the agent countered when he brought forward a bundle, half-wrapped in newspaper. "Found this downstairs." He peeled away the remainder of the covering and displayed a soldier's ensemble. A black fitted jacket with gold epaulets, matching straight leg pants and purple waist sash hung from his fingers.

At Rose's hesitation Harris offered, "Uniform appears recently cleaned and pressed, wouldn't you say?"

More humming.

"Miss McNally, the United States is trying to *defeat* the enemy, not welcome them with laundry service and a domicile."

The agent draped the outfit over his arm when a wallet-size photo eased loose from the upside-down jacket. He hunched over and retrieved the picture of a young Japanese girl perhaps seven or eight years of age. He glimpsed back to employees standing nearby and asked, "How many Orientals work at the Music Box?"

"Five," Rose answered, "Number Two thru…"

"I see that only four are present."

Rose verified the count. "Six is probably around here someplace. Anyone seen…"

"And would that by any chance be his quarters below in the boiler room?"

"Yes, but you're not suggestin' that he had anything to do with…"

"Thank you for your patience, Miss McNally," and he handed over the ensemble to her before tucking away the pic of the girl into his breast pocket. He tapped the brim of his Fedora and exited the theater onto O'Farrell Street where his sedan held the festering Fredericks.

Chapter Thirty-four

The Chevy rolled into the driveway. The father cut the engine and lowered his hands to his lap. "What an evening." A spark showed itself. "The surprise on Fredericks's face when you stepped in for another blow." He slid his vision sideways. "Where'd ya learn to punch like that—that straight-arm jab like a piston?"

"It's a specific movement in dancing. There is the first *port de bras*, the second *port de bras*, and so on. Sometimes used instead of a *cambré*."

Elmer put a theatrical slap to his forehead. "How stupid of me."

Anne pushed open the passenger door and told him not to dally, that the house lights shown from the uncovered windows.

"Holy crap," he said, pouring it on, "how'd that happen?"

He stepped from the car with his fatigue and followed her toward the stoop, stopping along the way to gather up the usual smattering of newspapers. Anne held open the door and motioned for him to get his rear-end in gear.

"Fast as she goes, sweetheart," the father said.

"I'll get you a beer."

"Not gonna change my mind as to your Jap friend."

On their travels home, Anne had conceded that there was more to Number Six than she had let on. She figured her father would find out anyways, no reason to hide the truth. Better they straighten things out now while other deceits had been exposed. She revealed his true name, his true country of origin. Her involvement with Nobuo had become part of her personal bygone, one more pair of slippers for her to wear. If her father agreed with her position on the matter, fine. If not, at least he might better understand the *why* of her.

"With some of the Grays on the loose, Nobuo still confronts great danger," Anne said.

"Such danger should visit him at the Presidio," Elmer argued.

"Have you forgotten who came to my aid in the alley the other night?"

"Doubt ya needed any assistance."

"And when he gave you that warning regarding Curly?"

"Didn't ask for the Jap's help. Besides, the redhead would've ended up on his backside one way or another."

They continued to bicker as they stamped around preparing the bungalow for the night. Each offered opinions on the fate of the foreigner—she promoting the notion that Chief Delaney was the only one who took a neutral position on the issue; he saying it was a military matter. Worn down from the debate, the father made his way to his rocker and fingered the dial of the Philco until Count Basie announced his presence:

Well I'm drifting and drifting

"Ya exhaust me, woman."

Like a ship out on the sea

"The trouble is that your heart can't hold in all the love you have for me," Anne said as she handed him his drink. "You just need to air out your feelings every so often."

Well I ain't got nobody

"Don't patronize me with your new fangled talk," he said before sipping his beer.

In this world to care for me.

Anne hawked the area rug as if following its braided pattern to an answer before starting in again about Nobuo. Elmer waved her off and went back to his libation when the electricity shut down and turned the house black. He told Anne to stay put.

Out the front and down the stoop and along the gravelly path he went when an oddity arrived. From the slit of a neighbor's shade, a soft glow showed. Curious, he thought. He circled around past the hydrangeas to the electrical panel. He flipped up its lid and with the aid of a full moon inspected the circuits. The main switch had been pulled. What the hell?

The window above the shrubs stood ajar. Sounds of men from inside made their way to him and he flopped to the ground.

*   *   *

Anne heard the rattling of dishes in the kitchen sink. At the sight of multiple beams crisscrossing each other, she realized something was amiss. She snatched a hearth's stoker from its resting place and tiptoed inside a coat closet, leaving the door open a crack. Shafts of light soon skittered past her to silver the radio and the rocker and the brick fireplace. With the weapon raised, she hardened her resolve. The rusty yawning from an auto, however, drew one of the intruders toward the entrance. He pinched back a window's covering and glanced out. Nothing seen, he locked the front door and rejoined his fellow conspirator who was picking his way to the bedrooms.

*   *   *

Elmer started to lift the Chevy's trunk when ancient hinges sounded his presence. He ducked behind the vehicle. He saw spots of light dancing upon the bungalow's window curtain. With their withdrawal he scouted the trunk, shuffled aside tools, a first aid kit and a spare tire. He plucked a rifle from under a sleeping bag and slid two cartridges into the chamber.

*   *   *

Anne withdrew deeper into the closet when she stumbled over an object. Both knees landed with a thud upon the hardwood floor. Damn.

"Did you hear that?" said one of the hooded men as he put up his hand to halt the other. They stilled themselves, perking up an ear. The second masked man, after a moment, dismissed the worry and continued his search of the bedchamber while his partner retraced his steps.

A distant creak from the hallway's fir planks warned Anne. With a hasty plan, she slinked from her hiding place, swung the door wide and slid in behind it. Someone came to the edge of the living room and fanned his vision toward his left, toward the kitchen. Everything seemed as before. His beacon moved in a clockwise direction, to the fireplace, to the rocker. The coat closet came into view, its entrance fully exposed. With caution he treaded closer and leaned in. Anne came around and caught the man full on the back of the head with her stoker. Her muscular leg cushioned his fall, lowering him to the floor in silence. She dragged him into the cloakroom, eased shut the door, and used his flashlight to scour through her duffle bag for a roll of medical tape. With the finding of a second familiar object, she smiled a knowing smile and brought the item to her voice.

*   *   *

Elmer hurried to the porch steps and put one foot in front of the other along the extreme side where the boards would be most solid. With stealth he jiggled the doorknob, but it wouldn't budge. In the belief that time was short, he cocked his .22 and took aim at the deadbolt.

From behind, a voice said, "Stop...stop right there."

Elmer felt a pistol's barrel against his spine. "Thought you'd be in Mexico by now."

"Had…had unfinished business to attend to." Jones snatched the gun from Klausen and tossed it onto a nearby woodpile.

The father jerked around.

"Easy," Jones said as he fixed his .45 on the sergeant before rapping his knuckles upon the entry. "Open up."

A figure in dark tights and a ski mask soon appeared. Jones studied him and then steered his examination further inside. "Don't see your buddy."

"He was just here," the accomplice said with a shrug.

Jones pushed Klausen through the living room and into the rocking chair. "Where…where's your little whore of a daughter who dances down at the strip joint?"

"Not a *strip joint*. A burlesque club."

The Gray brought his sidearm backwards, spring-loaded and ready for a swat, when another, dressed in black, came forward from the coat closet. In fluid and rhythmical movements, the person diverted Jones's intention and punched Klausen across the jaw with a straight-arm, piston-like punch.

"That…that's some wallop you got there," Jones said.

No response.

"We were wondering where you went," and then he turned back to Klausen and spied him grinning at his assaulter. Jones looked back and forth between the two, not sure what to make of the exchange.

The toe of a saddle shoe tapped with methodical gestures upon the floor. One…Two…and Elmer bolted up and jabbed at Jones's scar with sharp thrusts. Dazed, the pistol dangled at the Gray's side. His flashlight fell to his boot. Shapes came and went as the beam banged underfoot every which way. A hooded person dashed forward to assist Jones when another in the same disguise swept him off the floor with a hardened instrument of some kind. A knife fell to the carpet and two sets of inky figures dove after it, rolling around, slugging each other. Without warning, a shot echoed through the room.

"What the hell?"

Jones recovered his beacon and fixed it upon the injured Klausen before sliding it to where two persons had been fighting. Only one lay there now. Jones spun around when the tip of a hearth's tool found his mouth, sending him to the floor alongside his half-conscious confederate.

"Damn, that felt good," Anne said as she removed her hood. She was hand-brushing her matted hair when a stench of banana-scented sunscreen assaulted her. She flared out her nostrils, sniffing, and went to the stink and peeled off his mask. Red strands of hair squirted loose.

"Curly?" Anne said.

"It's Sean," he said with weakness, up on one knee. "Sean McG…"

And she kneed him across the cheek. He whined, which annoyed her, and she swung into the fifth position of a *developpe* and extended her heel ninety degrees into his chest. He returned flat to the hardwood.

Anne left the floundering reject and went to her father. "Are you all right?"

"Been better," and he winced at the showing of a puddle of blood at his shoe.

Anne untied his footgear and eased the gory mess off. She turned his ankle to and fro.

"Hey, take it easy."

"Quit your sniveling," and she jiggled his leg again. "Just a flesh wound," and dropped it to the floor.

At that point the house rose up in a sudden brilliance. The crunch of footsteps made their way from the path to the front entrance. A man in a black fedora perused the scene before him.

"Seems as if I've missed the party," Agent Harris said.

"See you got my message," Anne responded.

"Yeah, a kid got a call over his walkie-talkie and phoned in an emergency to the station. Gave this address."

"So that's where my radio went," Elmer complained to his daughter.

Anne shot a look to her father as if that was all he cared about before saying to the Fed, "You'll find their associate in the closet."

The agent stepped over Jones and Curly and strolled to the walk-in. An ugly puss of a man lay next to a duffle bag, dressed in nothing but his underwear. White medical tape bound his ankles and wrists. Harris guided him to his feet and hopscotched him to the middle of the living room.

Wart-Nose, after the sticky wrap was ripped from his mouth, pushed his glare to Anne. "Bitch."

She sauntered over and brushed some lint from his bare shoulder. "There is no need for such behavior," and she head-butted him. A brown stained tooth fell out.

Harris brought him back up before handing him over to a couple of policemen. Within the wake of the departing officers, he said to the Klausens, "Found some very telling evidence at Jones's place. Had a stockpile of shun knives stored in a cellar along with several copies of *War Commentary and Freedom* and a Trotskyite manual entitled *Anarchy and Chaos*. It appears that authority irritated the man. In addition, photos of every Italian and German Republican Gray adorned the walls, red **X**'s drawn thru two of them." He slid his attention to Elmer and said, "Next week's date was scripted on the bottom of a likeness of you. Due to the debacle at the Music Box, I suspect that Jones felt compelled to move up your execution."

Anne hefted the Gray partway up by his shirt collar to check the scar on the bridge of his nose. "I remember you telling me, dad," she said pivoting part way around, "concerning the deaths of Ponti and Schmidt. I'd bet my last G-string that they never suspected Jones to be the enemy. He used his trust to get close. That might explain why there wasn't much resistance."

"Yeah, you're right," the father said, "and the fraternity pins…"

"…torn off their dead bodies to strip them of any further belonging to the militia outfit," Harris added.

At that point another approached from the stoop, entered and marched across the living room. "Why'd you do it?" Fredericks said, taking his woozy subordinate from Anne, shaking him.

Jones gazed up at his commander, coming around. His hand, which held his bloodied mouth, muffled his wording. "You were mo-more worried about your place in history than...than shaping it."

Fredericks stood his former lieutenant to his full length, pressed him against the wall and prepared to strike. His fist hung in mid air.

"You always said there was no diff-difference between Japs and Wops and Krauts," Jones said. "Couldn't wait for that German prison to be built down in Texas, remember?"

"Yes, but this, killing your own men?" Fredericks said, his paw still balled up.

"It would seem that we've got ourselves an old fashion cleansing," the agent guessed as he turned to Jones. "Purify the ranks of the Republican Grays and march underground to do the bidding of the self-ordained, that about the size of it?"

"Can't wage a decent fight with half-breeds." He spoke with full clarity.

"The Fourth Army and Wright gave him a green light to harass the Japanese," Anne suggested. "Must've rose up like nirvana to old Jonesy."

"Given a two-fer-one," the agent added. "Eliminate the ethnic scum from the organization while blaming it on the Black Dragons. Then the bubble burst and Jones couldn't contain his hatred."

"Had a brother and son killed by two wars," Jones retorted. "Japs and Krauts, don't need either of them."

Fredericks released his hold, disgusted.

"Klau-Klausen here is worse than any of those Heinees," Jones persisted, slouching. "Pretended to be Dutch, nothing but a lying coward."

"No longer," Anne said as she regarded her father. "From now on we go by our birth names—Elmer and Anne Klause. Correct, daddy dearest?"

"Ah, you're no fun."

The law returned and started to usher the remaining two renegades along with Fredericks to waiting squad cars. Harris called out to the Gray's commander and thanked him for his aid in the search at Jones's.

Oscillating red and blue globes vacated the block. The agent glanced at his wristwatch and said, "Wish this war kept normal hours."

He passed to the porch where he saw an oblong object standing against a woodpile. He palmed it with interest and said to Klause, "This yours?" He took a peek at the chamber. "Loaded, too."

Embarrassed, the father accepted the rifle and fumbled out a fabrication. "Forgot all about the darn thing."

"Next time, might want to bring it to the fight."

"Thanks for the tip."

Chapter Thirty-five

S.F. CLEAR OF ALL JAPANESE

"For the first time in 81 years, not a single Japanese is walking the streets of San Francisco. The last of them, 274 in all, were moved yesterday to the Tanforan Assembly Center in San Bruno. Japantown lays empty. Its stores vacant, its windows plastered with 'To Lease' signs. There were no guests in its hotels, no patrons nibbling on sukiyaki or tempura. A colorful chapter in San Francisco's history has closed forever."

S.F. *Chronicle*
May 20, 1942

Miss Adelaide Pinkerton danced across the stage to a makeshift office carrying her six-month-old baby, Trouble. Oboes and violins strummed up from the orchestra pit. In a silk turquoise kimono, Cho-Cho-San made her introduction as she fawned over Miss Pinkerton's child. The exchange, however, started to take on a morbid tint. Cho-Cho-San teared up, continuing to pass her hand over Trouble, her strokes becoming more and more aggressive. Uncomfortable with the mysterious turn of emotions, Miss Pinkerton withdrew her infant in *á la seconde*, a quick spin sideways, and used an *allegro* to bounce toward the exit. A Japanese naval officer in his black fitted jacket with matching epaulets, standing collar and straight leg pants stood in the doorframe. Miss Pinkerton motioned hello to her lover in an *arabesque penchée,* her body balanced on one foot, her other leg extended behind her. He guided her chin upward to meet his gaze and went to kiss her when she lifted the swaddled bundle in presentation. The officer quaked at the news that the child was his. Cho-Cho-San quick-stepped to him and slapped her unfaithful husband. Ladies and child retreated together. With their newfound bond, mistress and wife glared back at the brash philanderer, all the while protecting the infant from his reach. Rejected, the Japanese naval officer performed a *pas de bourrie,* which took him back across stage to a clothes rack. He plucked off a hanger, shaped it to a point and stabbed himself repeatedly, but his attempts at seppuku were pathetic. The women giggled their embarrassment, whisked to his aid and assisted him to his ending as stage lights faded to black.

Taken aback, the audience's shock fell below their chatter. Lieutenant General John Wright crunched up his expression in disbelief. He eyed the police chief as if seeking definition but none resided there as well.

Not waiting for applause, the performers skipped out from behind the curtain. Dirty Martini in a Western style business skirt stepped forward with a gentleman in a foreign uniform on her arm. They raised their coupled hands to the nonplus audience. The actors moved aside as they gestured for Anne. Dressed in her kimono, she came to the edge of the stage and bowed in the direction of the musicians.

Agent Harris straightened up from a pillar and leaned to better appraise the Oriental dancer. A suggestion came to him and he picked a photo from his pocket, eyed it and headed backstage.

At their customary front row accommodations, the VIPs called for the owner to join them. Police Chief Delaney pulled back a chair, saying, "Rest a spell."

"Classy stuff, huh, boys?" Rose said as she plopped down on the cane-bottom chair.

"Very interesting," the chief said with diplomacy.

"Didn't care much for the American lady having a child by the Jap," Commander Wright said. "She came across like some secondhand call girl. Enjoyed the other version of *Madame Butterfly* better... where the foreign woman leaped to her death."

"You boys aren't gonna sull up on me, are ya?" she said.

"There's no room in this war for such self-deprecation, let alone on stage for everyone to see," the lieutenant general said. "Bad for morale."

"Don't be such a grump. Do ya some good to poke a little fun at yourselves."

The Music Box returned to its usual faire with Lollipop and Fifi gyrating and singing to Alveno Rey's "Deep in the Heart of Texas". Chaps, cowgirl hats and cutaway vests were all that clothed them.

"Now this is more like it," Wright said with a rush of smoke from his cigar. "Seems familiar."

The stars at night are big and bright...

"Oughta," she confirmed. "Performed the act at the fair."

Deep in the heart of Texas.

The McNally Nude Ranch was the main attraction along Treasure Island's "Gayway" at the '39 Golden Gate International Exposition. The spectacle brought flesh out into the open with plenty of epidermis on display. Other than an occasional snicker and the haughty attitude of feminists' organizations, the local authorities quietly supported the stag shows.

Rose hoisted up her dress, the curves of her legs catching the lieutenant general's interest, and displayed an FP-45 pistol tucked under her garter. "Had a chance to flash your present the other night. Didn't seem to scare the Gray much, though.

Anyways, the sentiment's much appreciated," and leaned over and gave him a wet one on the cheek.

"While it's only a single shot, the gun seems to be a big hit with the various resistance movements overseas," Wright said. "We're dropping 'em all over Europe," and he sucked on his cigar when another thought came to him. "Heard of the incident in the alley. Sorry your girl came under attack. She all right?"

"One measly vigilante can't put the hurt to Annie. She'll be fine."

"Seems that most of the militia have either resigned themselves to the authority of the State Reserve or are visiting our stockade," Chief Delaney added.

"Can't believe how such a stuttering excuse of a soldier could wreak so much havoc," Commander Wright said.

Delaney reminded him of the man's name—Jones—and how he had duped many of his fellow Grays, including his own commander.

"Almost stonewalled Operation Dragon," Wright said. "No telling what Jones was capable of. Got the paperwork to ship his sorry ass to the loony bin up at Napa. That way he'll carry little credibility with the media. Gotta keep a lid on this thing."

"And Fredericks?" Delaney asked.

"Had to consider the FBI's comments regarding how he helped with the capture of the remaining renegade Grays. To shut his mouth, I promised him a Reservist unit, same as Klausen's."

"They've switched back to *Klause*," Rose corrected. "Guess they figured they weren't foolin' anyone."

"I got trouble enough keeping Japs and Chinks separated in my head," Wright said. "If the damn Germans and Italians and the what-have-yous start switching things up, I'll need a program to keep track of this war."

"Did I hear you right, Fredericks is in charge of Klause's new outfit?" Rose asked. With a nod from across the table, she added, "Poor ol' Elmer, can't catch a break even when he's gone straight." She veered away and circled her finger in the air for another round of drinks.

"Here's to the ouster of the last of the Japs from the City," Commander Wright said, raising his glass.

Gentlemen, I do believe there's one more left, Rose thought with a smirk.

*   *   *

The cubicle's curtain remained open to accommodate the well-wishers. Benny traded pleasantries with Anne and her Oriental dancing partner while Dirty Martini took a seat on Harry's knee, making herself comfortable, petting the black lab at her feet.

"After a little drama, were we, ladies?" Harry asked.

A sinister grin showed on Anne. "Just wanted to entertain the folks with the improbable, switch it up some."

"Wanted to play with the mucky-mucks in the front row," Harry insisted, "bend their brains with your friend here prancing around in that Japanese uniform."

"Farce is a natural companion of satire," the Oriental volunteered. "*Kyōgen* comedy is centuries old."

"In any event," Harry said, "the performance was sublime. Particularly enjoyed the smooth transition from the *tendu* to the *chasse*. Very nice."

"Look at you," Benny said, "all cultured up with ballet talk and stuff," and smiled at Harry.

"Is that such a surprise? There's still a bit of refinement in me."

"Bet I can fix that," Dirty Martini said with a tickle to his cheek.

"You go, girl," the bus driver said and laughed a throaty laugh.

"Benny," Anne interjected, "I've got a proposition for you."

"Already been propositioned, betrothed for life."

"I was hoping you might be able to help out Hajime and Number Six. There's a bonus in it."

"Number Six?" Benny asked. A recognition soon came to him and he said, "Oh, you mean Little Guy. Sure, glad to help. I owe him for those herbs he recommended for the wife."

In the middle of Anne's solicitation, the sound of an authoritative voice spilled down the hallway. She told everyone to stay put and went to investigate. At the kitchen's glass portal, a scene appeared before her with serious implications. Worried, she hurried back to the dressing room.

*   *   *

"I'd like everyone to step forward," Harris said as he scotched an imaginary line across the floor with the tip of his Oxford.

Four looked to Rose for reassurance before moving to the gestured demarcation along with the rest of the kitchen help. With the photo drooping from the end of his outstretched hand, the agent paraded up and down, comparing the black-and-white features of a young Japanese girl to that of the staff, trying to catch a likeness in their faces.

"I will approach you individually with a question or two," Harris said. "Please answer in your native tongue."

For Numbers Two thru Five the routine was the same: the FBI man asked where they were born and when did they immigrate to the United States. All answered in Cantonese. Satisfied with the responses, the agent slid sideways to the last man.

"Where were you born?"

The employee swallowed a wad of saliva. Within his hesitation, Rose started forward, yapping, but the agent was quick to silence her.

"I repeat, where were you born?"

A person in a Japanese officer's suit entered as the swinging door flapped behind him. Agent and performer stood there, gazes fastened onto each other.

Without any explanation but with plenty of dread, the alien darted back out into the hallway and bolted toward the rear exit. Harris gave chase, yelling for him to halt. Waiters lost the handle on serving trays while Anne and others glimpsed from the row of cubicles.

In the dimly lit alley the suspect tripped over a wooden crate and tumbled to earth. Before he could rise to his feet, the agile agent was upon him.

"You've cost me many a sleepless night," Harris said as he pushed his captive to the turf.

"What do you want?" the Oriental said.

"I don't think we've been properly introduced. I'm Agent Harris with the Federal Bureau of Investigation. And you are?"

"Nice to meet you. Must go," and the alien attempted to stand.

The agent put his full weight onto him and brought out a pair of restraints. "Let's try these on for size."

"If I were a betting man," Harris continued, staring downward, cuffing him, "I'd wager you can't speak any Cantonese, or Mandarin for that matter."

"Don't speak Chinese at all," the accused answered as he tried to break loose.

"Speak Japanese by any chance?"

"Speak Japanese very well."

"Aha, now we're getting someplace."

A groan.

"You're not an American citizen, are you?" Harris pressed.

"No, I am Nisei."

"What a minute," the FBI man said as he squinted within the darkness, "I know you."

"My name is Hajime Ishigawa. You delivered me to Presidio, remember?"

"What's with the Japanese uniform? I woulda kept it if I'd known you were gonna…"

"Not uniform. This is costume."

Harris tightened his grip.

284

"I am performer and soldier and chef. I am very talented," and a twinkle showed upon Hajime's countenance.

"Got any I.D. on you?"

"I know what I.D. means now. I take English classes. I speak good. Very talented." With his bound hands, he struggled to produce a laminated card from his pants pocket.

Harris inspected the identification, MILITARY INTELLIGENCE SERVICE written in bold letters above a photo. "What do you do for M.I.S.?"

"Well, I could tell you, but then I must kill you." Another grin. "From a Charlie Chan movie—the one where he educates a fish."

Irritated, the agent started in again, but each time the same answer was tendered—that Mr. Ishigawa's mission was classified, that he couldn't reveal where he was stationed or the nature of his training. Nothing.

"How convenient," the agent said. He thumbed the edge of the I.D. while sizing up his prisoner.

Harris lit a cigarette and drew on it long and slow. "Tell me, why did you run away when you saw me back there in the kitchen?"

"I thought commander recognized me on stage. He is very strict. Not allowed to leave base for many weeks." Hajime had rehearsed the alibi before he left Anne's dressing room. He didn't know how it would go, but the agent's reaction pleased him. "Had to blow off much steam. I use *steam* correctly?"

Harris relaxed his facial muscles and took another pull on his Chesterfield.

"You not report me, okay?" Hajime constructed up a pair of sad eyes.

Harris flexed his head. "Son, I don't owe you any favors. Already did that when you saw your wife and daughter off," and he sent a Music Box employee standing nearby on an errand.

A moment later a barrel-chested individual entered the alley with a frown. "What's so important, agent?" Commander Wright said.

"Excuse the interruption, sir, but this man claims to be under your command."

"Is that you, Ishigawa, in that imposter's uniform?"

"Yes, sir. Theater shorthanded and I just…"

"You were the one on stage tonight?"

"Yes, sir."

"Can't say that I approve," Commander Wright said.

"No, sir."

"We'll talk later." The commander turned his attention back to Agent Harris and said, "You can release this man into my custody."

Harris uncuffed the Oriental and handed back his I.D. The private and the lieutenant general left together. At the sound of the rear door closing, the agent found himself alone. The fog started to roll in. The lane took on the eerie sheen of a Hollywood whodunit. A vision flashed before him as his brain went back to the scene at the kitchen, to the last Oriental in line, to Number Six.

"Well, I'll be," and he stubbed out his cigarette on the brick wall, heaved up a laugh and disappeared into the mist.

*   *   *

Women whispered behind their raised hands as Elmer made his way backstage. Ever since his close encounter with mortality, he had been an emotional junkyard. Usually possessed with enough confidence to charm the hide off a heifer, uncertainties had laid claimed to his thinking. He couldn't get the image out of his head—an X drawn across a pic of himself. Jones's maniacal intentions loomed up before him. The thought that he was next in line for an express ticket to Holy Cross Cemetery unnerved him. His future without his daughter, without anyone, crowded him. He slugged to an office and knocked under a hanging "Open" sign.

"Can't ya read?" hollered a female's voice from inside.

Another rap on the door.

"This better be good," and Rose marched to the entrance. She pulled back her expression at the kneeling Elmer and said, "Whaddya doin' down there?"

"Marry me."

"Are ya touched or somethin'?" With hands on hips, she released a sigh and said, "Put some sense back into that skull of yours and get up."

She ushered him inside. A moment later a wispy arm reached back out and twisted the sign around, which now read "Go away", and the lock clicked into its casing.

*   *   *

The Chevy churned up Liberty Street. From the passenger seat, Anne noticed several red stains on her father's face.

"Appears somebody got mugged by a pair of runaway lips," she said. With a moistened thumb, she reached over and started to rub off the track of crimson marks, which ran from his forehead down to his shirt collar.

He pulled into the driveway, continuing to swat away her efforts. Well on their way to their evening tizzy fight, father and daughter argued about relationships, adulthood and the future. He switched off the ignition and set the brake. The pair emerged from the vehicle when a SFPD cruiser slowed down and honked its horn. Anne waved back and called out a thank you.

Elmer didn't understand his daughter's sudden familiarity with the local police and said, "What was that?"

She plucked up a *Chronicle* from the crabgrass. "Here's your paper."

He snatched the periodical from her and insisted on an answer.

She cleared her throat. "Nobuo can't stay at the Music Box anymore. Not alone, anyways."

"What's that got to do with the patrol car?"

"Do you mind?" Anne said.

The father huffed.

"Miss McNally—you remember her—the one with lips the size of snow cones."

"Miss Anne Klause!"

"Ah, you used my real name. How sweet."

A glare.

"All right, all right," and she paused, buying time to construct her next thought. "Rose needs Nobuo desperately, but if he worked there unprotected, bodily harm might come to him. Someone might even try to shoot him and that would be bad for business."

"Can live with all that."

"Can you live with your girlfriend's eternal rage?"

Elmer gestured to acknowledge the truth before him. "I'll give ya that one, but there aren't a lot of options here."

"Hajime wanted Nobuo to live at his home," Anne said, "and watch over the place."

"Little Tokyo houses the displaced Negro workers from the shipyard," the father added. "The Oriental would stick out like a bad rash."

"That's exactly what I said. So we settled on a compromise. Benny and his family will move into the three-bedroom while Hajime serves his time with M.I.S."

"Benny all right with that?"

"With three kids and one on the way? You betcha. They could use the extra space."

"What 'bout the Feds? After all, this Nobuo fella belongs to the enemy."

"Rose struck up a deal with Chief Delaney and Lieutenant General Wright. In exchange for her silence regarding certain liberties the men have taken with female performers, they have consented to place Nobuo under house arrest. The paperwork to have him reassigned to a federal prison will be delayed, of course."

Anne unlocked the front door and the two crossed the threshold when Elmer asked where Nobuo was now.

"Well, that's what makes this thing so intriguing, daddy dearest."

Not another *daddy dearest*.

"Nobuo will be escorted by the California State Military Reserve from his new place of residence to the Music Box each day," and she brushed his uniform, not to clean but with higher meaning.

Elmer grew tight at her gesture and started to ask for clarification when he heard a loud voice alongside a round of thuds from outside. He doubled back to the porch and bent an ear toward the rear of the Chevy. More banging.

"What's that?"

"I do believe that is your new prisoner," Anne said.

"Oh no, ya don't," and he stomped after his daughter.

From the auto's trunk, muffled cries went unattended. "Anyone there? Hello?"

HISTORICAL NOTES

Sally Rand's Music Box shut out its lights at the end of the war. The theater on O'Farrell Street in the Tenderloin went into ignominious decline until 1972 when it reopened as the Great American Music Hall. Sally became an American entertainment icon with her renowned "fan dance". She rose from being an acrobat with Ringling Brothers Circus to owning her own burlesque club to starring in several Hollywood movies including "Bolero". Cecil B. DeMille gave her the name based on a Rand McNally atlas. The dancer was arrested four times for indecent exposure at the 1933 Chicago World's Fair. She also organized Sally Rand's Nude Ranch at the Golden Gate International Exposition in 1939. She died at age 75 in 1979. Sally Rand is not Rose McNally.

In 1890 a group of Sunday school boys formed a military club. They soon adopted the natty uniform of West Point. It is rumored that the California Grays helped the local authorities clear out the riffraff from San Francisco's Barbary Coast for the 1915 Panama-Pacific International Exposition. Their involvement in the dock strikes of the thirties and Japantown raids during World War II is hazy. They still exist today and are headquartered in San Francisco. The California Grays are not the Republican Grays.

Lt. Gen. John L. DeWitt commanded the Fourth Army at the San Francisco Presidio as well as the Western Theater of Operations. He was mainly responsible for the sending of 120,000 Japanese to internment camps. After the war, the media vilified him for his racial comments. He was held responsible for the worst abuses of civil liberties in the history of the United States. He died in 1962. Lt. Gen. John L. DeWitt is not Lt. Gen. John L. Wright.

Little Tokyo in San Francisco was razed and leveled by hungry realtors and conniving politicians who used slum clearance ordinances as justification. African-Americans moved into the vacated neighborhood and many occupied low-income housing. Today the area is known as the Fillmore District (eastern segment of the Western Addition). The Japanese community holds onto a foothold at the northern end near Geary Boulevard.

Hundreds of Japanese Americans served as code breakers during WW 11. With this added ability, the U.S. defeated the Japanese at Midway. Later, M.I.S. intercepted the flight plan for Admiral Yamamoto's private plane and killed the designer of Pearl Harbor and Japan's top military strategist. Many in the M.I.S. joined the 100th Infantry Battalion from Hawaii, which later became part of the 442nd Regimental Combat Team, an all Japanese-American unit. The outfit is the most decorated regiment in the history of the United States, including twenty-one Medal of Honor recipients. In honor of certain requests, the true identity of Hajime Ishigawa shall remain confidential.

"The Great Los Angeles Air Raid" is the name given by contemporary sources to the imaginary enemy attack and subsequent anti-aircraft artillery barrage that took place February 24th and 25th of 1942. Initially, the source of the aerial invasion was thought to be part of the same Japanese fleet that ravaged Pearl Harbor. The U.S. Office of Air Force History has since attributed the event to a case of "war nerves" likely triggered by lost weather balloons and exacerbated by stray flares and shell bursts from adjoining batteries.

The I-25 was a submarine aircraft carrier of the Imperial Japanese Navy that took part in the attack on Pearl Harbor as well as recon missions of the Aleutian Islands in preparation for an invasion. The sub's plane carried out the first aerial bombing on the continental United States during the so-called "Lookout Air Raid" near Brookings, Oregon. The purpose of the strike was to start a massive forest fire to draw U.S. military attention away from the Pacific Theater and the impending invasion of Midway.

I-25's deck gun also fired on Fort Stevens, Oregon. In 1943 several submarine aircraft carriers were lengthened to four hundred feet, able to carry three aerial bombers. Anthrax devices were being considered as potential weapons upon American cities.

Nobuo Fujita was a Warrant Flying Officer who flew a floatplane from the deck of the I-25 submarine. In 1962 he visited Brookings, Oregon, after receiving assurance that he would not be tried as a war criminal. He carried his samurai sword with the intention of committing seppuku if all did not go well. The town, however, made him an honorary citizen (not without controversy). His family's 400-year-old sword now resides in the local museum. Mr. Fujita started a student exchange program between Brookings and Tokyo and planted a tree at the bombsite as a gesture of peace. He passed away in 1997. Nobuo Fujita is not Nobuo Akita.

Elmer DeGraf, the author's grandfather, created the 49 Mile Scenic Drive in San Francisco and worked for several mayors as the City's official greeter for foreign dignitaries. He was a member of the California Grays and served in WWI. As a member of the California State Military Reserve, he helped guard the Golden Gate Bridge during WWII. A week after V-Day, a Japanese stranger mysteriously and suddenly appeared as Mr. DeGraf's personal chef. Elmer DeGraf is not Elmer Klause.

Anne DeGraf's photo was in the 1937 issue of *Life* magazine as the youngest member of the San Francisco Ballet and Opera Company at age fifteen. Her instructor, Merishio Ito, was wanted as a spy but escaped to Japan. When WWII arrived, she auditioned for Sally Rand's Music Box, but her father refused to allow such silliness. Ms. DeGraf turned down a scholarship to the Ballet Russe de Monte Carlo at the insistence of John Hilary McCarty, her fiancée at the time. Anne settled down in San Francisco to devote herself to her husband and three children, the eldest of which is yours truly. Anne DeGraf is not Anne Klause.

ALSO BY JOHN MCCARTY

Memories That Linger is a coming-of-age adventure about fourteen-year-old Sean McGinnis and his two buddies along the banks of the Russian River in northern California. Apple Ripple, marijuana, and carnal cravings provide newfound horizons as the trio explores the rural hamlet of Rio Nido. Then one day a gut-wrenching crisis makes an uninvited visit to the McGinnis clan, and Sean flees downriver to escape the heartache. His pals catch up, but a nine-foot water creature, government Black Coats and a mysterious island waylay them. With renewed resolve, Sean scraps his way back to Rio Nido only to discover that his family's plight has deepened. Homeless and with few financial resources, Sean navigates his mother and younger siblings through the tumultuous summer of 1953.

"*Memories* is a nostalgic trip back to the day when the Big Band sound did battle with Rock 'n' Roll. A grand accomplishment."
-Benny Barth, drummer for Peggy Lee and Mel Torme

"One of the fine accomplishments of John McCarty's novels is his rendering of the tough and unsentimental way of talking you can hear in these parts (Russian River Valley)."
-Bob Jones, *Sonoma West Times and News*

"John McCarty realizes the power of nostalgia and how people are hungry to go back to the good ol' days."
-*The Windsor Times*

*   *   *

In the Rough is a farcical contemporary issues novel. Eddy Peters drifts into the backwater town of Monte Rio in northern California on the run from booze, civilization and authority. The military veteran shirks the solicitations of a masseuse in her fight against the construction of a nearby treatment plant. But a defrocked priest and a pot grower soon sweep him up into battle with the hope of saving their rural way of life from the evils of progress. Not to be outwitted by a band of buffoons, a deep pocket Bohemian and a self-absorbed chamber president conspire for the redevelopment of the town. Beaten down but not defeated, Eddy and his alliance pave a twisted path upon which greed and fate speed both sides to an unexpected ending.

"Great characters live in John McCarty's *In the Rough*. This novel is a little gem. Lots of local color and a fun read."
-Sonoma County Gazette

"*In the Rough* is the best mix of eclectic characters since *On the Road*. John McCarty's wild ride through the anti-establishment denizens of the Russian River in Sonoma County is a throwback treat."
-Mike Reilly, former president of California Coastal Commission

"*In the Rough* captures the heart of local politics in its most basic and repugnant form. A must read."
-Gil Loescher, professor of international politics at Oxford University, England.

For further information regarding John McCarty's novels, go to www.johnmccarty.org.

John Michael McCarty is a fourth-generation San Franciscan and retired educator. He was a history instructor at Earl Shilton Community College in England and at St. Mary's College in Moraga, California. A member in good standing with the San Francisco Historical Society and the Fulbright Association, John has written two previous novels. *Memories That Linger* and *In the Rough* are zany tales of the famous and not-so-famous who reside along the banks of the Russian River in northern California.

Made in the USA
Las Vegas, NV
03 October 2022

56512766R00167